WHEN I WAS YOUR AGE

WHEN I WAS YOUR AGE

Original Stories About Growing Up

✦

edited by

AMY EHRLICH

CANDLEWICK PRESS

VOLUME ONE

Introduction copyright © 1996 by Amy Ehrlich
"All-Ball" copyright © 1996 by Mary Pope Osborne
"The Great Rat Hunt" copyright © 1996 by Laurence Yep
"Everything Will Be Okay" copyright © 1996 by James Howe
"Why I Never Ran Away From Home" copyright © 1996 by Katherine Paterson
"Reverend Abbott and Those Bloodshot Eyes" copyright © 1996 by Walter Dean Myers
"Muffin" copyright © 1996 by Susan Cooper
"Taking a Dare" copyright © 1996 by Nicholasa Mohr
"Flying" copyright © 1996 by Reeve Lindbergh
"Scout's Honor" copyright © 1996 by Avi
"Blue" copyright © 1996 by Francesca Lia Block

VOLUME TWO

Introduction copyright © 1999 by Amy Ehrlich
"In the Blink of an Eye" copyright © 1999 by Norma Fox Mazer
"Food from the Outside" copyright © 1999 by Rita Williams-Garcia
"Interview with a Shrimp" copyright © 1999 by Paul Fleischman
"The Long Closet" copyright © 1999 by Jane Yolen
"How I Lost My Station in Life" copyright © 1999 by E. L. Konigsburg
"Bus Problems" copyright © 1999 by Howard Norman
"Pegasus for a Summer" copyright © 1999 by Michael J. Rosen
"Learning to Swim" copyright © 1999 by Kyoko Mori
"Waiting for Midnight" copyright © 1999 by Karen Hesse
"The Snapping Turtle" copyright © 1999 by Joseph Bruchac

First paperback edition in this format 2012

The Library of Congress Cataloging-in-Publication Data is available.

Library of Congress Catalog Card Number 95-4820

ISBN 978-0-7636-1034-0 (paperback; volume one)
ISBN 978-0-7636-1734-9 (paperback; volume two)

ISBN 978-0-7636-5892-2 (paperback bindup)

12 13 14 15 16 SHD 10 9 8 7 6 5 4 3 2

Printed in Ann Arbor, MI, U.S.A.

This book was typeset in Fairfield and Perpetua.

Candlewick Press
99 Dover Street
Somerville, Massachusetts 02144

visit us at www.candlewick.com

ＥＮＴＳ

✦ ✦

VOLUME ONE

When I Was Your Age

VOLUME ONE

INTRODUCTION

"Tell me a story of when you were a little boy," I used to ask my father, when I was a little girl. Because he happened to be a writer, the stories he told were more romantic than fairy tales, more exciting than TV adventure dramas. Maybe they were even true!

That's what we did when we put together this collection: We sent letters to all of the writers, asking them for stories. "If you are interested in this project (we said) the story you might choose to tell doesn't have to be literally true in every detail but should be located in time and space in your own childhood. It can be dramatic or serious or funny—whatever tone is right for the characters and plot."

Each story that came back amazed us. Each was completely different from the others and yet they had so much in common. Perhaps this is because all these writers (and the rest of us too) share childhood itself—a rich and important time in a human life.

Time moves more slowly in childhood. That's probably hard to realize when you are living through it, but think for example how long a summer seems between one school year and the next. The quality of what you see and feel is more vivid too in childhood. When you are very happy or very sad, those emotions color everything.

Some of the experiences you are having, even right now, may remain with you always as memories.

Several of the stories in this collection take place more than half a century ago. Television had not yet been invented, and radios and phonographs were the only entertainment in people's homes. There was no MTV, no video arcades, no malls. World War II was going on, yet children played without fear on city streets. Life was very different, but through the lens of the storyteller, you can see what it felt like to be a child in this vanished world.

Walter Dean Myers's "Reverend Abbott and Those Bloodshot Eyes" will take you to Harlem in New York in the late 1940s, when every mother on the block would keep an eye on all the children and holler if anyone misbehaved. And with the boys in Avi's story "Scout's Honor," you can take the subway all the way from Brooklyn to Manhattan and walk across the George Washington Bridge, afraid not of muggers but only of dishonoring yourself in front of your friends.

For all the writers in this collection, the places they describe so vividly are the places where they grew up. These are special places yet ordinary; taken for granted at the time but etched and glowing in memory. Quite simply, they are home.

Listen to Mary Pope Osborne in her story "All-Ball" describe the army posts of the 1950s: "I loved the neat lawns, clean streets, trim houses, and starched uniforms. I loved parade bands, marching troops, green jeeps, tanks, and transport trucks. . . . Living on an army post in those days was so safe that in all the early summers of our lives the children of our family were let out each morning like dandelions to the wind."

Just as home is the place known best, so are children's families the center of the world in these stories. In fact, more than half of them are about a child's intense love for another family member—mother, father, sister, brother. Most often, this beloved person understands the child's longings and responds in a full and loving way.

Beneath the humor of Laurence Yep's "The Great Rat Hunt" is the poignant story of a boy's relationship with his father. The child narrator, who has asthma, cannot impress his father with his athletic ability; and yet his father lets the boy know that he is loved for who he is. What could be a more important gift from a parent to a child?

In Reeve Lindbergh's "Flying," another kind of understanding is involved. When her aviator father tries to teach his children about airplanes by taking them up in a small plane on Saturday afternoons, the lesson instead is about what flying means to *him*.

Brothers and sisters too—particularly older ones— can be a powerful influence on children. In Katherine Paterson's "Why I Never Ran Away from Home," set in wartime China, it is her bullying big sister Lizzie—

prettier and more talented (or so the narrator thinks) — who stops her from doing something disastrous.

But a family's love can also be destructive. In some of the stories, children are very needy and vulnerable, and the writers show that if parents or brothers or sisters ignore this, the child can be badly hurt.

In Francesca Lia Block's "Blue," a girl's father, sad and distant since his wife deserted them, does not see his daughter's despair until it is almost too late. And in James Howe's "Everything Will Be Okay," a boy's longing for a stray kitten collides hard with his brother's code about toughness.

In fact, the need to be tough is a strong undercurrent to many of the stories in this collection. Despite environments that are often safe and welcoming, the cruelty of other people—particularly people their own age— exposes children to danger and sometimes makes toughness the only possible response.

Taunts like "Crybaby," "Stupid," "Wacko," and "Sissy"; and phrases like "I felt lonely," "I was scared," "I couldn't stop crying" come up in these stories repeatedly. Childhood can be a harsh and friendless time.

In Susan Cooper's wartime story "Muffin," a schoolyard bully called Fat Alice scares Daisy, the heroine, far more than the bombs falling in England during the Blitz. Fat Alice is truly evil; her meanness has no apparent motive or cause. She kicks, trips, shoves, and pinches while the adults are busy elsewhere.

What is a child to do against such terrorism? Resourcefulness is certainly required. But so too is real certainty and self-confidence. Throughout this collection, the question of identity—what it is and how you get it—comes up over and over again.

In the stories, children define themselves by their similarities and differences to their siblings and parents. In Nicholasa Mohr's "Taking a Dare," for example, it takes real nerve for the narrator to find her own path between her mother's intense and unquestioning Catholicism and the atheism of her socialist father.

But there are times when children, for their survival, must move away from their families and carve out new identities all their own, and this is a process that does not seem to come easily.

In fact, most of the stories in *When I Was Your Age* have some emotional pain in them. Their child heroes are self-conscious or ill at ease in the world. Some suffer at unfair circumstances (such as the death or disappearance of a parent), while others are just simply filled with pain—crying and miserable and alone. *Different.*

What is the answer? What can children do aside from learning to be tough, which is only a temporary or at best a partial answer? I believe that an uncanny number of the stories in this collection show another more creative path—the transformation of suffering through art.

Clues to it are everywhere in the stories. But perhaps the clearest comes from Francesca Lia Block's "Blue." In the end, it is only when the heroine, La, writes about her vanished mother that her terrible pain stops. The words she writes also have the effect of connecting other people to her:

> "Daddy," La said.
> When she handed him the story, his eyes changed.
> "It's about Mom," La said, but she knew he knew. . . .
> "Thank you, honey." He looked as though he hadn't slept or eaten for days. But he took off his glasses then, and La saw two small images of herself swimming in the tears in his eyes.

· · ·

Where does writing begin? What is it that shapes writers? If we want to look for the seeds of it in childhood, I think this collection makes it clear that they have probably been there for a very long time.

Isolation and separation can be bridged by language. Words can cross time and distance, connecting people of different generations and ages and experience. As you read the stories in *When I Was Your Age,* think of the grown-up writers who were once children. Here they are; this is what they saw and felt and remembered.

Listen carefully. They are telling you their stories.

— AMY EHRLICH

Mary Pope Osborne

ALL-BALL

~⦅~

M A R Y   P O P E   O S B O R N E

I remember the first time I got really bad news.

I was eight years old, and my family was living in white wooden army quarters at the edge of a thick pine forest in Fort Eustis, Virginia. All my life we had lived on military posts, and I loved them. I loved the neat lawns, clean streets, trim houses, and starched uniforms. I loved parade bands, marching troops, green jeeps, tanks, and transport trucks. I loved having military police at the entrance gate. When I was four, I dreamed that the M.P.'s guarding the gate chased away a couple of ghosts that tried to come onto our post. It is one of the most vivid dreams I've ever had, and to this day, it makes me feel good to remember it.

Living on an army post in those days was so safe that in all the early summers of our lives the children of our family were let out each morning like dandelions to the wind. My teenage sister went off with her friends while my brothers and I filled our time playing with our toy soldiers, including my favorite—a small silver statue of General Omar Bradley. We played "maneuvers" by carrying large cardboard boxes around the parade field, stopping every hundred yards to "bivouac" by making grass beds and napping inside our boxes.

At five o'clock, when the bugle played and the flag was lowered, we went home. Our return was often punctuated by the joyous sight of our dad stepping out of a chauffeured military car, his arms raised to embrace us.

But one spring night when I was eight, bad news changed everything. I remember my dad was helping me prepare my bath. I was sitting on the edge of the tub while the water ran, and Dad was standing in the doorway, wearing his summer khaki uniform. "Sis—" he always called me Sis or Little Bits—"in six weeks, Daddy is going to Korea."

I looked at him and burst into tears. I knew we wouldn't be going with him. Though the Korean War had ended eight years earlier, U.S. soldiers were still sent there for tours of duty—without their families.

"Don't cry," he said. "I'll only be gone for a year."

Only a year?

"While I'm gone, you'll live in Florida, in Daytona Beach, near the ocean."

Daytona Beach? Away from an army post?

"You'll have a wonderful time."

"No I won't!" I hated this news. And to prove it, I pushed him out of the bathroom.

Of course, I was right and he was wrong. A few weeks later, when Dad drove our family to Daytona Beach to get us settled, I didn't find our new life wonderful at all.

Our house was low to the ground, flamingo-pink, and made of stucco. There were no kids in the whole neighborhood. There were no real trees in our small yard—just a few scrubby ones. There was no wide open parade field to play on.

I recoiled from this new life—especially when I discovered lizards scampering across our cement driveway, a huge water bug scuttling across the floor of the TV room, and a gigantic black spider hovering in the corner of the garage. Such monsters didn't exist on army posts—neither did the crazy variety of houses, the litter, the tawdry seaside billboards.

Adding to the trauma of adjusting to life off a military post was the awareness that my dad was leaving in just three weeks. At first, I tried to manage my grief by taking a little time out of every day to cry. In those days, I was very organized. I kept a daily list of things to do like:

> *Wash hands*
> *Play with dolls*
> *Practice writing*
> *Practice running*

I added "Cry for Daddy" to the list. But as I counted

down the days till his departure, I began to cry even when it wasn't scheduled. Worse, I abandoned the other things on my list to keep a watch on my dad. I studied everything he did—from buying a vanilla ice-cream cone at the Dairy Queen to playing catch with my brothers—because I felt I had to store up enough memories of him to last through the coming year.

The pressure became unbearable and soon forced me into the strangest relationship of my life. Just thinking about this relationship now can bring tears to my eyes. Was it with a wonderful girl? Boy? Grown-up? Dog, cat, parakeet?

No. It was with a *ball*.

About two weeks before Dad left, he took my brothers and me to a Rose's Five & Dime store. He gave us fifty cents each to buy whatever we wanted.

This is the most precious fifty cents I will ever spend, I thought. Slowly, I wandered the rows of comics, coloring books, plastic dolls, and bags of candy, looking for an object worthy of the last-fifty-cents-my-father-gave-me-before-he-went-to-Korea.

When I came to the ball section, I saw, amidst a variety of balls, a truly unique specimen: a nubby rubber ball, bigger than a softball and smaller than a kickball. It was made up of swirling pastel colors—pink, blue, green.

I picked up the ball and bounced it.

It was the best bouncing ball I'd ever encountered. Barely did it touch the wooden floor before it sprang back into my hands. The ball felt friendly, spunky, and vibrant. It had such a positive and strong personality that I named it before we even got home: All-Ball.

For the next twelve days, All-Ball and I were inseparable. I bounced him on the driveway and on the sidewalk. Standing apart from everyone, deep in my own world, I bounced him for hours. And while I bounced, I talked to myself. I invented stories. Not dramatic stories of high-adventure. But stories about ordinary families— families in which everyone stayed together and everyone was safe and secure.

In these families, there was perfect order. The children all had names that began with the same letter— David, Danny, and Doris; Paul, Peter, and Patsy; Anne, Alice, Adam, and Ace.

I gave the children ages, personalities, and dialogue. I played all the parts. I was John joking with Jane; Jane laughing with Jack; Adam telling a story to Ace; Alice describing her school outfits to Anne.

I lived in different families morning, afternoon, and twilight. I could only create these worlds with All-Ball's help. His sprightly, joyous attitude gave me confidence. The sound of his rhythmic bounce banished my fears. His constant presence eased the sorrow of Dad's leaving. In fact, whenever Dad tried to engage me in conversation or play, I turned away from him. I stopped paying attention to him altogether.

I had fallen in love with a ball.

Though everyone in my family must have thought my behavior odd, they adjusted quickly. Within a day or two, they were treating "Sis's ball" sort of like a family pet.

No one, however, was fully aware of the depth of my attachment until the morning All-Ball was destroyed.

It was a hot, bright July morning—just two days before Dad was to leave for Korea. I was outside before everyone else, bouncing All-Ball on the sidewalk, inventing a family with a neat number of years between each child. I liked the children to be ten, eight, six, four. Boy, girl, boy, girl. John, Jane, Jed, Joy.

While I was bouncing All-Ball in the early warm air, a small black dog wandered down the sidewalk to see what was up, a little dog I paid no attention to—until it was too late. And then everything happened so fast, I couldn't stop it.

I fumbled a bounce. The black dog charged and grabbed All-Ball in his mouth. He punctured the rubber skin with his teeth, then shook the deflated ball with glee, tearing it to pieces. I started to scream. I screamed and screamed.

Everyone rushed out to their yards—old people from all the quiet, lonely houses. My parents, brothers, sister. I couldn't stop screaming as I ran around, picking up all the torn patches of All-Ball. I clutched them to my chest and howled at the top of my lungs.

My mother explained to the neighbors that my ball had popped. My brothers and sister watched me in horror—my father in confusion. "We'll get you another ball," he said.

He couldn't have uttered crueler words. There was no other ball like All-Ball. Not in the whole world. Not with his spirit, his bounce, his steadfastness. I screamed "No!" with such rage that everyone retreated.

I ran inside, and, clutching the pieces of All-Ball, I went to bed, yelling at everyone to leave us alone. I kissed the pastel-colored nubby skin and sobbed and sobbed.

I did not get up all day. I grieved for the death of All-Ball with all the grief my eight years could muster. I was brought lunch, cool drinks, newspaper comics, wet washcloths for my head, children's aspirin. But nothing worked. I would not get up. I would not let go of the torn pieces of the ball.

At twilight, I could hear the family having dinner in the dining room. My mother had the decency to allow me to work out my sorrow on my own. I don't think she even allowed anyone to laugh.

As light faded across my room, I could hear sprinklers spritzing outside, and an old woman calling to her cats. By now, my eyes stung and were nearly swollen shut.

My throat burned. My heart had not stopped hurting all day.

"Little Bits?" My father stood in my doorway. He was holding a ball. It was mostly white with a little bit of blue.

I moaned and turned my face to the wall as he walked toward the bed.

"You won't let me give you this new ball?" he said.

"No!" I said, gasping with another wave of grief. "Go away!"

"This ball's pretty nice," he said.

Closing my eyes, I shook my head emphatically, furious he did not understand the difference between the ball he held and All-Ball. "I hate it! Go away!"

He didn't. He sat on the edge of the bed.

But I would not look at him. My burning eyes stared at the wall. My body was stiff with anger.

"I like your barrette," he said softly.

He was referring to a pink Scottie dog barrette locked onto my tangled hair.

I didn't speak.

He cleared his throat. "I hope you'll wear that the day I come home."

I blinked. The truth was I hadn't thought much about his coming home. Only about his leaving.

"I'll bring you a ring when I come back," he said.

I didn't move. Just blinked again.

"What kind of ring would you like?"

I mumbled something.

"What?" he asked.

"A pearl," I said hoarsely.

"A pearl ring. Okay. On the day I come home, I'll bring you a pearl ring. And a music box. How's that? I'll hide in the bushes, and when you ride up on your bike, home from school, I'll jump out and surprise you. How's that?"

He cleared his throat again. I turned just a little to look at him. I saw he had tears in his eyes. I didn't want him to feel sad too. That was almost worse than anything.

I reluctantly rolled over onto my back. I looked at the ball he held. It was still a stupid ball, no doubt about that. But I mumbled something about it being pretty.

"Will you play with this one?" he said.

I touched it with my finger. I let out a quivering sigh, then nodded, accepting the complications of the moment. All-Ball would know that he could never be replaced. Ever. He was the one and only ball for me. But I could pretend to like this other one. Even play with it. For Dad's sake.

He handed me the white ball and I embraced it and smiled feebly.

He smiled back. "Come eat some dinner with us now," he said.

I was ready. I wanted to leave my room. The light of day was nearly gone.

"Come on." He helped me off the bed, and, clutching pieces of All-Ball along with the new white ball, I joined the family.

My dad left soon after that. We entered a new school. Ball-bouncing was replaced with friends, homework, and writing letters to Korea. Still—and this is weird, I'll admit—I slept with a torn piece of All-Ball under my pillow for the next year, until after my dad came home.

Notes from

MARY POPE OSBORNE

"I decided to share the story of All-Ball with young readers because I think it speaks to the hardest thing about being a child: the fact that most things in your life are out of your control. On the other hand, it also shows one of the best things about being a child: the fact that you can use your imagination to help ease your troubles.

All the games I once played—from talking to All-Ball, to playing with my dolls, to pretending to be a cowboy or a soldier with my brothers—helped me become a writer. And one of the great joys of being a writer is that every day I can still use my imagination to help ease my troubles. The spirit of All-Ball now lives in my writing tools, instead of in a beloved rubber ball."

Laurence Yep

THE GREAT RAT HUNT

LAURENCE YEP

I had asthma when I was young, so I never got to play
sports much with my father. While my brother and
father practiced, I could only sit in bed, propped up by
a stack of pillows. As I read my comic books, I heard
them beneath our apartment window. In the summer, it
was the thump of my brother's fastball into my father's
mitt. In the fall, it was the smack of a football. In the
winter, it was the airy bounce of a basketball.

Though my father had come from China when he
was eight, he had taken quickly to American games.
When he and Mother were young, they had had the
same dances and sports leagues as their white school-
mates—but kept separate in Chinatown. (He had met
Mother when she tripped him during a co-ed basketball
game at the Chinatown Y).

Father was big as a teenager and good at sports. In

fact, a social club in Chinatown had hired him to play football against social clubs in other Chinatowns. There he was, a boy playing against grown men.

During a game in Watsonville, a part-time butcher had broken Father's nose. It never properly healed, leaving a big bump at the bridge. There were other injuries too from baseball, basketball, and tennis. Each bump and scar on his body had its own story, and each story was matched by a trophy or medal.

Though he now ran a grocery store in San Francisco, he tried to pass on his athletic skills to my older brother Eddy and me. During the times I felt well, I tried to keep up with them, but my lungs always failed me.

When I had to sit down on the curb, I felt as if I had let my father down. I'd glance up anxiously when I felt his shadow over me; but he looked neither angry nor disgusted—just puzzled, as if he could not understand why my lungs were not like his.

"S-s-sorry." I panted.

"That's okay." He squatted and waved his hat, trying to fan more air at me. In the background, Eddy played catch with himself, waiting impatiently for the lessons to begin again. Ashamed, I would gasp. "Go on . . . and play."

And Father and Eddy would start once more while I watched, doomed to be positively un-American, a weakling, a perpetual spectator, an outsider. Worse, I felt as if Eddy were Father's only true son.

And then came the day when the rat invaded our store. It was Eddy who first noticed it while we were restocking the store shelves. I was stacking packages of pinto beans when Eddy called me. "Hey, do you know what this is?" He waved me over to the cans of soup. On his palm lay some dark drops. "Is it candy?"

Father came out of the storeroom in the rear of our store. Over his back, he carried a huge hundred pound sack of rice. He let it thump to the floor right away. "Throw that away."

"What is it, Father?" I asked.

"Rat droppings," he said. "Go wash your hands."

"Yuck." Eddy flung the droppings down.

While Eddy washed his hands, I helped Father get rid of the evidence. Then he got some wooden traps from a shelf and we set them out.

However, the traps were for mice and not for rats. The rat must have gotten a good laugh while it stole the bait and set off the springs.

Then Father tried poison pellets, but the rat avoided them all. It even left a souvenir right near the front door.

Father looked grim as he cleaned it up. "I'm through fooling around."

So he called up his exterminator friend, Pete Wong, the Cockroach King of Chinatown. While Pete fumigated the store, we stayed with my Aunt Nancy over on Mason, where the cable cars kept me up late. They always rang their bells when they rounded the corner. Even when they weren't there, I could hear the cable rattling in its channel beneath the street. It was OK, though, because my cousin Jackie could tell stories all night.

The next day, when we went back home, Father searched around the store, sniffing suspiciously for deadly chemicals. Mother went upstairs to our apartment over the store to get our electric fan.

She came right back down empty-handed. "I think he's moved up there. I could hear him scratching behind the living room walls."

Father stared at the ceiling as if the rat had gone too far. "Leave it to me," he said. He fished his car keys from his pocket.

"Where are you going?" Mother asked.

Father, though, was a man of few words. He preferred to speak by his actions. "I'll be back soon."

An hour and a half later he returned with a rifle. He held it up for the three of us to examine. "Isn't it a beaut? Henry Loo loaned it to me." Henry Loo was a pharmacist and one of Father's fishing buddies.

Mother frowned. "You can't shoot that cannon off in my house."

"It's just a twenty-two." Father tugged a box of cartridges out of his jacket pocket. "Let's go, boys."

Mother sucked in her breath sharply. "Thomas!"

Father was surprised by Mother's objection. "They've got to learn sometime."

Mother turned to us urgently. "It means killing. Like buying Grandpop's chickens. But you'll be the ones who have to make it dead."

"It's not the same," Father argued. "We won't have to twist its neck."

Buying the chicken was a chore that everyone tried to avoid at New Year's when Mother's father insisted on it. To make sure the chicken was fresh, we had to watch the poulterer kill it. And then we had to collect the coppery-smelling blood in a jar for a special dish that only Mother's father would eat. For a moment, I felt queasy.

"You're scaring the boys," Father scolded her.

Mother glanced at him over her shoulder. "They ought to know what they're getting into."

I didn't believe in killing—unless it was a bug like a cockroach. However, I felt different when I saw a real rifle—the shiny barrel, the faint smell of oil, the decorated wooden stock. I rationalized the hunt by telling myself I was not murdering rabbits or deer, just a mean old rat—like a furry kind of cockroach.

"What'll it be, boys?" Father asked.

Taking a deep breath, I nodded my head. "Yes, sir."

Father turned expectantly to Eddy and raised an eyebrow.

From next to me, though, Eddy murmured, "I think I'll help Mother." He wouldn't look at me.

Father seemed just as shocked as Mother and I. "Are you sure?"

Eddy drew back and mumbled miserably. "Yes, sir."

Mother gave me a quick peck on the cheek. "I expect you to still have ten toes and ten fingers when you finish."

As we left the store, I felt funny. Part of me felt triumphant. For once, it was Eddy who had failed and not me. And yet another part of me wished I were staying with him and Mother.

Father said nothing as we left the store and climbed the back stairs. As I trailed him, I thought he was silent because he was disappointed: He would rather have Eddy's help than mine.

At the back door of our apartment, he paused and said brusquely, "Now for some rules. First, never, never aim the rifle at anyone."

I listened as attentively as I had the disastrous times he'd tried to teach me how to dribble, or catch a football, or handle a pop foul. "I won't." I nodded earnestly.

Father pulled a lever near the middle of the gun. "Next, make sure the rifle is empty." He let me inspect the breech. There was nothing inside.

"Yes, sir," I said and glanced up at him to read his mood. Because Father used so few words, he always sounded a little impatient whenever he taught me a lesson. However, it was hard to tell this time if it was genuine irritation or his normal reserve.

He merely grunted. "Here. Open this." And he handed me the box of cartridges.

I was so nervous that the cartridges clinked inside the box when I took it. As I fumbled at the lid, I almost felt like apologizing for not being Eddy.

Now, when I got edgy, I was the opposite of Father: I got talkier. "How did you learn how to hunt?" I asked. "From your father?"

My father rarely spoke of his father, who had died before I was born. He winced now as if the rat had just nipped him. "My old man? Nah. He never had the time. I learned from some of my buddies in Chinatown." He held out his hand.

I passed him a cartridge. "What did you hunt? Bear?"

"We shot quail." Father carefully loaded the rifle.

I was uncomfortable with the idea of shooting the cute little birds I saw in cartoons. "You did?"

He clicked the cartridge into the rifle. "You have to be tough in this world, boy. There are going to be some times when nobody's around to help—like when I first came to America."

That was a long speech for Father. "You had your father." His mother had stayed back in China, because in those days, America would not let her accompany her husband.

"He was too busy working." Father stared back down the stairs as if each step were a year. "When I first came here, I got beaten up by the white kids. And when the white kids weren't around, there were the other Chinese kids."

I furrowed my forehead in puzzlement. I handed him another cartridge. "But they were your own kind."

He loaded the rifle steadily as I gave him the ammunition. "No, they weren't. The boys born here, they like to give a China-born a hard time. They thought I'd be easy pickings. But it was always a clean fight. No knives. No guns. Just our feet and fists. Not like the punks nowadays." He snapped the last cartridge into the rifle. "Then I learned how to play their games, and I made them my friends." He said the last part with pride.

And suddenly I began to understand all the trophies and medals in our living room. They were more than awards for sports. Each prize was a sign that my father belonged to America—and at the same time, to Chinatown. And that was why he tried so hard now to teach sports to Eddy and me.

When I finally understood what sports really meant to my father, it only magnified the scale of my ineptitude. "I'm not good at fighting." As I closed the lid on the box of ammunition, I thought I ought to prepare him for future disappointments. "I'm not much good at anything."

Careful to keep the rifle pointed away from me, Father unlocked the door. "I said you have to be tough, not stupid. No reason to get a beat-up old mug like mine."

I shook my head, bewildered. "What's wrong with your face?"

Father seemed amused. He stepped away from the door and jerked his head for me to open it. "It's nothing that a steamroller couldn't fix."

"But you have an interesting face," I protested as I grabbed the doorknob.

"Are you blind, boy? This mug isn't ever going to win a beauty contest." He chuckled. "I've been called a lot of names in my time, but never 'interesting.' You've got a way with words."

The doorknob was cold in my hand. "I do?"

Father adjusted his grip on the rifle. "I wouldn't buy any real estate from you." And he gave me an encouraging grin. "Now let's kill that rat."

When I opened the door, our home suddenly seemed as foreign to me as Africa. At first, I felt lonely—and a little scared. Then I heard Father reassure me, "I'm with you, boy."

Feeling more confident, I crept through the kitchen and into the living room. Father was right behind me and motioned me to search one half of the room while he explored the other. When I found a hole in the corner away from the fireplace, I caught Father's eye and pointed.

He peered under a chair with me and gave me an approving wink. "Give me a hand," he whispered.

In silent cooperation, we moved the chair aside and then shifted the sofa over until it was between us and the rat hole. Bit by bit, Father and I constructed an upholstered barricade. I couldn't have been prouder if we'd built a whole fort together.

Father considerately left the lighter things for me to lift, and I was grateful for his thoughtfulness. The last thing I wanted was to get asthma now from overexertion. When we were done, Father got his rifle from the corner where he had left it temporarily.

As we crouched down behind our improvised wall, Father rested the rifle on it. "We'll take turns watching."

"Yes, sir," I said, peering over the barrier. There wasn't so much as a whisker in the hole.

While I scanned the hole with intense radar eyes, Father tried to make himself comfortable by leaning against the sofa. It made me feel important to know Father trusted me; and I was determined to do well. In the center of the living room wall was the fireplace, and on its mantel stood Father's trophies like ranks of soldiers reminding me to be vigilant.

We remained in companionable silence for maybe three quarters of an hour. Suddenly, I saw something flicker near the mouth of the hole. "Father," I whispered.

Father popped up alertly and took his rifle. Squeezing one eye shut, he sighted on the rat hole. His crouching body grew tense. "Right." He adjusted his aim minutely. "Right. Take a breath," he recited to himself. "Take up the slack. Squeeze the trigger." Suddenly, he looked up, startled. "Where'd it go?"

As the gray shape darted forward, I could not control my panic. "It's coming straight at us."

The rifle barrel swung back and forth wildly as Father tried to aim. "Where?"

I thought I could see huge teeth and beady, violent eyes. The teeth were the size of daggers and the eyes were the size of baseballs, and they were getting bigger by the moment. It was the rat of all rats. "Shoot it!" I yelled.

"Where?" Father shouted desperately.

My courage evaporated. All I could think of was escape. "It's charging." Springing to my feet, I darted from the room.

"Oh, man," Father said, and his footsteps pounded after me.

In a blind panic, I bolted out of the apartment and down the back stairs and into the store.

"Get the SPCA. I think the rat's mad," Father yelled as he slammed the door behind him.

Mother took the rifle from him. "I'd be annoyed too if someone were trying to shoot me."

"No." Father panted. "I mean it's rabid." We could hear the rat scurrying above us in the living room. It sounded as if it were doing a victory dance.

Mother made Father empty the rifle. "You return that to Henry Loo tomorrow," she said. "We'll learn to live with the rat."

As she stowed the rifle in the storeroom, Father tried to regather his dignity. "It may have fleas," he called after her.

Now that my panic was over, I suddenly became aware of the enormity of what I had done. Father had counted on me to help him, and yet I had run, leaving him to the ravages of that monster. I was worse than a failure. I was a coward. I had deserted Father right at the time he needed me most. I wouldn't blame him if he kicked me out of his family.

It took what little nerve I had left to look up at my father. At that moment, he seemed to tower over me, as grand and remote as a monument. "I'm sorry," I said miserably.

He drew his eyebrows together as he clinked the shells in his fist. "For what?"

It made me feel even worse to have to explain in front of Eddy. "For running," I said wretchedly.

He chuckled as he dumped the cartridges into his shirt pocket. "Well, I ran too. Sometimes it's smart to be scared."

"When were you ever scared?" I challenged him.

He buttoned his pocket. "Plenty of times. Like when I came to America. They had to pry my fingers from the boat railing."

It was the first time I'd ever heard my father confess to that failing. "But you're the best at everything."

"Nobody's good at everything." He gave his head a little shake as if the very notion puzzled him. "Each of us is good at some things and lousy at others. The trick is to find something that you're good at."

I thought again of the mantel where all of Father's sports trophies stood. Eddy gave every promise of collecting just as many, but I knew I would be lucky to win even one.

"I'm lousy at sports," I confessed.

His eyes flicked back and forth, as if my face were a book open for his inspection. He seemed surprised by what he read there.

Slowly his knees bent until we were looking eye to eye. "Then you'll find something else," he said and put his arm around me. My father never let people touch him. In fact, I hardly ever saw him hug Mother. As his arm tightened, I felt a real love and assurance in that embrace.

Shortly after that, the rat left as mysteriously as it had come. "I must've scared it off," Father announced.

Mother shook her head. "That rat laughed itself to death."

Father disappeared into the storeroom; and for a moment we all thought Mother had gone too far. Then we heard the electric saw that he kept back there. "What are you doing?" Mother called.

He came back out with a block of wood about two inches square. He was carefully sandpapering the splinters from the edges. "Maybe some day we'll find the corpse. Its head ought to look real good over the fireplace."

Mother was trying hard to keep a straight face. "You can't have a trophy head unless you shoot it."

"If it died of laughter like you said, then I killed it," he insisted proudly. "Sure as if I pulled the trigger." He winked at me. "Get the varnish out for our trophy will you?"

I was walking away when I realized he had said "our." I turned and said, "That rat was doomed from the start." I heard my parents both laughing as I hurried away.

Notes from
LAURENCE YEP

"I had no intention to be a writer, but a chemist as my father had wanted to be. However, under the prodding of a high school English teacher, the Reverend John Becker, I began submitting stories to magazines. Much to my surprise, I sold my first story to a science fiction magazine when I was eighteen.

I had all the material I needed for future stories in my family, neighbors, and friends. The story I've told here is a much-cherished family story. Though my father was born in China, he came over here as a boy and learned all sorts of American sports. In fact, before we had the store, he was a playground director and basketball coach in San Francisco's Chinatown.

Unlike my athletic older brother, I never mastered the vagaries of dribbling a basketball or catching a pop fly, despite years of practice. Even so, my father did his best to hide his disappointment. Later, he took great pride in my books; and, in lieu of athletic trophies, he displayed the various plaques, bowls, and medals that I received for my stories."

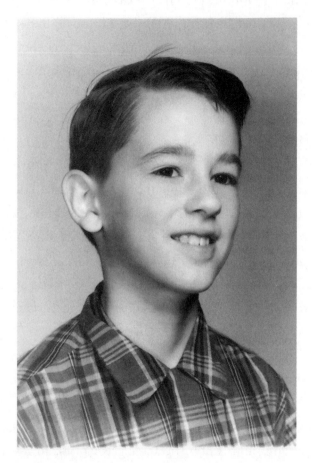

EVERYTHING WILL
BE OKAY

꘍

J A M E S   H O W E

The kitten is a scrawny thing with burrs and bits of wood caught in its hair, where it still has hair, and pus coming out its eyes and nose. Its big baby head looks even bigger at the end of such a stick of a body. I found it in the woods at the end of my street where I play most days with my friends. This time I was alone. Lucky for you I was, I think to the kitten. Otherwise, David or Claude might have decided you'd be good practice for their slingshots. Those two can be mean, I think to myself. I don't like playing with them really, but they live at the end of the street and sometimes you just play with the kids on your same street, even if they're mean, sometimes even to you.

The kitten makes a pitiful noise.

"Don't worry," I tell it, stroking its scabby head until the mewing is replaced by a faint purr. "Everything will be okay. I'm going to take you home, and my mom will give you a bath and some medicine."

I tuck the kitten under my jacket and run out of the

woods, across the street, down the sidewalk toward my house. I feel the warmth of the kitten through my shirt and start thinking of names.

I'm only ten, so it will be five or six years before I work for Dr. Milk. My two oldest brothers worked for him part-time and summers when they were teenagers. Now my other brother, Paul, works there. Dr. Milk is the vet out on Ridge Road. He takes care of our dogs, and he will take care of my kitten.

I never had a pet that was my very own. A couple of years ago, my father got a new beagle to replace the old one who had died, Patches was his name. He called the new one Bucky and said that Bucky could be mine. But saying a thing is so doesn't mean it is.

Bucky lives in a kennel out back, keeping his beagle smell, which my mother hates, far away from the house. I feed Bucky some days and play with him, but I am not allowed to bring him inside to sleep at the end of my bed or curl up next to me while I do my homework. Bucky is an outdoor dog; he is a hunting dog.

He is my father's dog, really.

When I am older, I will go hunting with my father the way my brothers have done. I try not to think about this. I want to go, because I want my father to like me. But I don't want to kill animals.

One time when my father and three brothers went hunting, one of my brothers killed a deer. Most times they kill rabbits or pheasants if they get lucky. Most times they don't get lucky. But this time one of my brothers, I don't remember which one, killed a deer.

The deer was hung by its feet from a tree just outside the kitchen. I could see it hanging there when I sat at my place at the table. My father urged me to eat my venison and talked about the slippers he was going to have made from the hide. I couldn't eat. The thought of the venison made me want to throw up.

I could see the deer's eyes, even from the kitchen table. There was life in them, still. Only the deer and I knew that there was life the bullet had missed. It was in the eyes.

I pushed the venison away.

My father said, "That's a waste of good meat."

My brothers teased me. One of them called me a sissy.

My mother said, "You don't have to eat it," and took the slab of gray meat off my plate.

My mother reaches into my jacket and removes the kitten by the scruff of its neck. She tells me to go down to the cellar and take off all my clothes and put them in a pile next to the washing machine.

"This animal is filled with disease," she says. "We can't let it touch anything in the house."

"We'll take it to Dr. Milk," I say. "He'll make it better."

"We'll see," she says, pushing me toward the cellar stairs, the kitten dangling from one of her hands.

I can feel tears welling up. "But that kitten is *mine*," I say. "I found it and it's going to be my pet."

She doesn't say anything. Looking up from the cellar stairs, I see her shaking her head at the kitten. Its eyes are clamped shut. I can see the pus oozing out of them.

"You are a sorry sight," she tells the kitten in the same soothing voice she uses with me when I'm sick. "A sorry sad sight."

I feel in the pit of my stomach what the future of that kitten is. The feeling spreads through me like a sudden fever. Down in the cellar taking off my clothes, I cry so hard my body shakes.

When I return upstairs, my mother wraps me in my bathrobe and holds me until I can speak.

"Where's the kitten?" I ask.

"Out on the back porch in a box. Your brother will be home soon."

Paul will be going to college in the fall. Right now he's a senior in high school. I can't decide if I'm going to miss him or not. He's the brother I know best because he's been around the longest. The others left home when I was even younger.

Paul is the brother who taught me to ride my bicycle and the one who spent an entire Saturday with me and not his friends building a real igloo out of snow and ice. He's the brother who tells me how to be a man.

He is also the brother who plays tricks on me and sometimes the tricks are cruel. When I get angry, he says I don't have a sense of humor. He twists my arm behind my back sometimes until I say I'll do what he wants me to do. He makes promises he doesn't keep.

Paul is seventeen. He shaves every day and kisses girls right in front of me like it was nothing. He works at Dr. Milk's part-time and summers.

I am sitting on the back porch waiting for Paul to come home and talking to the box next to me.

"Don't worry, Smoky," I tell the kitten inside. "I won't let anything bad happen to you, I don't care how sick you are. My big brother will take you to Dr. Milk's and give you shots and medicine and stuff and you'll get better, you'll see. My big brother can fix anything."

The kitten is awfully quiet. I wish it would make even a pitiful noise.

We sit in silence. I daydream that I am seventeen. I am big and strong like my brother and I can make Smoky better. I see myself driving to Dr. Milk's out on Ridge Road, carrying the kitten in its box into the back room (which I have never seen, really, only heard my brothers tell stories about), giving it some medicine, reassuring it . . .

"Everything will be okay, Smoky, everything will be okay."

In the kitchen behind me I hear my brother and mother talking in low voices.

Dr. Milk is not there when my brother pulls the car into the parking lot. It is after hours. My brother has a key. I am impressed by this.

"Come on," Paul says in his take-charge voice, "get that box now. Bring it on in here."

He flicks on the light in the waiting room. "You're coming in back with me," he commands. "I'll need your help."

"What are you going to do?" I ask. I am holding the box tight against my chest. I feel Smoky moving around inside.

"What do you think?" he says. "You heard your mother. That kitten is sick, bad sick."

"She's your mother, too."

"Well, she happens to be right," Paul tells me. "With an animal that far gone, you don't have a choice. It's got to be put to sleep."

I think the tears I jam back into my body are going to kill me. I think if I don't let them out they will kill me. But I won't let them out. I won't let Paul see.

"You *do* have a choice" is all I say. I hug the box for dear life and move to the door. Paul moves faster.

"Come on now," he says, gently taking hold of my arm, "be a man."

"I'm not a man," I tell him. "I don't want to be."

"You've got to do what's right. That kitten is half dead as it is."

"Then it's half alive, too."

He shakes his head. "You always have to one-up me, don't you?" he says.

I don't know what he means, but I do know that no matter what I say he is going to do what he wants to do.

A few minutes later, we are in the back room. The box is empty. Smoky is inside a big old pretzel can with a hose attached, clawing at the can's sides as my brother pumps in the gas. He is telling me it is good for me to watch this, it will toughen me up, help me be more of a man. Then he starts to lecture me about different methods of putting animals out of their misery, but all I can hear is the scratching. And then the silence.

At the supper table that night, I don't speak. I don't look at my brother's face or my father's or my mother's. I look at the tree branch outside the kitchen window where the deer once hung. My brother is saying something about taking me to the driving range tomorrow. He will teach me to hit a golf ball.

I won't go with him. I don't want him teaching me anything anymore.

In the fall he will go off to college. I will be eleven. I will be alone with my parents, alone without my brothers.

I get up from the table and no one stops me.

In the living room which is dark I sit for a long time thinking. I think about my kitten. I think about the pretzel can. I think about what it will be like not having any brothers around. I feel alone and small and frightened. And then all of a sudden I don't feel any of those things. All of a sudden it's as if Paul has already left and I am on my own and I know some things so clearly that I will never have to ask an older brother to help me figure them out.

I will never work for Dr. Milk.

I will not go hunting with my father.

I will decide for myself what kind of boy I am, what kind of man I will become.

❧

Notes from

JAMES HOWE

"When I was asked to write a story based on my childhood, I wasn't sure how or where to begin. I was surprised that my thoughts kept coming back to a long-forgotten episode involving a kitten I found one summer when I was ten. Slowly, the events and feelings came into sharper focus—and while I can't swear that every moment of this story really happened, I know that every feeling is true. And in time, I came to understand that the reason for writing this story had less to do with the kitten and more to do with my brothers and myself.

As I was the youngest, my three brothers were very important in my thinking about who I was and who I would be when I grew up. All my brothers were interested in the arts and at one time or another planned on arts-related careers. As it turned out, I was the only one who actually realized that particular dream.

But my entire family was instrumental in my becoming a writer. We were a word-loving family. Our house was full of books and games; no dinner conversation was complete without jokes and wordplay. My mother recognized my talent as a writer early on and encouraged me to consider it as a profession. It took me a long time to follow her advice, but when I did, it was like coming home. Writing has always been a natural part of who I am."

Katherine Paterson

WHY I NEVER RAN AWAY FROM HOME

KATHERINE PATERSON

My daughter Mary doesn't like for me to tell this story. "It's too sad," she says. "It was a sad time," I say. "I'm very happy now." "But I want my mommy to be happy when she's little," she says. "It has a happy ending," I say. "It tells why I never ran away from home."

"Guess what?" That's all my nine-year-old sister Lizzie had to say to get me excited.

"What?"

"You'll never guess," Lizzie said. And I wouldn't. Lizzie was too smart for me. She'd skipped second grade, the one I was stumbling through. Everyone praised Lizzie. Momma depended on her to help with our two baby sisters. Complete strangers would stop Momma to say how pretty Lizzie was. "Such darling freckles," they'd say. Lizzie would frown. She didn't think freckles were darling, but I did. I wanted to be just like Lizzie. Smart, dependable, pretty. Even our brother Sonny thought she was terrific, and Sonny was twelve years old.

"What?" I asked again. "What? What? Tell me."

"We're going to see a moving picture show. The mothers are going to take us into Shanghai to see *The Wizard of Oz.*" Lizzie knew all about *The Wizard of Oz.* She'd read the book.

We lived in China when I was seven, and I'd never seen a movie. Well, actually, I had seen part of one, but I got scared and began crying so loud that Momma had to take me out before it was half over.

"You mustn't yell this time," Lizzie warned. "You'll ruin it for everyone."

"Okay," I promised, already thrilled and scared.

"If it gets too scary for you, you can close your eyes, and I'll punch you when it's okay to watch again, all right?"

I nodded solemnly and promised myself that no matter what happened I would not cry. I knew Lizzie thought I was a crybaby. I was born on Halloween, so she and Sonny often called me "Spook Baby." They could count on me to burst into tears every time they did. If I called Lizzie "Lizard," she'd ignore me or just look at me and laugh.

As excited as I was about going to see *The Wizard of Oz,* I was frightened by the trip into the city. True, there were no bombs falling, no enemy soldiers standing about with guns and bayonets as there were in other Chinese cities where we'd lived. But Shanghai beyond the safe walls of the American School was crowded with desperate people.

Outside the school gate, the mothers herded our little group of American children into rickshas to go to the theater. While they did so, Chinese children no bigger than I was crowded around us. These children wore rags for clothes. I could see that their faces and bodies were covered with sores, as they pushed their dirty hands at my face, begging for coins.

I wished for my Daddy. I was never as frightened when our tall, funny father was with us. But all the fathers were far away. Ours was back home with our Chinese friends in Hwaian, near the worst of the fighting. I knew I was supposed to be happy that God needed Daddy there working with Pastor Lee to help people who were hungry and hurt by the war. But I wasn't happy; I was jealous of those people. I wanted Daddy to be with us.

Once the movie began, though, I was swallowed up in its magic. The real world of war and homesickness and fear seemed to disappear. Even I was changed. I was no longer an ordinary-looking seven-year-old crybaby. In my soul, I knew that I looked exactly like Judy Garland.

True, I missed a lot of the cyclone, most of the flying monkeys, and only got a few deliciously scary glimpses of the Wicked Witch of the West. But Lizzie kept her promise. She poked me when it was safe to watch again, so I didn't miss too much of the movie, and I only cried after Dorothy was safely home in Kansas.

The management was selling phonograph albums of the music in the theater lobby. Patty Jean White's mother bought one. I longed to have one for my own, but the White's dormitory room was right near ours. Surely Patty Jean would let the rest of us listen. Besides, we'd lost our record player when the soldiers looted our house in Hwaian.

For the next several days, the seven of us who had seen the movie gathered in the Whites' room and listened to the record. I loved those songs, especially "Somewhere Over the Rainbow." I longed to go over the rainbow. It sounded more like heaven than the place we sang hymns about every day and twice on Sundays. Besides, when I sang that song, I knew I sounded just like Judy Garland.

"Let's play Oz," Lizzie said one day while we were listening.

We looked at her in astonishment. "There's no room," someone said.

"Not indoors, silly. Outdoors in the quadrangle." We got excited. The Shanghai American School buildings surrounded a rectangle of huge green lawn. The quadrangle would make a wonderful Land of Oz.

"I'll be Dorothy," I offered.

Everyone turned and stared. "I'm supposed to be Dorothy," I said, a bit anxiously. Couldn't they see I was born to be Dorothy? Besides, I knew all the words. I was getting more agitated. Couldn't they understand? No one could sing those songs with more feeling.

Lizzie was the first one to speak up. "No," she said. "And stop jumping up and down. Patty Jean will be Dorothy. She has the right hair."

It wasn't fair. Patty Jean was an only child. Her mother had nothing better to do than brush and braid her long blonde hair. No one ever brushed my short brown hair but me, and I usually forgot.

"You have to be pretty to be Dorothy." Lizzie continued. Patty Jean began to priss up her mouth at that. "Besides —" and this was the worst blow of all — "besides," Lizzie said, "Patty Jean can sing."

I was crushed. I could imagine one of the other kids saying something that mean, but my very own sister? She and Sonny could laugh at me in our room, but right in front of everybody? I was working so hard at not crying that before I knew it, all the good parts were gone.

"You're small for your age," Lizzie was saying. "You can be a Munchkin."

"Lizard," I muttered under my breath. "Lizard. Lizard. Lizard." Lizzie pretended not to hear me.

I wanted to complain to Momma when we went

back to our room that afternoon, but Sonny was visiting, playing with the little girls so Momma could write Daddy a letter. Even with Sonny staying in the big boys' dormitory, our room was so crowded with beds that you could hardly walk around them.

Sitting on her bed writing, Momma looked worried. She always looked worried in those days, especially when she was writing to Daddy. Would he be hurt out there where the war was going on? Would he be killed? Would we ever see him again?

If my mother was worried, I was terrified. What would I do without my wise father? I was terribly homesick for him. I wrote letters to him whenever I could. We were never sure he would get our letters, but we sent them anyway.

"I'm going to write a letter to Daddy," I announced, as soon as I realized that no one was in a mood to listen to me whine. I slid across the bed on my knees to look over Momma's shoulder. I liked to copy the grown-up way my mother wrote. "Lovingly, Mary." That's the way she signed her letters.

"Look at this!" Lizzie yelled when I proudly showed her the letter I had written. She made her way between the beds to show it to Sonny. Sonny snorted. They both laughed.

"Give it to me," I said, trying to grab back my letter. But they passed it back and forth over my head.

Momma tried to get them to calm down. "But, Momma," Lizzie said. "Look how she signed it!"

"I signed it just like Momma does."

"No you didn't. You said 'Lovely Katherine.' Lovely Katherine," she repeated, her voice ending in a squeak. Then she and Sonny doubled over in hysterical laughter. Even Momma was trying hard not to smile.

For a while, Lizzie and Sonny called me "Lovely Katherine" instead of "Spook Baby." I tried not to cry, but I couldn't help it. It was mean of them. I knew that no one thought I was lovely. Momma was lovely. Lizzie was lovely. Even prissy Patty Jean was lovely. I was a Munchkin.

I was, as it turned out, the only Munchkin. I did my best. I sang "Follow the Yellow Brick Road" through my nose as loud as I could, hoping that Susan or Margaret (I'd given up on Lizzie) would take note of my superior acting ability and promote me to a better role. It didn't work. Not only did I not get a promotion, I didn't even get a solo. After a few bars, the older girls decided that it was stupid to have just one Munchkin singing. I would *be* the Munchkin, but everyone would have to help with singing "Follow the Yellow Brick Road."

So they all sang with me, but when Patty Jean, with her stuffed bear that played Toto, and Susan and Margaret and Billy left Munchkinland, my career as Munchkin was over.

"What am I supposed to do now?" I asked, ever hopeful.

"Sit down and be the audience," said Margaret. I looked to Lizzie, but she had forgotten me. She was having a wonderful time. She was the Wicked Witch. She even had a costume. She'd tied Momma's purple shawl around her shoulders like a cape. There were no trees in the middle of the quadrangle to hide behind, but Lizzie didn't need trees. She huddled on the ground, completely hidden by her witch cape. She lay still for a long time, waiting until the others were in the middle of a song or deep in conversation about the wonders of Oz and then *POOF!* she leaped right into their path, cackling away. Everyone would jump and scream each time as though it had never happened before.

That gave me an idea. Wouldn't it be great—just when the four friends plus stuffed bear were most downhearted—wouldn't it be great to have a friendly Munchkin poof into the action? Surely the magical appearance of a Munchkin would cheer them up and send them on down the yellow brick road with renewed courage.

"Don't forget!" I cried, bursting into a nasal song. "You're off to see the wizard—the wonderful—" The Scarecrow, Lion, and Tin Man dragged me out of their path back to the audience spot (I was also the entire audience) and sat me down. Lizzie just stood there and watched without saying a word. I could see the smirk on Patty Jean's face, which proved how unworthy she was to play Dorothy. Judy Garland would never smirk at a humiliated Munchkin.

I didn't cry. Only babies cried, and babies weren't allowed to play with the big kids. If I dared cry, I would be sent to play with the little ones.

I can't remember how many weeks our chief entertainment was *The Wizard of Oz*, but eventually Lizzie and the others tired of it. Besides, the big boys of our families had started a new game.

During the day, workmen were digging a trench across the wide green quadrangle to install new pipes. When we left the school dining room after supper, it was not quite dusk. Sonny and some of his friends invented a game called "Snake in the Gutter." One of the twelve-year-olds, the bigger the better, would be the snake. Everyone else would have to jump across the ditch while the snake ran up and down trying to grab you. If the snake touched you, you were dead.

I had thought anything would be better than being a Munchkin, but I was wrong. At least there was music and imagination and longing in that game. In Snake in the Gutter, there was only twilight terror and certain death. Patty Jean's mother took one look and refused to let her darling play. I sneered at that. The ditch was only two feet deep and about that wide. And it wasn't really dark. But without Patty Jean in the game, I was the youngest, the slowest player. Every night, I was always the first to be caught and killed.

One day that spring, Lizzie and I came back to our dorm room after school to find a lady we didn't know visiting with Momma. There was no room for chairs, of course, so the women were each sitting on the edge of a bed. As usual, Momma had the two little ones falling off her lap onto the bed beside her. She introduced Lizzie and me to her visitor as her two older daughters. I hardly had time to be proud that I was one of the older ones when the woman started looking us up and down as though she was shopping for a piece of furniture.

Finally, she smiled at Lizzie. "Isn't she lovely," she said. "What charming freckles." Then she turned and stared at me again. "Now, Mary," she said, "you can't tell me this one belongs to you. She doesn't look a bit like the rest of the family." She laughed as though she had said something funny. "Where on earth did you pick up this little stranger?"

My mother was sputtering in protest. She reached out and put an arm around me, but it didn't help. I had heard the visitor's pronouncement, not my mother's denial. So that was it. My parents had adopted me, but my mother was too kind to tell me that I wasn't really theirs. It seemed to explain everything—why my mother hardly had time even to brush my hair, why Lizzie wouldn't take up for me in front of the others, why I wasn't beautiful like my mother or clever like my father . . .

That night, after the snake bit me, I just started to walk away. It wasn't worth the fight. I wasn't thinking about what lay in the gathering darkness outside the walls of the school—war, crime, beggar children with their dirty hands stretched out—that was all forgotten. I was leaving.

I got to the edge of the quadrangle, nearly to the gate, when suddenly I realized that Lizzie had left the game and was chasing after me. When she caught up, she was panting from running so hard.

"Where do you think you're going?" she demanded, holding her side while she tried to catch her breath.

"I'm running away," I said. I felt perfectly calm. I hadn't considered for a moment that when you run away, you need some place to run to. I was just walking out.

"What do you mean, 'running away'?" She grabbed my arm. She was clearly angry. "It's nearly dark out there."

"I know," I said, shaking off her hand. "I don't care." I started walking again.

"Don't be stupid," she said.

"I'm not stupid," I said calmly. "But it's no use staying here. Nobody likes me, and I know I'm adopted, but Momma's too nice to tell me."

Lizzie really grabbed me now. She whirled me

around, and although it was nearly night, I could see fire in her eyes. "You can't run away. I won't let you. And if you even try, I will never speak to you again as long as you live."

Since that night, many people have told me that they loved me, but perhaps never quite so effectively. I thought about running away off and on for several years after that, but I would immediately discard the notion. After all, I couldn't run away. Lizzie wouldn't let me. It was a very comforting thought.

Notes from
KATHERINE PATERSON

"When I tried to think of a story to tell for this collection, I was nearly stumped. I could remember plenty of anecdotes from my past, but a real story with a beginning, middle, and end seemed hard to come by. The story I have told seemed closest to having a plot, but there was a problem: It was as much my older sister's story as my own—what if she hated it?

With fear and trembling, I sent Elizabeth

(we now call her Liz, not Lizzie) a copy of what I'd written. She wrote me back a postcard. 'Not to worry,' she said. 'I liked it.' Whew! But if you've read the story, you already know what a great person Lizzie is and aren't the least bit surprised that she's still helping her little sister through frightening situations.

Although I loved to read and often fantasized about growing up to be powerful and famous, it never occurred to me as a child that someday I would be a writer. In the sixth grade I did achieve a measure of fame as a dramatist. I wrote plays that my friends and I practiced during recess and were occasionally allowed to act out for the class. Creative writing wasn't a part of 'real schoolwork' in those days. Writing meant penmanship—dipping your pen into the inkwell and inscribing loops and slants on the page. Since I nearly always dropped a large blob of indelible ink on the paper, my grades in writing tended to be poor.

It wasn't until I was in college that my professors suggested that I might have some writing talent. I didn't take the idea seriously until after I was married and had the first of our four children."

Walter Dean Myers

REVEREND ABBOTT AND THOSE BLOODSHOT EYES

WALTER DEAN MYERS

When I was a kid in the late forties, I thought the whole world was like Harlem, full of life and colors and music that spilled out onto the streets for all the people to enjoy. Life was a constant adventure, although some moments were a lot more adventuresome than others. Take, for example, the fight between the kids on our block and Reverend Abbott, our visiting minister. We didn't have anything against Reverend Abbott because he was white, and I don't think he had anything against us because we weren't. In fact, he was probably a good man, and I'm sure he didn't deserve to have so much trouble during his first summer serving the Lord.

Reverend Robinson, our regular minister, was away for the summer trying to raise money for the church's upstate camp, Rabbit Hollow. That left Reverend Abbott just about in charge, or at least he thought he was.

Actually, if Reverend Abbott hadn't tried so hard to help us, things might have been different. Take the time he tried to protect us from Sugar Ray Robinson, the greatest fighter in the world. We used to play a game called Skullies. You drew numbered boxes in the middle of the street and you shot bottle caps or checkers from one number to the other until you became a "killer," and then you knocked out all the other bottle caps. One day, about four of us were really involved in a game of Skullies and didn't notice the long, almost pink Cadillac cruising down the street. The driver of the Caddy was Sugar Ray Robinson, welterweight champion of the world. In those days, a lot of athletes either lived in or hung out in Harlem. Sugar Ray would often come around and play with the kids, the same way that Willie Mays, the baseball all-star, did when he came to New York.

OK, so Sugar Ray yelled at us, asking why we were blocking his car. Then he got out and challenged us to a fight. Now, we knew that Sugar Ray Robinson was the welterweight champion and would not hurt any of us, but Reverend Abbott didn't know anything of the sort. All he saw was a man getting out of his car and challenging the kids. He came out yelling at Sugar Ray and telling him that he had better get back into his car.

Sugar Ray took one look at the tall, thin man in front of him, shook his head, and got back into his Caddy.

We tried to explain to Reverend Abbott that you didn't jump up into the face of Sugar Ray, but he didn't seem to get it. He just kept insisting that fighting was wrong and that we should learn to turn the other cheek. It was clear to us that the good reverend was trying to mess things up for us.

Being a kid in Harlem wasn't the easiest way to live. We didn't have much of a crime problem in those days, but we did have to worry about the Window Watchers and the Root Ladies. We certainly didn't need anybody else to look out for.

The Window Watchers were the biggest pain because there were more of them. They were the women who used to bring their pillows to the windows and watch what was happening on the block. Sometimes they would talk to each other from the windows, or order up collard greens from the vegetable man who brought his truck around in the afternoons. But mostly, they would watch what was going on and report to your mother if you did anything they considered wrong.

I remember one time Johnny Lightbourne threw a candy wrapper on the sidewalk in front of the church. A Window Watcher spotted him from the fourth floor and called down to another Watcher on the first floor. Johnny's mother knew about it before he got home.

This was bad, but the Root Ladies were worse. The thing was, you didn't mess with Root Ladies. Not that you actually believed that they could do anything with their roots and candles and mumbo jumbo, but there was no use taking chances. When you went over to La Marketa, you saw them sitting with rows of colored candles and twisted little roots that Fat Butch said looked like dried-up shrunken people, and you saw that they looked a little strange, and you crossed the street. No big deal—unless somebody threw a snowball at one of them and they looked at you with the evil eye. All you had to do if a Root Lady gave you the evil eye was to hold up a mirror and shine it back at her. You had to know how to protect yourself when you were a kid. In a cigar box in my closet, I kept a small mirror for Root Ladies, a crucifix for vampires, and a ground-up peach pit to throw on dogs with purple tongues.

You also had to know some of the rules. You didn't play handball against a Root Lady's house, walk in her shadow, or bring a broom near her. If you followed the rules, you didn't have to worry—even if she could make her eyes glow and send them out at night to get you just when you were about ready to fall asleep.

What the Watchers and the Root Ladies did like was that all of the kids in the neighborhood went to church. In fact, most of our lives were centered around the church. I started Sunday school at about four and received my first book, *Stories for Every Day of the Year*, as a prize in the Tots Parade when I was five. In the summers, we went to Bible school, which was more like a summer camp than a religious school. Every kid in the neighborhood had made a wallet in Bible school.

We also learned to play basketball in the church gym. The ceiling in the gym was low and you could tell who played ball in our church because they had flat jump shots. The church also had dances for teenagers, and that really seemed to upset Reverend Abbott.

The dances had chaperones who carried fans advertising local funeral parlors. The chaperones would go through the crowd and put the fans between the couples dancing and tell them to "make room for the Holy Ghost."

When Reverend Abbott saw his first dance and the thirteen-and-up crowd doing their thing, he was upset. There was no room for such goings-on in the Presbyterian church. So he made an announcement that there would be no more dances while he was in charge. What he wanted to do was to substitute relay races and Bible quizzes for the dances. We didn't have MTV in those days, or video game arcades, and the dances were about our only social event. Somebody suggested a compromise: We would have relay races and square dancing. Reverend Abbott was pleased.

The next Friday was the first square dance. The

chaperones stayed on the small stage and looked on approvingly. Then Reverend Abbott went to his study, and somebody put on a mambo record. It was hard to tell exactly who had put on the mambo record because it went on a second after the lights went out. The chaperones, mostly mothers and big sisters, immediately started for the light switches. They weren't that upset. But when Reverend Abbott opened the door and saw a host of healthy young bodies swinging to a frantic Latin beat in the eerie dimness of the red emergency lights, he was beside himself. The names of all the teenagers present were taken and their parents were notified the next morning by a committee of church ladies.

OK, so Reverend Abbott wanted a fight. We decided to give him one.

We had had young ministers like Reverend Abbott before. They would work for a few months in the church, then go on to another area or, if they were lucky, to their own church. We found out that Reverend Abbott was scheduled to give his first sermon on the second Sunday after breaking up our dance.

We also found out that there was going to be an important funeral in the church later that same day. Sam Johnson, the numbers man and Bar-B-Que King of Eighth Avenue, had died. Mr. Johnson was famous for his girth, his gold tooth, his promptness in paying off when you hit the number, and his barbecue sauce.

It was rumored that his funeral would be attended by every big-time gangster in Harlem. There would even be, the story went, some Italian gangsters from East Harlem coming over.

So Reverend Abbott was going to have not one but two chances to show his stuff: He would give the morning sermon at 9:30 and then conduct the funeral at 12:00. He wanted to get them both right. Several sisters said that whenever they passed the minister's study, he was either sweating over his message or down on his knees, praying. It was to be his big day.

It was going to be our big day too.

The kids were divided into two groups—the "littles," of which I was one, and the teenagers. It was the teenagers who came up with the plan to undermine Reverend Abbott. But the littles were part of the plot.

Sunday school started in our church at 8:00 and was over at 8:45. At 9:15, the recorded caroling bells would start, calling all the worshipers to Sunday morning service.

At 9:00, Reverend Abbott was in his study, making last-minute changes in his sermon. Girls with ribbons on their braids and Vaseline rubbed into their faces and knees were out in front of the church. Some of the boys were planning to go to the West End Theater, which was showing three features and a serial. But some of the littles knew what was going to happen, and one of them had already sneaked upstairs and found out that it was Mrs. Davis who was going to put on the record that would summon everyone to church. Her favorite hymn was "What a Friend We Have in Jesus," and its version of recorded bells sounded very nice. The little who discovered Mrs. Davis in the sound room went out and relayed the message to the big kids.

At three minutes to nine, the telephone on the first floor rang. There was a breathless voice on the wire: an urgent message for Mrs. Davis. Mrs. Davis was a pillar of the church. A tall woman with broad shoulders, a wide, dark face, and eyes that turned up ever so slightly, she had been one of its earliest members. Now she was being called downstairs with the word *emergency* ringing in her ears.

Emergencies in those days did not mean that your cat was in a tree or your car had a flat. An emergency in Harlem meant one of two things, either a death in the family or a fire.

Mrs. Davis rushed from the sound room, grasping the railings heavily as she made her way down the stairs toward the first floor telephone. The sound of her feet on the steps could be heard all the way down the hall.

Much to her surprise, there was no one on the phone when she answered it.

The sneakers on the teenager who ran into the sound

room could hardly be heard. The record on the player was removed and another put in its place. The volume was turned up slightly. The door was closed and a padlock was put in place—not, mind you, the same padlock that was usually there and for which Mrs. Davis still held the key in her hands.

Then the teenager disappeared on his sneakered feet, down the stairs and out the side door onto 122nd Street.

The record could be heard all over the neighborhood.

"OOOOOO-EE! DON'T ROLL YOUR BLOOD-SHOT EYES AT ME!"

Heads turned, mouths dropped opened, eyes widened. People couldn't believe what they were hearing!

The lyrics were less than elegant. The song, about a man who had been out all night carousing and whose eyes are bloodshot in the morning, wasn't that original. But coming from the church sound system, amplified for the glory of God and the amusement of the entire neighborhood, it would long be remembered.

Reverend Abbott himself flew up the stairs, two at a time, sweat popping off his brow, only to find the heavy door hopelessly locked.

Mrs. Davis followed to find him banging on the padlock with his fist. She took a look, saw the padlock had been changed, and turned and rushed back down the stairs in search of the church janitor.

The record played over and over until the janitor was located and the lock broken. By the time the record was removed and the proper one put on in its place, the entire church was in an uproar. Some people were upset, and others suppressed smiles. We littles went into the back alley and told each other what records we would have put on if we had had the chance. We also stuck our fingers with a pin and swore in blood that we wouldn't tell who had done it, even though only a few of us knew which teenager had actually been in the sound room.

Reverend Abbott started his sermon by talking about how some people didn't realize how lucky they were to have a nice church like ours. Then he tried to get into his regular sermon, which was about all the work that Noah put in when he built the ark and why we should all work for God. But he was so nervous that he forgot most of it.

The funeral went a lot better. Because Fat Butch's mama was Sam Johnson's goddaughter, he had to go to the funeral with her. He said that Reverend Abbott went on about how it wasn't always easy to tell a good man from a bad man and how we shouldn't judge people without seeing their true hearts. All the gangsters at the funeral liked this a lot and one even cried.

The next Sunday, Reverend Abbott put two teenagers in charge of making sure the right record was on, which stopped all the hopes of the littles that "Open the Door, Richard" would call the faithful to church.

On Reverend Abbott's last Sunday, he thanked the congregation and said that he thought he was ready to face any challenge that God might put before him. He was probably right.

Notes from

WALTER DEAN MYERS

"When I was a child, I was too busy working at childhood to notice if I was having a good time of it or not. In thinking back, it seems as if I must have enjoyed myself most of the time. Judging from what was important to me — Stoop Ball, Kick-the-Can, Scullies, and other games — it's clear that I wasn't worried that my family was poor, which we were, or about neighborhood violence.

As a young boy, I belonged to the Presbyterian church on the corner of my block, and the church and its teachings belonged to me as well. The church was just an extension of our homes, or so it seemed. We drew our values, and our strengths, from that community and that church. It told us that life was good, and so were we. I'd like to recapture that feeling for young people today.

The church has traditionally played an important part in the lives of African Americans, both for regular churchgoers and for the community at large. Many activities — religious, social, and at some times, political — had their beginnings and often their focal point in the church. Our leadership came most often from the pulpit as well. Consider Martin Luther King, Jr., or Malcolm X, or Adam Clayton Powell—all ministers, all leaders.

My grandfather was a great storyteller. He could bring his stories, almost all taken from the Old Testament, to life in a way that would make me tremble. My stepfather used to tell stories too. His were usually scary stories, and sometimes funny. Like my stepdad and my grandfather, I tell stories too, only I write mine down."

Susan Cooper

MUFFIN

SUSAN COOPER

When a war has been going on for more than a third of
your life, you feel it's always been there. It seemed normal, to the children of Cippenham Primary School, that
there were air-raid shelters on the school playground,
long, windowless concrete buildings half sunk into the
ground, and that they should all sit inside, singing songs
or reciting multiplication tables, whenever the bombers
came rumbling their deadly way overhead. It seemed
normal that every signpost in the country should have
been removed; normal that the streets were fringed with
huge concrete barriers called "tank traps," to make life
difficult for the invading enemy if the Germans should
ever manage to cross the English Channel.

Daisy and her friends took all this for granted, like
the fact that they'd never seen a fountain or a steak or
a banana. They didn't recognize that they were living
through World War II; it was just "the war." It was part
of life.

Fat Alice was part of life too, unfortunately. She was the boss of the school playground: a big, pasty-faced girl with short straight hair and an incongruously shrill voice. A group of hangers-on drifted in her wake, notably Pat and Maggie, two wispy, wiry girls who hovered about her like pilot fish escorting a shark. As prey for her little gang, Fat Alice chose a particular victim at the beginning of each term. This term she had chosen Daisy.

It was a Monday morning in a blossoming spring, but Alice, Pat, and Maggie were not paying attention to the daffodils. The three of them had Daisy cornered against the fence just inside the playground gate. It was a rough wooden fence, put up to replace the elegant old wrought-iron railings that had been taken away for the War Effort, to be melted down and used for guns, or ammunition, or bombs. A splinter drove deep into Daisy's arm, where it was pushed against the wood by Maggie's mean little fingers.

"Ow!" said Daisy. "Ow-ow-ow!"

"Shut up," said Fat Alice, in her high, whiny voice. "Walk along the line like I said, and don't step off it or you'll get punished."

Fear was making Daisy breathe fast. She felt sick. She teetered along the chalk line they had drawn on the ground, and because of her fear she lost her balance, and lurched to one side. Shrieking with delight, the other three fell on her, pulling her blonde braids, shoving her to the ground so that Fat Alice could grab her hand and scrape the back of it over the gravel-studded asphalt. This was Alice's favorite torture; she had learned it from her brother, who ruled the boys' end of the playground.

Daisy squealed. Her hand was bleeding. She aimed a furious kick at Fat Alice's bulging leg as her three tormentors scattered, and the kick was seen by Mrs. Walker, one of the "dinner ladies" who not only served meals but also kept watch during recess, to prevent the children of Cippenham Primary School from murdering each other. "Daisy Morgan!" screeched Mrs. Walker. "I seen that! No kicking! I'll tell your teacher!"

But a dog was barking fiercely on the other side of the fence, a little gray terrier with sharp-pricked ears and tail, and beside him stood the old lady who lived in the house next to the school. Daisy didn't know her name. She was standing very upright, wearing a shapeless brown cardigan and skirt, and she was shaking her stick at Mrs. Walker.

"It wasn't the girl's fault!" she called, in a clear, authoritative voice. "She was defending herself! I saw the others attacking her!"

The bell rang, and Daisy fled for school. Mrs. Walker sniffed suspiciously as she passed, but she didn't report her.

At dinnertime, Daisy slid a piece of meat from her

plate into her handkerchief, even though it was—for once—good-tasting meat instead of rubbery gristle, and she hid it in her pocket. On the way home after school, she paused by the fence.

The old lady and her dog were standing on their doorstep like sentries, watching the shouting hundreds of children flood untidily by. Daisy called out, "Please may I give him a piece of meat?"

"I'm sure he'd be delighted," the old lady said in her strong clear voice. "Muffin! Show your manners!"

Muffin barked, twice, deliberately, before bolting the limp gray square that Daisy tossed to him. Beaming, Daisy waved, and ran home.

"Alice Smith did it," she said, sitting at the kitchen table, wincing as her mother dabbed antiseptic on her scraped hand. "Alice Smith is a *Nazi!*"

Daisy's mother spent most of her time worrying about Daisy's father, who was in a destroyer somewhere in the North Atlantic, chasing enemy submarines. She said softly, "I don't think so, darling. Not quite."

But Alice and Pat and Maggie were on the attack again next day at recess, chasing Daisy into a corner and lashing at her bare legs with thin whippy branches torn from the old lady's front hedge. Daisy heard Muffin barking indignantly at them and knew that the old lady was watching, but she was running too fast to be able to ask for help. Instead she took the perilous step of complaining to her teacher about her persecution. Her teacher spoke reproachfully to Fat Alice for thirty seconds, and Fat Alice sat next to Daisy in the shelter during the next air-raid practice and pinched her silently and viciously for half an hour.

Daisy's arm was black and blue. She felt desperate. There was no escape. All her life she was going to be made miserable by the Alice gang, and nothing she did could make the slightest difference. After school that day, on a wild impulse, she ran down the sidewalk and in through the old lady's front gate. Beside the front door, a forsythia bush was blooming like a great yellow cloud.

Daisy knocked at the door. "Please," she said when it opened, "please—" and to her horror she burst into tears.

"Oh dear," said the old lady. "This won't do. Come in and have a cup of tea with Muffin and me."

It was a house filled with framed old-fashioned photographs and hundreds of small ornaments; it felt friendly. Muffin lay with his chin across Daisy's feet. Over a cup of comforting weak tea with milk and sugar, and two digestive biscuits, Daisy asked the old lady if she would mind speaking to her teacher, to describe what she had seen Fat Alice do. If a grown-up gave witness, perhaps there was a chance the tormenting might stop.

"Of course I will!" the old lady said briskly. "Bullies must always be stopped, by any means possible. That's what this war is all about. I shall speak to your teacher tomorrow."

But before the morning came, the village of Cippenham was given a very noisy night. Daisy was woken in the darkness, as so often before, by the chilling up-and-down wail of the air-raid siren, agitating the night from a loudspeaker on the roof of the local police station. She pulled on her raincoat over her pajamas, slung her gas-mask case over her shoulder, and followed her mother and her sleepy four-year-old brother Mike out to their air-raid shelter, the little turf-roofed, metal-walled cave sunk into the back lawn. The night was cold, and the bright beams of searchlights groped to and fro over the dark sky. There was already a faint rumble of aircraft engines in the air.

"Quickly, darlings!" Her mother hurried them to the shelter door, behind its barricade of sandbags. It was hard to see anything; flashlights were forbidden in the blacked-out nights of wartime England, where the windows of every house were covered closely by black curtains, or by strips of sticky brown tape that would also keep glass from scattering if the windows were blown in by blast.

Daisy could hear shells bursting in the sky, fired from the long guns of the anti-aircraft post at the end of the street. Then the bombs began falling, with their unmistakable dull *crump* sound, vibrating through the earth.

She had never been much afraid of the bombs, not with the intense personal terror she felt when Fat Alice and her friends jumped out at her. But this time, the bombs sounded closer than ever before—a sequence of huge crashes, louder and louder, shaking the shelter so that the single lighted candle jumped and flickered on the earthen floor. Daisy buried her head in her mother's lap.

It was a long night, before the single steady note of the all clear sang out through the sky, and they could go back to bed.

When Daisy set out from home next morning, she found a crowd of excited children milling in the road near her school, and behind them a fluttering orange tape strung as a temporary barrier across the road. Behind the tape was a huge hole. Broken pipes jutted from the clay-brown soil; the earth had been sliced as if it were a cake.

"What is it?" Daisy said to the nearest familiar face.

"It's a bomb crater, stupid! Jeff found three super bits of shrapnel!"

"A whole stick of bombs fell last night." This was a chunky, confident boy called Fred, who always came top of Daisy's class. "Our two were the first, that's why they're closer together."

"Our two?" Daisy said.

"The other one's right by the playground. Just our luck it didn't hit school."

"Jerry can't shoot straight!"

"Look, there's all the teachers! They're sending everyone home!"

Daisy wasn't listening. She was edging along what was left of the sidewalk, past the crater, past houses whose windows were blank and empty, their glass all blown in by the bomb. Assorted grown-ups frowned at her and called her back, but not before she had reached the playground gate—splintered now, and hanging from one hinge. She saw the playground littered with bricks and broken glass and strange pieces of metal. And beside it, she saw an unfamiliar gap. The old lady's house was no longer there.

Daisy rushed forward, into the playground, ignoring the shouts behind her, until she stood at the edge of the ruin where the house had been. It was a mass of rubble, of broken brick and splintered beams; she saw a piece of carpet jutting from underneath a pile of roofing tiles. There was a strong smell of dust.

A hand took hold of her shoulder; it was the elderly policeman who watched the road crossing before and after school.

"Come on, love. You can't come here—it's dangerous."

"The old lady," Daisy said urgently. She looked up at him. "The old lady?"

"Did you know her?" said the policeman.

"Sort of," Daisy said.

The policeman hesitated, then sighed. "She was killed by the bomb. Direct hit. She can't have known a thing about it."

Daisy stared at him, stunned. Yesterday the old lady had given her tea and digestive biscuits. Today she didn't exist. It wasn't possible.

The policeman said again, gently, "Come on."

As Daisy turned to go with him, a movement in the ruins of the house caught her eye. She paused, peering, and saw Muffin, cowering behind a heap of rubble. He seemed to be unhurt, but he was coated with dust and dirt, and he was shivering—shaking all over, violently, as if he were terribly cold.

"Muffin! Here, boy! Muffin!" She tried to get his attention, but he wouldn't look at her. She wondered if he could hear.

"It's the bomb," the policeman said. "That her dog, is it? England's full of dogs and cats like that, these days. Lost their people. Shell-shocked, like. Come on then, boy!" He moved toward the dog, hand outstretched, but Muffin turned away abruptly and fled.

"We'll keep an eye out for him," the policeman said.

Before she went home, Daisy stopped at the tiny general store opposite the school. Its windows had all been blown in, but it was still open; indeed there was a cheerful notice lettered on the plywood which had already been nailed over the windowframe, reading:

MORE OPEN THAN USUAL. With some pennies she found in her pocket, Daisy bought a bun, and when nobody was looking she threw it into the ruins of the old lady's house. Muffin would be back, and he would be hungry.

And Muffin did come back. Before long, the playground was cleared of rubble, the road was repaired, the remains of the old lady's house were flattened, and school began again. And the children began to notice Muffin, sometimes, lying on the ground where his house had been. He was thin and dirty, and his ears and tail were no longer as perky as they had been before. Some of the children tried to call him, or catch him, but he always ran away.

Only once, when Daisy was alone and called, "Muffin! Muffin! Show your manners!"—then Muffin came trotting to her and licked her hand, and let her pat him. But even then he leaped away when she tried to take hold of his collar. There was no sign of him afterward, for days.

Fat Alice had been distracted from her usual pursuits by the excitement of the bomb craters, and the prestigious bits of shrapnel that could be collected, or taken away from the collections of smaller, weaker boys or girls. She had not forgotten Daisy, however. She began now a quiet campaign of small intermittent cruelties, with no reason or pattern. At unexpected times of the day, in classroom or playground or corridor, she would appear suddenly at Daisy's side and give her a quick fierce kick or pinch, vanishing afterward with a speed remarkable in one so large. Daisy began to feel constantly nervous, like a hunted animal.

Sometimes she felt angry with herself for doing nothing to combat the maliciousness of Alice Smith. But what was there to do? She was outsized and outnumbered, and the little gang of bullies took care never to do anything that might catch the attention of a teacher. Now that Daisy had lost the old lady, the only grown-up she could enlist as saviour was her mother. But that had been tried last term, by Molly Barnes, a placid, amiable girl even fatter than Alice, who was the butt of the gang for so long that she seemed to be constantly in tears. Molly's mother had come to school to complain—and close on her heels had come Alice's mother, a tough, aggressive lady who was heard, through the headmaster's closed door, angrily shouting a number of words Daisy had never heard uttered before.

So the headmaster had not known which mother to believe, and the reign of Fat Alice had gone on undisturbed. And Daisy said nothing that would bring her own mother to the school, because she knew the result would be just the same.

It was a Friday, four weeks after the bombs fell, when Alice did the worst thing of all. Daisy liked Fridays, not only because they marked the end of the week, but because the last class of the day was art. She loved drawing and painting, more than anything. Even though, in their overcrowded school, her class had to double up with Alice's class for art—giving Alice easy opportunities for poking Daisy with one end of a paintbrush, or dabbing paint on her skirt with the other—even so, it was Daisy's favorite class.

And this Friday was even better than most. Their teacher said, "Think of the best story you've ever heard from your mother or father, and paint me a picture of it."

Daisy thought of the last time her father had come home on leave, after he had been sailing to the north coast of Russia on what he called "the Murmansk run," and she painted what he had described. She painted his destroyer, as she often did at home, but she showed it encrusted all over with ice, with men muffled up in heavy jackets and gloves chipping the ice away from spars and guns and rails. She painted the gray angry sea and the big waves, and a patchy blue sky, and a huge, white jagged iceberg rearing up in the background. She particularly liked the iceberg.

"That's wonderful, Daisy!" said her teacher, and she held it up in front of the class. She said Daisy should take the picture home to show her mother, and then bring it back next week to be shown to the whole school in morning assembly.

Daisy set off cheerfully for home, in the noisy

bouncing crowd pouring out of the playground. But a figure came running and pushed her sideways, and then another, and she found herself nudged and shoved out of sight of everyone else, behind the air-raid shelters. Alice, Pat, and Maggie closed around her, bright-eyed, grinning.

"She did *ever* such a nice painting!" said Alice, shrill, jeering. "She's so stuck-up, she thinks she's the cat's meow — here, I'll show you her *lovely* painting!"

She grabbed the rolled-up paper from under Daisy's arm.

"Give it back!" Daisy yelled. But Pat and Maggie were holding her arms, and she couldn't get free. She struggled, feeling her eyes blur with angry tears, and she saw Fat Alice unroll her beautiful painting and drop it deliberately face-down into a muddy puddle. Then Alice lifted her foot and trod on it.

Daisy let out a great sob, and kicked at Alice. She felt her shoe hit Alice's shinbone, hard.

Fat Alice shrieked with pain. Her face twisted with fury and venom, and she advanced on Daisy. "Just you wait!" she hissed.

But behind her, there was a sudden astounding noise, halfway between a roar and a shriek, and out of the wasteland that had been the old lady's house, Muffin came rushing. He looked very small, and very dangerous. He flung himself at Fat Alice, growling and snapping; then whirled at Pat and at Maggie, nipping their ankles, jumping up at them, teeth bared. A small dog had become a small tornado, a whirling flurry of danger and menace. The three girls screamed and backed away, but Muffin came after them, snarling, biting, until they scattered and ran.

"Mad dog!" Alice howled. "Mad dog . . ." Her voice faded as she disappeared down the road.

Muffin came back to Daisy. He looked up at her, panting, his tongue lolling, and she crouched beside him and fondled his small dirty head. Muffin licked her face.

"Let's go home, Muffin," Daisy said.

Muffin barked, deliberately, twice.

Daisy picked her painting out of the puddle. It was a blurred, muddy, unrecognizable mess. She crumpled it up and dropped it again, and she turned and ran out of the playground, through the streets, home. Muffin ran at her heels.

Bursting through the kitchen door, breathless, Daisy found her mother peeling potatoes. "Mum," she said, grasping for the words she had been rehearsing as she ran. "Mum, I have a friend, he's been bombed out, please can he stay?"

Daisy's mother looked down at Muffin.

"Dad says every ship should have a mascot," Daisy said.

Her mother smiled. She said, "You just have time to give him a bath before tea."

Notes from
SUSAN COOPER

"My story 'Muffin' is set in England during World War II, because that's where I was when I was your age. I once put all that part of my life into a book called *Dawn of Fear*, a war story which is pure autobiography except that I turned myself into a boy called Derek. Don't ask me why.

The main character in 'Muffin,' Daisy, is not me, but she goes to the same school as Derek/Susan, and the bombs that she hears fall are the same ones Derek hears in *Dawn of Fear*. I found myself wondering the other day whether Derek ever met Muffin. It's sometimes hard for writers to remember where real life ends and story begins.

I began life as a passionate reader and pretty soon realized I was a writer as well. When I edited my school magazine, I found it was much easier to write things than to persuade other people to write them, and I still own a rather embarrassing issue in which eleven contributions (and two pictures) are signed by Susan Cooper. I've been scribbling away ever since."

TAKING A DARE

⁄⁄⁄

NICHOLASA MOHR

It all started the day my friend Casilda dared me. All my friends were hanging out in the schoolyard at St. Anselm's. It was around seven o'clock on Saturday evening. Casilda, Wanda, Mary, and little Ritchie had already confessed earlier.

Now we were just watching people leaving church after confessing. The kids began to talk about how confession made you feel different—pure and holy. ". . . so then the next day when you receive Communion," explained Casilda, "you become clean and without no sins." She looked up at the sky all dreamy-eyed, like she had just done something so perfect.

The fact was, all my friends—except for Joey who was Pentecostal—had already made their First Communion. Even little Ritchie, who was only eight, had made his Communion last year in Puerto Rico. I was ten years old and I still had not made my First Communion. Every Saturday, it was the same. Me and Joey had to wait until the rest of them confessed; then we had to hear how they all felt pure and terrific. More and more, I began to feel left out, like I was a stranger instead of their friend.

Here I was again, listening to them sound off. Blah, blah, and blah, bragging like they knew it all. I was really getting annoyed and decided to let them know just how I felt.

"It don't sound like a big deal to me," I told them.

"That's because you don't know what you are missing." Casilda went on boasting, paying me no mind. But I had already heard enough! I was going to show them what I thought of them and their holy selves.

"I think I'm gonna receive Holy Communion and without no confession," I blurted out.

"But you can't!" argued Wanda. "You have to go to confession and tell the priest all the bad things you done. Then the priest gives you prayers to say so that God will forgive your sins."

"That's right," added Mary. "That's called penance. You gotta say penance first to prepare for Holy Communion."

"Or else it's a sin—a big sin—and you could go to hell!" declared Casilda.

I enjoyed looking at their shocked expressions and decided to go even further. "But I don't believe in no confession. Anyway, my father says there ain't no hell and no heaven either. He says heaven and hell are right here on earth. Heaven is for the rich and hell is for the poor."

"That's a bad thing to say," shrieked Mary.

"You better not talk that way," warned Wanda.

"Yeah," agreed little Ritchie, "I think that's a real bad *sin* to say."

I just shrugged at their attempts to stop me. Actually, I was pleased to be getting all their attention.

"All right, since you act like it's no sin and you ain't scared, go on!" shouted Casilda loud and clear. "I dare you to receive Holy Communion tomorrow." I hesitated, but Casilda wouldn't let up. "Well Big Mouth, are you gonna do it or not?"

Everybody became quiet, waiting to see what I would do. So how could I back off? Especially the way Casilda got right into my face. No way was she going to make me look chicken in front of my friends.

"Well?" she shouted, standing with her hands on her hips and her chin pointing my way. "You said you were gonna do it. It's tomorrow or forget about it."

"Tomorrow for sure," I answered, trying to sound unconcerned and confident. "Unless you got a problem, girl, I'll see your face there too." I could hear the *oohs* and *aahs* from the others. But I stood my ground, because tomorrow at ten o'clock Mass, all my friends were coming to see me take Casilda's dare.

· · ·

My mother blamed my attitude about religion and the Catholic Church on my dad. And in more ways than one, she was right. You see, I never went to Catholic school like some of the other Catholic kids. The main reason was because we couldn't afford the fee. I was the youngest of seven children, and the only girl. Money was always scarce in our household. But even if we'd had the funds, my dad would have refused to pay for parochial school. He was an avid socialist and was opposed to organized religion, especially the Catholic Church.

So I was sent instead to catechism. Two afternoons a week I was let out early from public school to attend religious instruction at St. Anselm's Catholic school. But most of the time, I never got there like I was supposed to. Instead, I skipped catechism and played outside until it was time to go home. Or I'd go farther down to Third Avenue where the big stores were, and I'd window-shop.

When I did manage to attend catechism, I hardly paid attention. I found it all very boring. But now as I look back, I can see my dad's influence at work. "Don't be superstitious like your mother," he'd warn me. He told me to question everything the nuns taught me. My dad told me it was the bosses in our dominant society who wanted all workers to be obedient. Then the workers would never fight for justice or their rights. It was the Church's way, and the way of capitalism too, he told me.

When I asked him if he believed in God, he'd snap

back, "There is no God. There is humankind and only the here and now!"

He would never tell me these things in front of my mother. She was quite religious and always had a lit candle in a red glass holder in front of a holy picture of St. Lazarus. My mother often prayed at her small altar for the salvation of my father's soul.

But I wasn't so sure my dad was right. For instance, sometimes I'd sneak into St. Anselm's by myself, especially on the afternoons when I was supposed to be in religious instruction. If I heard or saw a priest, nun, or any grown-up, I would duck down behind one of the pews and remain out of sight.

I loved inhaling the fragrance of melted wax and incense. Sitting and just thinking in the silent, almost empty church had a comforting effect on me. Carefully, without making a sound, I would visit the stations of the cross and all the holy statues. I'd examine the details of each station and the carving of the snake beneath the sacred Virgin's feet. It was at once both mysterious and marvelous.

Occasionally, I tried to feel pious by staring at the faces of the large statues. I hoped to see them blink an eye or move a muscle. I waited for a signal that would prove their power. But they continued to stare blankly into space and never moved an inch. Still, I got to know each one and even developed a fondness for them. I had two favorites: the Sacred Heart of Jesus and the Immaculate Conception. I lit candles to them but never bothered to put a cent in the money box. Most of the time, I had no money. When I did get a few cents, it went to buying candy, which I was not about to give up for anybody or anything.

Whenever I was tempted to make a wish, I thought about my dad and felt like a traitor. I knew I was doing wrong by taking the candle in the first place. But since I didn't make a wish and asked for nothing, I figured it wasn't too terrible a sin.

But tomorrow, according to my friends, I *would* be committing a terrible sin. If my mom knew, she would surely give me a bad punishment. If I was caught, my dad wouldn't defend me either. For sure he'd say I got what was coming to me for playing silly games. No matter which way I figured it, I was risking deep trouble.

Besides, during my solo visits to St. Anselm's, I had bonded with my church. In fact, I figured how I probably knew it better than Casilda, Wanda, Mary, and her cousin Ritchie did! I knew each corner and just about every carving there. Even though I wasn't religious like my friends, I knew that the Communion wafer was supposed to be the body of Christ. Now *that* was a scary thought!

As much as I loved and respected both my parents, it was hard to figure out which one of them was right. I listened to my dad, but I also prayed just like my mom. Usually, I prayed to God. When I wanted something or got scared, I was not above pleading with God. I'd pray with all of my might: God let this happen or God don't let that happen. It seemed I always called on God when I needed help. During those times of need, prayers came naturally to me.

Tonight was no exception. I prayed real hard that something would happen to stop my going through with the dare. I also prayed that if I did go to church tomorrow, none of our neighbors would see me there, especially not nosy Mrs. Melendez. She was always watching out of her front window so she could gossip about everybody on our block. That whole night, I could hardly sleep. My stomach did flip-flops, and I tossed and turned until the sun came up.

I ate my breakfast on Sunday morning, well aware that it was customary to fast from confession until one received Holy Communion. "You gotta have a clean stomach to eat the body of Christ," Wanda had warned. "Maybe you better not eat breakfast."

"I'll eat all I want for breakfast," I had told her. Now, I could hardly chew my cereal or drink my milk.

I was grateful that no one in my family went to early Sunday Mass. My mother always told us she preferred to go on weekdays when there were few people and she could commune better with God. My older brothers never attended Mass, except for Easter Sunday and other high holy days. My aunt Maria went to afternoon Spanish Mass at one o'clock.

My mother gave me her blessing, as she did every Sunday, and sent me off to meet my friends. We were all going to attend ten o'clock Mass as usual.

I tried to act really calm when I saw everyone. I was surprised that even Joey was there. His folks didn't allow him to go inside our church. Joey was taking a chance disobeying them, so I knew he was there to see the action. There was no way I was gonna back out now.

"Are you really gonna do it?" asked Joey.

"Sure," I answered. "Why not!"

"You can still change your mind, you know."

"It's all right if she's chicken," said Casilda with a big phony smile. "It don't matter to me none."

"Look, girl," I snapped back, "I'm going through with it. So it don't matter what you want. I even had me a big breakfast—bacon and eggs." I lied. "And they tasted great. So, be cool . . . fool!"

When we arrived at church, we went right up to the front pew, because everyone except Joey was receiving Communion. I sat still during Mass, not daring to turn around. If anybody saw me, I sure didn't want to see them. Then the time came for Communion. Slowly but surely Casilda turned and stared into my eyes. As she walked up to the altar, she was followed by Wanda, Mary, and Ritchie. At first, I sat there feeling too numb to move. Maybe my friends wouldn't notice and I could stay put. But I knew I had no choice, so I stood and followed behind Ritchie.

I watched carefully and copied whatever Ritchie did. I knelt down at the altar and put my palms together and closed my eyes, as if in deep prayer. But I made sure to peek out of my right eye so I could see the priest. He was getting closer and closer. Then it was my turn, and the priest stood before me and made the sign of the cross. I stuck out my tongue and tasted the wafer, as thin and sticky as a postage stamp. I was amazed that it had no flavor at all. My heart was pounding so hard I couldn't move. But I took a deep breath and managed to open my eyes. Then I got to my feet and followed the others back to our pew.

As I sat down, I felt a sharp poke in my side. It was Casilda. "Now you'll go to hell for sure," she whispered.

"Stop chewing," Wanda warned me. "You're not supposed to chew the sacred body of Jesus, you know. Let it melt in your mouth!"

They both scared me half to death. I sat and silently prayed for mercy while I waited for something terrible to happen to me. But Mass continued and nothing unusual occurred.

Outside, the sun was shining and people stood

around talking to each other. I was glad that no one had stopped me or recognized me. Secretly, I thanked God for my good luck.

Joey was the first one to speak. "Wow!" he shrieked. "You did it, girl. I didn't think you would go through with it but—"

"Yeah!" interrupted Casilda. "But you committed a very big sin."

"For sure," agreed Mary. "And when you make your real Communion, you're gonna have to confess it."

"That's right." Wanda nodded. "And you're gonna have to do a lotta penance. Girl, I wouldn't want to be in your shoes for nothing!"

I felt pretty victorious now and ignored their warnings. After all, I had taken the dare and won.

"It don't bother me none," I smugly answered. "You see I ain't never going to confession. And I ain't never taking Communion again! Never!"

"Then you will just go to hell for absolute sure," said Casilda.

"Remember, my father says there ain't no hell!" I responded.

"But what does your mother think?" asked Casilda. "Tell us that!"

I couldn't answer with the truth, because I knew exactly what my mother thought. She would probably punish me worse than God. "I don't worry about that,"

I lied, then shrugged. "Anyway, I'm entitled to my own opinion, you know. This is a free country!" It was a favorite phrase from my older brother Gilbert.

As we walked along, the argument dwindled and we got to talking about other things. We spoke about school, and the end of the latest serial of the Green Hornet in the movie theaters, and the most recent Batman and Robin comic book.

Soon after, my mother took me to task and made sure I attended religious instruction. And about a year and a half later, I made my First Holy Communion. It was then that I finally owned up to most of my sins. These of course included lighting candles without contributing to the money box and receiving Communion without confession. I expected to be doing penance for at least a year. To my surprise, the priest mildly rebuked me and gave me a reasonable penance.

Afterward, I admitted to myself that it was a great relief to be able to confess and remove those dreaded sins from my conscience. But I never once admitted my relief to Casilda, Wanda, Mary, and little Ritchie, or even Joey. After all was said and done, I had won the dare. My newfound clean conscience remained my secret.

Notes from
NICHOLASA MOHR

"From the moment my mother handed me some scrap paper, a pencil, and a few crayons, I discovered that by making pictures and writing letters I could create my own world . . . like 'magic.' In the small, crowded apartment I shared with my large family, making 'magic' permitted me all the space, freedom, and adventure that my imagination could handle. Drawing and painting were my first loves. Then, I began to write and to paint pictures with words.

When I was asked to write a story for this anthology, I decided to describe an event in my childhood that had tested my religious beliefs and my regard for authority figures. The incident I wrote about forced me to make some important decisions at an early age. Because my parents had such conflicting views about religion and spiritual beliefs, I had to find my own way. Upon reflection, I realized that my rebelliousness had a purpose. By taking my friends' dare, I was able to act independently, without taking either parent's side.

To this day, I continue to have a solid

spiritual belief in a divine order very much like my mother's. I also strongly believe in many of the practical things my father taught me. Like him, I think that people must work hard and respect each other on this planet. Good deeds and faith in the capacity of our fellow human beings are necessary for our survival."

Reeve Lindbergh

FLYING

➤

REEVE LINDBERGH

When I was your age, I was flying. I wasn't flying all the time, of course, and I didn't fly by myself, but there I was, nonetheless, on Saturday afternoons in the 1950s, several thousand feet in the air over the state of Connecticut, which is where I grew up. I sat in the back cockpit of a small airplane and looked down at the forests and the fields and the houses and the roads below me from an intense, vibrating height and hoped that my father, in the front cockpit, would not notice that I had cotton balls stuffed in my ears.

I always flew with my father, who had been a pioneer aviator in the 1920s and '30s. I think that he wanted to share his love for the air and for airplanes with his growing family, the way sports-minded fathers took their children to ball games on Saturdays and taught them to play catch afterward. My father took his children to the airport instead and taught them to fly.

Though he was the pilot on these flights, he did

not own the airplane. It was a sixty-five-horsepower Aeronca, with tandem cockpits, that he rented from a former bomber pilot whose name was Stanley. Stanley managed the airport, including the huge loaf-shaped hangar that served as a garage for repairs and maintenance to the aircraft, and he leased out the group of small planes tethered near the building like a fleet of fishing boats clustered around a pier.

It was Stanley, most often, who stood in front of the airplane and waited for my father to shout "Con-TACT!" from the cockpit window, at which time, Stanley gave the propeller a hefty downward shove that sent it spinning into action and started the plane shaking and shuddering on its way. The job of starting the propeller was simple but perilous. My father had warned us many times about the danger of standing anywhere near a propeller in action. We could list almost as well as he did the limbs that had been severed from the bodies of careless individuals "in a split second" by a propeller's whirling force. Therefore, each time that Stanley started the propeller, I would peer through its blinding whir to catch a glimpse of any pieces of him that might be flying through the air. Each time, I saw only Stanley, whole and smiling, waving us onto the asphalt runway with his cap in his hand and his hair blowing in the wind of our passing—"the propwash" my father called it.

My sister and my three brothers flew on Saturdays too. The older ones were taught to land and take off, to bank and dip, and even to turn the plane over in mid-air, although my second-oldest brother confessed that he hated this—it made him feel so dizzy. The youngest of my three brothers, only a few years older than me, remembers my father instructing him to "lean into the curve" as the plane made a steep sideways dive toward the ground. My brother was already off balance, lean-ing *away* from the curve, and hanging on for dear life. For my sister, our father demonstrated "weightless-ness" by having the plane climb so steeply and then dive so sharply that for a moment she could feel her body straining upward against her seatbelt, trying to fight free, while our father shouted out from the front seat that one of his gloves was actually floating in midair.

"See the glove? See the glove?" He called to her over the engine noise and explained that if this state of weightlessness could continue, everything inside the plane would go up in the air. My sister nodded, not speaking, because, she told me later, everything in her stomach was going up in the air, too, and she did not dare open her mouth.

My oldest brother took to flying immediately and eventually got a pilot's license, though he ended up joining the navy and becoming a "frogman," spend-ing as much time underwater with an aqualung and a wetsuit as he ever had spent in the air. What he secretly yearned to do during the flying years, though, was to jump right out of an airplane altogether, with a parachute. Finally, many years later, he had his chance and told me about it afterward. He stood at the open door of the airplane, with the parachute strapped to his back, wobbling back and forth at first, like a baby bird afraid to leave the nest. Then he jumped, fell about a hundred feet through the air, and only then pulled the cord that caused the chute to blossom around him like a great circular sail. Swaying under it, he floated toward the ground until he landed, fairly hard. I listened with astonishment; my brother's daring thrilled me to the bone.

My father on the other hand, along with most of the early aviators, was not impressed by the growing enthusiasm for parachute-jumping as a sport. Young daredevils like my brother could call it "sky-diving" if they wanted to, but the aviation pioneers referred to it disgustedly as "jumping out of a perfectly good airplane." In their day, a pilot only jumped when he had to: if it was absolutely certain that the airplane was headed for a crash and the parachute was his only hope for survival.

I was considered too young for aerial adventures when I flew, so I did not get dizzy or sick or worry about whether my parachute would open. It was only the noise that gave me trouble. I have never shared other people's enthusiasm for loudness. I don't like sudden sounds that make you jump with alarm, like the noises of fireworks or guns, or endless sounds that pound in your head so hard you can't think about anything else, like the commotion made by jackhammers and the engines of small airplanes. My sister felt exactly the same way. In fact, she was the one who showed me how to stuff cotton balls in my ears, secretly, for takeoff—when the engine noise was loudest—and for as long during the flight as we could get away with it.

Our father frowned upon the cotton balls. If he saw them, he would make us remove them. He claimed that they diminished the experience of flying and were in any case unnecessary: The engine noise was not so terribly loud that one couldn't get used to it; he certainly had done so. But my sister and I agreed that the only reason he and the other early aviators had "gotten used to" the noise of airplane engines close to their ears was that they had been deafened early on. We were not about to let this happen to us!

My mother, who had also flown back in the early days, always told us that she had loved her experience as a glider pilot best, because there was such extraordinary quiet all around her. In the absence of the usual aircraft engine noise, she could hear the songs of birds and sometimes even the trilling of insects, crickets or cicadas, on the grassy hillsides below. She said that because there was no noise, she could actually feel the power of air, the way it could push up under the wings of a glider and keep it afloat—like a boat on water—with the strength of unseen currents. She talked about "columns of air," stretching like massive tree trunks between earth and sky. "Just because you can't see the air doesn't mean there's nothing to it," she said. "Most of the really important things in our lives are invisible, anyway."

When it was my turn to fly with my father, I sat in the back cockpit and enjoyed the view all around me while he, in the front cockpit, flew the plane. I had a duplicate set of controls in back, with rudder pedals, a stick, and instruments, so that if I had been a true student pilot, I could have flown the plane myself, if called upon to do so. But since I was too young to understand or even to reach most of the controls in my cockpit, I just watched them move as if by magic, with no help from me at all, in response to my father's direction and will.

It looked easy. The stick in front of me, exactly like the one in front of my father in the forward cockpit, looked like the gearshift on our car. If it moved backward suddenly (toward me), it meant that my father had decided we were going up. There would be a rushing in my ears, in spite of the cotton, and as I looked over my father's head, through the front window of the aircraft, I would imagine that we were forcing our way right into heaven, higher and higher through ever more brilliantly white banks of cloud. I sometimes daydreamed of bumping into angels, assembled on one of these cloud banks with their halos and their harps, or startling St. Peter at the pearly gates, or God himself in his sanctuary.

But then, as I watched, my stick would point forward again, toward what I could see, over the front pilot seat, of the back of my father's neck, with its trim fringe of gray hair and a khaki shirt collar. Then the airplane would nose down, giving a cockeyed view on all sides of blue sky and wooded hillsides and little tiny roads with buglike cars creeping along them, so very slowly. When we were flying, I was struck always by the insignificance of the world we had left behind. Nothing on the ground had speed, compared to us. Nothing looked real. Once I had climbed into the airplane, all of life seemed concentrated inside the loud space of it, shaking but steady, with my father's own hand on the controls. We were completely self-sufficient, completely safe, rock-solid in the center of the sky.

It was also a bit monotonous. My father did the same things and said the same things, loudly, over and over. I knew by heart that a pilot had to fly with a steady hand, with no sudden or jerky movements, just a little throttle here, a little wing dip there, always a light, even touch, always a calm approach. I knew all the stories about student pilots—those not already dismembered by propellers—who "froze" to the stick in a panic and could not let go, forcing the plane into a tragic nose-dive. There was no room in my father's lessons with me, his youngest and least experienced child, for soaring like the birds—no wind in the hair, no swooping and circling. We just droned along, my father and me.

And then, one Saturday afternoon, we didn't. I don't remember now exactly what made me understand there was something wrong with the airplane. I think there may have been a jerking sensation that repeated itself over and over. And I think too that there was a huge stillness in the air, a silence so enormous that it took me a moment to realize that it was actually the opposite of noise and not noise itself. The silence was there because the engine had stalled. Perhaps the most profound moment of silence occurred when my father realized that it was not going to start again—no matter what he did. We were in the middle of the sky, on a sunny Saturday afternoon over Connecticut, in a plane without an engine.

I don't think there was any drop in altitude, not at first. What I noticed was my father's sudden alertness, as if he had opened a million eyes and ears in every direction. I heard him say something sharp on the airplanes's two-way radio to Stanley down below, and I could hear the crackle of Stanley's voice coming back. I knew enough not to say very much myself, although my father told friends later that I asked him once, in a conversational way, "Are we going to crash?" And when he told this part of the story, the part where I asked that question, he would laugh.

I don't remember being afraid of crashing. In fact, I don't remember fear at all, but I do remember excitement. At last something different was going to happen! I quickly took the cotton out of my ears because my father was talking. He told me that he was looking for a good place to land. We would have to land, he explained, because the engine wasn't working, and we could not land at the airport, because we were too far away to get there in time. (*In time for what?* I wondered.) He was looking for an open area to put the plane down in, right below us somewhere. We were now over a wooded hillside, dotted here and there with cow pastures: It would have to be a cow pasture. He spotted one that looked possible and circled down toward it.

There was nothing resembling a runway below us and no room to spare. He would have to tip the plane sideways and slip it into the pasture that way, somehow righting it and stopping its movement before it could hit any of the trees at the four edges of the field. We circled lower and lower, barely clearing the treetops, and then he told me to put my head down between my knees.

"Hold on!" my father said.

I didn't see the landing, because my head was down,

but I felt it: a tremendous series of bumps, as if we were bouncing on boulders, and then the plane shook and rattled to a stop. Then we took off our seatbelts and opened the doors and got out. I didn't see any cows in the pasture, but there were a bunch of people coming toward us from the road, and it looked as if one of them might be Stanley from the airport. I was careful to stay clear of the propeller.

Nobody could figure out how we had landed safely. They had to take the plane apart to get it out of the pasture, a week or more after that Saturday afternoon. But my father and I got a ride back to the airport with Stanley and drove home in plenty of time for dinner. We didn't talk much on the way home. My father seemed tired, though cheerful, and I was thinking.

I had found out something about him that afternoon, just by watching him work his way down through the air. I held on to the knowledge tightly afterward, and I still hold it to this day. I learned what flying was for my father and for the other early aviators, what happened to him and why he kept taking us up to try flying ourselves. As we came in through the trees, he was concentrating hard, getting the rudder and the flaps set, trying to put us in the best possible position for a forced landing, but he was doing more than that. He was persuading and coaxing and willing the plane to do what he wanted; he was leaning that airplane, like a bobsled, right down to where it could safely land. He could feel its every movement, just as if it were part of his own body. My father wasn't flying the airplane, he was *being* the airplane. That's how he did it. That's how he had always done it. Now I knew.

Notes from

REEVE LINDBERGH

"In the household where I grew up, writing was a kind of family habit, something the adults around me did every day without thinking too much about it, like taking a walk or brushing their teeth. I can't recall any time during my childhood when one of my parents was *not* engaged in writing a book. Most often, they were both busy writing books. This made us believe that the best thing you could do with an interesting idea or experience was to write it down. My sister Anne and I caught on to this notion early, and because of it, I think we both became writers before we grew up, though neither of us really believed we were writers until we had published books of our own, when we were parents ourselves.

I wrote this story about flying with my father because I remember it so clearly after all these years, but I've never told it, from my point of view, until now (though my father used to tell the story and others have too). When I became an adult, I found out how unusual it was to have had a 'forced landing' with Charles Lindbergh, this famous pioneer aviator I was related to, but at the time, it was just a little extra excitement during another Saturday afternoon of flying with my father. I wanted to write the experience down the way it really was, with the sense of excitement and the sense of normal everyday family life mixed up together. I think that's the way life really is."

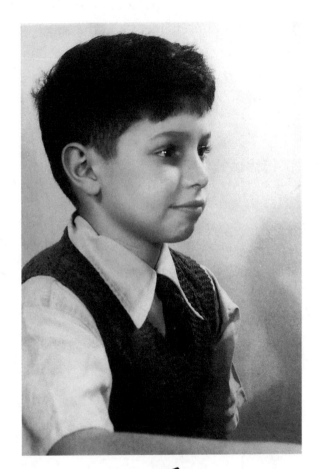

SCOUT'S HONOR

A V I

Back in 1946, when I was nine, I worried that I wasn't tough enough. That's why I became a Boy Scout. Scouting, I thought, would make a man of me. It didn't take long to reach Tenderfoot rank. You got that for joining. To move up to Second Class, however, you had to meet three requirements. Scout Spirit and Scout Participation had been cinchy. The third requirement, Scout Craft, meant I had to go on an overnight hike in the *country*. In other words, I had to leave Brooklyn, on my own, for the first time in my life.

Since I grew up in Brooklyn in the 1940s, the only grass I knew was in Ebbets Field where the Dodgers played. Otherwise, my world was made of slate pavements, streets of asphalt (or cobblestone), and skies full of tall buildings. The only thing "country" was a puny pin oak tree at our curb, which was noticed, mostly, by dogs.

I asked Scoutmaster Brenkman where I could find some country. Now, whenever I saw Mr. Brenkman, who was a church pastor, he was dressed either in church black or Scout khaki. When he wore black, he'd warn us against hellfire. When he wore khaki, he'd teach us how to build fires.

"Country," Scoutmaster Brenkman said in answer to my question, "is anywhere that has lots of trees and is not in the city. Many boys camp in the Palisades."

"Where's that?"

"Just north of the city. It's a park in Jersey."

"Isn't that a zillion miles from here?"

"Take the subway to the George Washington Bridge, then hike across."

I thought for a moment, then asked, "How do I prove I went?"

Mr. Brenkman looked deeply shocked. "You wouldn't *lie*, would you? What about Scout's honor?"

"Yes, sir," I replied meekly.

My two best friends were Philip Hossfender, whom we nicknamed Horse, and Richard Macht, called Max because we were not great spellers. They were also Scouts, Tenderfoots like me.

Horse was a skinny little kid about half my size whose way of arguing was to ball up his fist and say, "Are you saying . . . ?" in a threatening tone.

Max was on the pudgy side, but he could talk his way out of a locked room. More importantly, he always seemed to have pocket money, which gave his talk real power.

I wasn't sure why, but being best friends meant we were rivals too. One of the reasons for my wanting to be tougher was a feeling that Horse was a lot tougher than I was, and that Max was a little tougher.

"I'm going camping in the Palisades next weekend," I casually informed them.

"How come?" Max challenged.

"Scout Craft," I replied.

"Oh, *that*," Horse said with a shrug.

"Look," I said, "I don't know about you, but I don't intend to be a Tenderfoot all my life. Anyway, doing stuff in the city is for sissies. Scouting is real camping. Besides, I like roughing it."

"You saying I don't?" Horse snapped.

"I'm not saying nothing," I said.

They considered my idea. Finally, Horse said, "Yeah, well, I was going to do that, but I didn't think you guys were ready for it."

"I've been ready for *years*," Max protested.

"Then we're going, right?" I said.

They looked around at me. "If you can do it, I can do it," Max said.

"Yeah," Horse said thoughtfully.

The way they agreed made me nervous. Now I really was going to have to be tough.

We informed our folks that we were going camping overnight (which was true) and that the Scoutmaster was going with us—which was a lie. We did remember what Mr. Brenkman said about honesty, but we were baseball fans too, and since we were prepared to follow Scout law—being loyal, helpful, friendly, courteous, kind, obedient, cheerful, thrifty, brave, clean, *and* reverent—we figured a 900 batting average was not bad.

So Saturday morning we met at the High Street subway station. I got there first. Stuffed in my dad's army surplus knapsack was a blanket, a pillow, and a paper bag with three white-bread peanut butter-and-jelly sandwiches—that is, lunch, supper, and Sunday breakfast. My pockets were full of stick matches. I had an old flashlight, and since I lived by the Scout motto—Be Prepared—I had brought along an umbrella. Finally, being a serious reader, I had the latest Marvel Family comics.

Horse arrived next, his arms barely managing to hold on to a mattress that seemed twice his size. As for food, he had four cans of beans jammed into his pockets.

Max came last. He was lugging a new knapsack that contained a cast-iron frying pan, a packet of hot dogs, and a box of saltine crackers—plus two bottles. One bottle was mustard, the other, celery soda. He also had a bag of Tootsie Rolls and a shiny hatchet. "To build a lean-to," he explained.

Max's prize possession, however, was an official Scout compass. "It's really swell," he told us. "You can't ever get lost with it. Got it at the Scout store."

"I hate that place," Horse informed us. "It's all new. Nothing real."

"This compass is real," Max retorted. "Points north all the time. You can get cheaper ones, but they point all different directions."

"What's so great about the north?" Horse said.

"That's always the way to go," Max insisted.

"Says who?" I demanded.

"Mr. Brenkman, dummy," Horse cried. "Anyway, there's always an arrow on maps pointing the way north."

"Cowboys live out west," I reminded them. They didn't care.

On the subway platform, we realized we did not know which station we were heading for. To find out, we studied the system map, which looked like a noodle factory hit by a bomb. The place we wanted to go (north) was at the top of the map, so I had to hoist Horse onto my shoulders for a closer look. Since he refused to let go of his mattress—or the tin cans in his pockets—it wasn't easy. I asked him—in a kindly fashion—to put the mattress down.

No sooner did he find the station—168th Street— than our train arrived. We rushed on, only to have

Horse scream, "My mattress!" He had left it on the platform. Just before the doors shut, he and I leaped off. Max, however, remained on the train. Helplessly, we watched as his horror-stricken face slid away from us. "Wait at the next station!" I bellowed. "Don't move!"

The next train took forever to come. Then it took even longer to get to the next stop. There was Max. All around him—like fake snow in a glass ball—were crumbs. He'd been so nervous he had eaten all his crackers.

"Didn't that make you thirsty?"

"I drank my soda."

I noticed streaks down his cheeks. Horse noticed them too. "You been crying?" he asked.

"Naw," Max said. "There was this water dripping from the tunnel roof. But, you said don't move, right? Well, I was just being obedient."

By the time we got on the next train—with all our possessions—we had been traveling for an hour. But we had managed to go only one stop.

During the ride, I got hungry. I pulled out one of my sandwiches. With the jelly soaked through the bread, it looked like a limp scab.

Horse, envious, complained *he* was getting hungry.

"Eat some of your canned beans," I suggested.

He got out one can without ripping his pocket too badly. Then his face took on a mournful look.

"What's the matter?" I asked.

"Forgot to bring a can opener."

Max said, "In the old days, people opened cans with their teeth."

"You saying my teeth aren't strong?"

"I'm just talking about history!"

"You saying I don't know history?

Always kind, I plopped half my sandwich into Horse's hand. He squashed it into his mouth and was quiet for the next fifteen minutes. It proved something I'd always believed: The best way to stop arguments is to get people to eat peanut butter sandwiches. They can't talk.

Then we became so absorbed in our Marvel Family comics we missed our station. We got to it only by coming back the other way. When we reached street level, the sky was dark.

"I knew it," Max announced. "It's going to rain."

"Don't worry," Horse said. "New Jersey is a whole other state. It probably won't be raining there."

"I brought an umbrella," I said smugly, though I wanted it to sound helpful.

As we marched down 168th Street, heading for the George Washington Bridge, we looked like European war refugees. Every few paces, Horse cried, "Hold it!" and adjusted his arms around his mattress. Each time we paused, Max pulled out his compass, peered at it, then announced, "Heading north!"

I said, "The bridge goes from east to west."

"Maybe the bridge does," Max insisted with a show of his compass, "but guaranteed, *we* are going north."

About then, the heel of my left foot, encased in a heavy rubber boot over an earth-crushing Buster Brown shoe, started to get sore. Things weren't going as I had hoped. Cheerfully, I tried to ignore the pain.

The closer we drew to the bridge, the more immense it seemed. And the clouds had become so thick, you couldn't see the top or the far side.

Max eyed the bridge with deep suspicion. "I'm not so sure we should go," he said.

"Why?"

"Maybe it doesn't have another side."

We looked at him.

"No, seriously," Max explained, "they could have taken the Jersey side away, you know, for repairs."

"Cars are going across," I pointed out.

"They could be dropping off," he suggested.

"You would hear them splash," Horse argued.

"I'm going," I said. Trying to look brave, I started off on my own. My bravery didn't last long. The walkway was narrow. When I looked down, I saw only fog. I could feel the bridge tremble and sway. It wasn't long before I was convinced the bridge was about to collapse. Then a ray of hope struck me: Maybe the other guys had chickened out. If they had, I could quit because of *them*. I glanced back. My heart sank. They were coming.

After they caught up, Horse looked me in the eye and said, "If this bridge falls, I'm going to kill you."

A quarter of a mile farther across, I gazed around. We were completely fogged in.

"I think we're lost," I announced.

"What do we do?" Horse whispered. His voice was jagged with panic. That made me feel better.

"Don't worry," Max said. "I've got my compass." He pulled it out. "North is that way," he said, pointing in the direction we had been going.

Horse said, "You sure?"

"A Scout compass never lies," Max insisted.

"*We* lied," I reminded him.

"Yeah, but this is an *official* Scout compass," Max returned loyally.

"Come on," Max said and marched forward. Horse and I followed. In moments, we crossed a metal bar on the walkway. On one side, a sign proclaimed: NEW YORK; on the other, it said: NEW JERSEY.

"Holy smoke," Horse said with reverence as he straddled the bar. "Talk about being tough. We're in two states at the same time."

It began to rain. Max said, "Maybe it'll keep us clean."

"You saying I'm not clean?" Horse shot back.

Ever friendly, I put up my umbrella.

We went on—Max on one side, Horse on the other, me in the middle—trying to avoid the growing puddles. After a while, Max said, "Would you move the umbrella? Rain is coming down my neck."

"We're supposed to be roughing it," I said.

"Being in the middle isn't roughing it," Horse reminded me.

I folded the umbrella up so we all could get soaked equally.

"Hey!" I cried. "Look!" Staring up ahead, I could make out tollbooths and the dim outlines of buildings.

"Last one off the bridge is a rotten egg!" Horse shouted and began to run. The next second, he tripped and took off like an F-36 fighter plane. Unfortunately, he landed like a Hell-cat dive-bomber as his mattress unspooled before him and then slammed into a big puddle.

Max and I ran to help. Horse was damp. His mattress was soaked. When he tried to roll it up, water cascaded like Niagara Falls.

"Better leave it," Max said.

"It's what I sleep on at home," Horse said as he slung the soaking, dripping mass over his shoulder.

When we got off the bridge, we were in a small plaza. To the left was the roadway, full of roaring cars. In front of us, aside from the highway, there was nothing but buildings. Only to the right were there trees.

"North is that way," Max said, pointing toward the trees. We set off.

"How come you're limping?" Horse asked me. My foot *was* killing me. All I said, though, was, "How come you keep rubbing your arm?"

"I'm keeping the blood moving."

We approached the grove of trees. "Wow," Horse exclaimed. "Country." But as we drew closer, what we found were discarded cans, bottles, and newspapers— plus an old mattress spring.

"Hey," Max cried, sounding relieved, "this is just like Brooklyn."

I said, "Let's find a decent place, make camp, and eat."

It was hard to find a campsite that didn't have junk. The growing dark didn't help. We had to settle for the place that had the least amount of garbage.

Max said, "If we build a lean-to, it'll keep us out of the rain." He and Horse went a short distance with the hatchet.

Seeing a tree they wanted, Max whacked at it. The hatchet bounced right out of his hand. There was not even a dent in the tree. Horse retrieved the hatchet and checked the blade. "Dull," he said.

"Think I'm going to carry something sharp and cut myself?" Max protested. They contented themselves with picking up branches.

I went in search of firewood, but everything was wet. When I finally gathered some twigs and tried to light them, the only thing that burned was my fingers.

Meanwhile, Horse and Max used their branches to build a lean-to directly over me. After many collapses — which didn't help my work — they finally got the branches to stand in a shaky sort of way.

"Uh-oh," Horse said. "We forgot to bring something for a cover."

Max eyed me. "Didn't you say you brought a blanket?"

"No way!" I cried.

"All in favor of using the blanket!"

Horse and Max both cried, "Aye."

Only after I built up a mound of partially burned match sticks and lit *them,* did I get the fire going. It proved that where there's smoke there doesn't have to be much fire. The guys meanwhile draped my blanket over their branch construction. It collapsed twice.

About an hour after our arrival, the three of us were gathered inside the tiny space. There was a small fire, but more light came from my flickering flashlight.

"No more rain," Horse said with pride.

"Just smoke," I said, rubbing my stinging eyes.

"We need a vent hole," Horse pointed out.

"I could cut it with the hatchet," Max said.

"It's my mother's favorite blanket."

"And you took it?" Max said.

I nodded.

"You *are* tough," Horse said.

Besides having too much smoke in our eyes and being wet, tired, and in pain, we were starving. I almost said something about giving up, but as far as I could see, the other guys were still tough.

Max put his frying pan atop my smoldering smoke. After dumping in the entire contents of his mustard bottle, he threw in the franks. Meanwhile, I bolted down my last sandwich.

"What am I going to eat?" Horse suddenly said.

"Your beans," I reminded him.

Max offered up his hatchet. "Here. Just chop off the top end of the can."

"Oh, right," Horse said. He selected a can, set it in front of him, levered himself onto his knees, then swung down—hard. There was an explosion. For a stunned moment, we just sat there, hands, face, and clothing dripping with beans.

Suddenly Max shouted, "Food fight! Food fight!" and began to paw the stuff off and fling it around.

Having a food fight in a cafeteria is one thing. Having one in the middle of a soaking wet lean-to with cold beans during a dark, wet New Jersey night is another. In seconds, the lean-to was down, the fire kicked over, and Max's frankfurters dumped on the ground.

"The food!" Max screamed, and began to snatch up

the franks. Coated with mustard, dirt, grass, and leaves, they looked positively prehistoric. Still, we wiped the franks clean on our pants then ate them — the franks, that is. Afterward, we picked beans off each other's clothes — the way monkeys help friends get rid of lice.

For dessert, Max shared some Tootsie Rolls. After Horse swallowed his sixteenth piece, he announced, "I don't feel so good."

The thought of his getting sick was too much. "Let's go home," I said, ashamed to look at the others. To my surprise — and relief — nobody objected.

Wet and cold, our way lit by my fast-fading flash-light, we gathered our belongings — most of them, anyway. As we made our way back over the bridge, gusts of wind-blown rain pummeled us until I felt like a used-up punching bag. By the time we got to the sub-way station, my legs were melting fast. The other guys looked bad too. Other riders moved away from us. One of them murmured, "Juvenile delinquents." To cheer us up, I got out my comic books, but they had congealed into a lump of red, white, and blue pulp.

With the subways running slow, it took hours to get home. When we emerged from the High Street Station, it was close to midnight.

Before we split up to go to our own homes, we just stood there on a street corner, embarrassed, trying to figure out how to end the day gracefully. I was the one who said, "Okay, I admit it. I'm not as tough as you guys. I gave up first."

Max shook his head. "Naw. I wanted to quit, but I wasn't tough enough to do it." He looked to Horse.

Horse made a fist. "You saying I'm the one who's tough?" he demanded. "I hate roughing it!"

"Me too," I said quickly.

"Same for me," Max said.

Horse said, "Only thing is, we just have to promise not to tell Mr. Brenkman."

Grinning with relief, we simultaneously clasped hands. "No matter what," Max reminded us.

To which I added, "Scout's Honor."

Notes from
AVI

"I am a twin and that meant—and still means—sharing with my twin sister, Emily. For example, usually it's me who tells the jokes while she laughs. Or, if we're at a party together, Emily does most of the talking, while I tend to be the listener.

When we were kids, one of her jobs was remembering. Thus, though we were in the same class from nursery school through seventh grade, Emily remembers our classmates' and teachers' names. I recall just my friends' names. In short, my memories of childhood are only of those things I did without her.

So, when asked to write a story about when I was young, I recalled the time I was trying to be a Boy Scout, my first attempt at an overnight camping trip. Emily wasn't there.

Keep in mind that 'Scout's Honor' is a piece of fiction. Though I can't recall the actual words we spoke, much less the moment to moment events, the broad outlines of that fiasco are true. What's more, I recall that, even then, we thought it was all pretty funny.

At the age when this story takes place—

though I was a voracious reader—it had never occurred to me that I might become a writer. But I *was* an inventor of stories, which I—and my friends—acted out, much as described in my book *Who Was that Masked Man, Anyway?* Only during high school, when I was told I was a bad writer, did I decide to prove that I could write. As for my twin sister, she too is a writer. She writes poetry and nonfiction. So you see, we still divide things up."

Francesca Lia Block

BLUE

F R A N C E S C A   L I A   B L O C K

La's mother wasn't there, waiting in front of the school in the dusty white Volvo station wagon. La sat on the lawn and watched all the other mothers gathering their children. When the sun started to go down, she walked home along the broad streets lined with small houses, thick, white, leaflike magnolia blossoms crisping brown at the edges, deadly pink oleander, eucalyptus trees grayed with car exhaust. The air smelled of gasoline, chlorine, and fast food meat, with an occasional whiff of mock orange too faint to disguise much with its sweetness.

La walked up the brick path under the birch tree that shivered in the last rays of sun and went into the pale-blue wood frame house. She found her father sitting in the dark.

"Daddy?" she whispered.

He looked up, and his swollen, unshaven face made her step backward as if she had been hit.

"What's wrong?" La asked. "Where's Mom?" She wanted to say Mommy, but she didn't want to use baby words.

"Your mother left." He sounded as though there were wet tissues in his throat.

"Where's Mommy?" she asked again.

"How many times do I have to tell you?" He never raised his voice to her. "She left us. She's gone."

"Where did she go?"

"I don't know."

La took a step toward her father, but the look in his eyes made her back away into her bedroom and shut the door. She sat on her bed and stared at the wall she had helped her mother paint with wildflowers, pale and heathery; now they seemed poisonous. La looked at Emily, H.D., Sylvia, Ann, Christina, and Elizabeth sitting on the love seat. Her mother had named them after her favorite poets. They stared back with blank doll eyes.

La wanted to cry, but she couldn't. She felt like a Tiny Tears doll with no water inside.

"La," said a voice.

She jumped and turned around. The closet door was open a crack. La never left the closet door open. She was afraid that demons would come out and get her in the night.

"La," the voice whispered.

She held her breath.

The closet door opened a little more, and a tiny shadow tiptoed out.

Maybe, she thought later, Blue was really just her tears. Maybe Blue was the tears that didn't come.

The creature came into the light. It had thin, pale, slightly bluish skin. It blinked at La with blue eyes under glittery eyelashes.

"Who are you?" La felt a slice of fear. "Why are you here?"

"For you."

La rubbed her eyes. "Are you a demon?"

The creature looked about to cry. La shook her head, trying to make it go away.

"Now you should sleep, I think," and the creature reached out its tiny blue fingers with the bitten nails and touched La's forehead.

Almost immediately La was asleep.

She dreamed about the creature holding her mother's hand and running through a field of wildflowers.

"Blue," La's mother said in the dream. "Your name is Blue."

The house where La lived looked completely different now. When La's mother was living there, the garden had been wild, but a garden—now the flowers were burnt up; crabgrass stitched the dirt. There had been bread baking, bowls of fruit, Joni Mitchell singing on the stereo, light coming through the windows. Now, the only light in the living room was from the television's glow. La's father stopped writing the novel he had been working on. Every night after he got home from the college, he corrected papers and watched TV. La's mother had been a student in his English class, and he had fallen in love with her when he read her poetry. Wanting to protect her from a world that seemed too harsh, he had not understood how she dreamed of living in a commune, dancing barefoot in parks, and reading her poems, wearing silver Indian bells and gypsy shawls, even though these were the things that had drawn him to her.

La remembered when she was a little girl, how her mother had held her close and said, "Can you see the little dolls in Mommy's eyes?" La had seen two tiny Las there. As she got older, she still looked for herself inside her mother. Now she tried to find that La in her father, but his eyes were closed to her, dull and blind.

La fixed herself a bowl of cornflakes and went into her room to talk to Blue.

"Did you know my mother?" La asked

"I can tell you things about her."

"How do you know?" La was suspicious.

"I know because I know you."

"Like what?"

"She wrote poetry."

La thought about the journals with the stiff, creamy

paper and thick, bumpy black covers that her mother hid at the bottom of the closet. La had looked for them after her mother had left, but they were gone. She had tried to remember some of the poems her mother had read to her from the books. She had opened a tiny bottle of French perfume that was sitting on her mother's marble-top dressing table. As she put a drop to her throat, she remembered something about a girl dancing in a garden while a black swan watched her with hating eyes and one poem about a woman with black roses tattooed on her body. Something about a blue child calling to a frightened woman from out of the mists — begging.

"Did she want me?" La asked Blue.

"At first she was scared of you. You were so red and noisy, and you needed so much."

La could feel her eyes stinging, but Blue said, "Then she changed her mind. After a while, you were all she really cared about."

"Then why did she leave?"

Blue went and perched on the window sill. "That I don't know."

One day at lunch, Chelsea Fox came and sat next to La. Chelsea had shiny lemonade-colored hair tied up high in a ponytail, and she was wearing pink lip gloss that smelled like bubble gum. La thought she was the most beautiful girl she had ever seen. She made you want to give her things.

"Don't you have any friends?" Chelsea demanded.

La shrugged.

"Why not?"

La said, "I like to play by myself."

"I used to be that way," Chelsea said. "I started talking when I was real little, and the other kids didn't understand what I was saying. They just sat in the sandbox and stared at me. So I made up an imaginary friend I talked to. But my mother told me it wasn't healthy."

"I do have one friend." La had been wanting to talk about Blue so much. And now Chelsea Fox was asking! La's heart started to pound against her. She felt as if she were made of something thin and breakable, with this one heavy thing inside of her. "Blue is blue and lives in my closet."

Chelsea laughed, all tiny teeth like mean pearls. "You still have an imaginary friend?"

"Blue is real."

Chelsea made a face at La, flipped her hair, picked up her pink metal Barbie lunch box, and walked away. La crushed her brown paper bag with her fist on the lunch table where she sat alone now. Milk from the small carton inside the bag seeped onto the peeling, scratched table and dripped down.

After that, no one talked to La at all. Chelsea Fox

had a birthday party. La saw the invitations with the ballerinas on them. She waited and waited. But she was the only girl who didn't get one.

When Miss Rose found out, she asked La and Chelsea to stay after school. Miss Rose was a very thin, freckled, red-haired woman who always wore shades of green or pink.

"Chelsea, don't you think you should invite La to your birthday party?" Miss Rose said.

La looked down to hide her red face. She remembered what Blue had told her about how red she had been as a baby, how it had frightened her mother.

Chelsea shrugged.

"Go ahead, Chelsea, ask La. It isn't nice to leave her out."

Chelsea smiled so her small white teeth showed. They reminded La of a doll's. "La, would you like to come to my party?"

La was afraid to look up or move. She hated Miss Rose then.

"She doesn't want to," Chelsea said.

"I think she does," said Miss Rose. "Don't you, La?"

"Okay," La whispered, wanting her teacher to shut up.

"Why don't you bring an invitation in tomorrow?" Miss Rose said.

"Just don't bring any imaginary friends," Chelsea hissed when they were dismissed onto the burning asphalt. La imagined Chelsea spitting her teeth out like weapons. The air smelled grimy and hot like the pink rubber handballs.

La walked past some boys playing volleyball. The insides of her wrists were chafed from trying to serve at recess; her knees were scraped from falling down in softball; her knuckles raw from jacks. Sometimes her knees and knuckles were embedded with bits of gravel, speckled with blood. She had mosquito bites on her back.

"There goes Wacko," one of the boys shouted.

La felt chafed, scraped, raw, and bitten inside too.

La wasn't planning to go to Chelsea Fox's birthday party, but she saved the invitation anyway. La's father saw it. He hardly spoke to his daughter anymore, but that morning, he said, "Is that a party invitation?"

La nodded.

"Good," said her father. "It's about time you did something like that."

La went mostly because her father had seemed interested in her again and she wanted to please him—she wanted him to see her. But the next weekend, when he drove her to Chelsea's tall house with the bright lawn, camellia-and-rose-filled garden, the balloons tied to the mailbox, and the powder-blue Mercedes in the driveway, he was as far away as ever.

Maybe it is better that he doesn't offer to walk me in, she thought. *I don't want them to see him anyway.*

She wanted to go home and play with Blue, but instead, she jumped out of the car and went up to the door where a group of girls waited with their mothers.

Chelsea answered, wearing a pastel jeans outfit. The girls kissed her cheek and gave her presents. When it was La's turn, she gulped and brushed her lips against Chelsea's face. Chelsea reached up to her cheek and rubbed away the kiss with the back of her hand.

Inside, the house was decorated in floral fabrics — huge peonies and chrysanthemums — and lit up with what seemed like hundreds of lamps. Little pastel girls were running around screaming. There was one room all made of glass and filled with plants and leafy, white iron furniture. In the middle was a long table heaped with presents. La sat in a corner of the room by herself. After a while, Chelsea's mother came in, leading a chorus of "Happy Birthday" and holding a huge cake covered in wet-looking pink-frosting roses. Chelsea's mother had a face like a model on a magazine cover — cat eyes, high cheekbones, and full pouting lips. She was tall and slender, her blonde hair piled on top of her head, with little wisps brushing down against her long pearled neck. La watched Chelsea blow out eleven candles in one breath.

"I'll get my wish!"

She probably did get her wish, La thought, watching Chelsea's small hands tearing open the presents — Barbies, Barbie clothes, Barbie cars, stuffed toys, roller skates, jeans, T-shirts, a glittery magenta bike with a white lattice basket covered with pink plastic flowers.

La had brought the almost-empty bottle of perfume that had belonged to her mother. Even though the fragrance inside it was the only thing that seemed to bring La's mother back, La had decided to give it to Chelsea. Maybe it would make Chelsea like her, La thought. It was her greatest treasure.

When Chelsea opened it, she said, "What's this? It's been used!" and threw it aside.

Chelsea's mother let the girls stay up until midnight, and then she told them to get their sleeping bags. La's belonged to her father — blue with red flannel ducks on the inside. The other girls had pastel sleeping bags with Snoopy or Barbie on them. La put her bag down in a corner and listened to the sugar-wild giggles all around her.

Suddenly, she heard Chelsea say, "La, tell us about your imaginary friend. La has an imaginary friend."

"She gave you an imaginary present," Amanda Warner said.

Snickers. They sounded mean with too much cake. La was silent.

"Come on." The girls squealed. "Tell us."

La said, "No I don't."

"Your mom left because you are so weird," said Katie Dell.

"I think her mom was pretty weird too. She was a hippy," said Chelsea.

La buried down in the musty red flannel of her sleeping bag.

Blue, she thought, to keep herself from crying.

Near morning, when the other girls were finally quiet, warm thin arms the color of Chelsea Fox's eyes wrapped around La's waist.

"Write about it," Blue whispered. "Write it all."

That was the same thing Miss Rose said the next day in class. "I want us all to write about someone we love." She looked straight at La. La noticed for the first time how sad Miss Rose's brown eyes were.

La went home and shut the door of her room. She lay down on her belly on the floor, with a pen and a piece of paper. There was a creaking sound, and the closet door opened. Blue came out.

"What are you doing?"

"I'm supposed to write about someone I love. I want to write about my mom, but I'm afraid."

Blue began to whisper things in La's ear. She picked up her pen and wrote.

• • •

La wrote how she had been named La for the musical sound and also for the city they lived in—not for the dry, flat, chain-link-fenced, train-track-lined, used-car-lot-full valley where their house was, but for the city over the hill. In that city, La's mother—wearing a paisley dress, her long hair hanging to her waist—took La to eat honey-colored cornbread at a restaurant with a mural of an Indian temple on the outdoor courtyard wall and soft candle cubes flickering like chants on every table. She took La to the museum where they saw jewelry in the shapes of fairies with stained-glass wings; to a temple in the hills full of gentle-faced Buddha statues and people planting trees, the air almost lavender with clouds of incense. They walked around the lake tucked into the Hollywood hills, feeling the cool, wet air on their cheeks, looking out at the expanse of water and the small, magical bridge lined with white globes; La imagined a princess receiving her guests there. They rode wooden horses on the carousel at the pier, feeling the smooth, wooden horse flanks, caressing the ridges of wooden roses on the saddles, watching the circle of lights that seemed to make the tinkling music. On dusty trails, they rode real horses, and La's mother pointed out the wildflowers peeking at them from behind rocks. When they got home, they zigzagged handfuls of wild-flower seeds into the earth—primrose, columbine, lupine, and cornflower. They painted wildflowers on the walls of La's room—"So you will always have them," her mother said.

La wrote about her mother coming into her room at night sometimes, to read La poetry by Emily and H.D. in the pinkish light, the words like her mother's perfume wafting around them. Sometimes, La's mother read her own poems. La felt the secret of sadness bonding them together then.

"I will love you forever," La's mother had said. "No matter where I am on the planet, I am always loving you."

La wrote about all of that and about the perfume bottle shaped like a teardrop that had brought her mother back.

"This is wonderful, La," Miss Rose said. "Would you like to read it to the class?"

La shook her head, cringing, pressing her back against hard wood and metal.

"I really think you should," said Miss Rose.

Chelsea Fox said, "I'd love to hear your story." She said it so sweetly that for a moment La believed her. But then she saw Chelsea glance over at Amanda Warner, and a silent laugh swelled the air between them.

"Go ahead," Miss Rose said.

La couldn't breathe. She felt like throwing up.

But when she started to read, something happened.

She forgot about Chelsea Fox, Amanda Warner, and everyone else in the class. The words La and Blue had written cast their spell—even over La. She could smell the perfume and bittersweet wildflowers; she could hear Joni Mitchell's *For the Roses* playing softly.

When La was finished, she looked up. Everyone was silent, watching her.

"That was beautiful," Miss Rose finally said.

The bell rang, and everyone scattered. La went into the fluorescent-lit, brown and beigy-pink hallway. Her heart was beating fast but in a different way this time. She felt as if she had physically touched everyone in the room, as if she had played her favorite song for Miss Rose and lifted an open, tear-shaped bottle of fragrance to Chelsea Fox's face.

"Your mom sounds like she was cool," Chelsea said, catching up with La. "My mom isn't like that. She doesn't spend time with me except to go shopping and stuff." La looked into Chelsea's blue eyes. The pupils were big and dark. There was no laughter in them now. La nodded.

Chelsea tossed her hair and ran to catch up with her friends.

When La got home, she ran inside to tell Blue. Her father wasn't on the couch watching TV where La expected him. She heard his typewriter keys and peeked into his office. The windows were open and Vivaldi was playing; he had a cup of coffee at his fingertips.

"Daddy," La said.

When she handed him the story, his eyes changed.

"It's about Mom," La said, but she knew he knew.

"I'm writing something about her too," he said. He held out his hand, and she went to him. He sat up and kissed her forehead.

"Thank you, honey." He looked as though he hadn't slept or eaten for days. But he took off his glasses then, and La saw two small images of herself swimming in the tears in his eyes.

La went to her room to tell Blue. In the closet, there were only clothes and shoes and shadows now.

Notes from

FRANCESCA LIA BLOCK

"I wrote 'Blue' based on certain aspects of my childhood, although much of it is very far from my reality. I lived in a house like the one described in the story, and I had an active imagination that I used in my writing as a way to feel connected to others. The main difference between my life and the story is that my parents were always together and very supportive of me.

It was their love and encouragement that influenced my decision to become a writer. I was at first hesitant to present the parents in 'Blue' in a negative light, since the story was meant to be at least semi-autobiographical, but I made certain choices because I wanted to add drama to the piece. My father, who is no longer living, always told me to write whatever I needed to write and not to be afraid or inhibited as an artist."

When I Was Your Age

Your Age

VOLUME TWO

INTRODUCTION

When I Was Your Age, volume two, has given me the great pleasure of editing a second group of stories by children's authors about growing up. I've now worked on twenty of these—twenty stories about twenty childhoods, twenty different ways of seeing and being in the world.

It stands to reason that every single person is unique, but when you ask twenty authors the same question: "What was it like when you were a child?" and get answers that are so wildly different in content and tone, it makes you look at other people in amazement. How have we come to be together? How do we even manage to communicate?

But the ten stories in *When I Was Your Age,* volume two (and those in the first volume as well), chart a clear and certain path through the forest of human differences. It is simply this: we are *all* different, we are *all* human, and if we tell the truth, we *will* be understood.

The authors in this collection have been honest and generous. They have shown us how they've managed not only to survive their childhoods but to treasure and even to laugh at them. If you read the notes at the end of each story, I think you will see an almost seamless connection between the authors' stories and the rest of their lives. These people—these children who grew up to be authors—write because they need to. By exploring the past with words, they can give form and meaning to their own experiences.

And what are these experiences? I think I can tell you a bit about each story without giving too much away. Rather than attempting to analyze anything, I'd rather tell you what I most love about each author's writing. That way, I'll be able to enjoy it all over again, and perhaps you will too.

Norma Fox Mazer's "In the Blink of an Eye" pulls us right into her world. Here is Norma, vivid from the very first sentence, all her nerves jangling: "In the gutter, a lit cigarette butt catches my eye. I swoop for it, stick it in my mouth, and take a puff. It tastes like dirty straw; still, I suck deeply, as I've seen my father do." Outside in the street Norma is tough, a tomboy, but at home she can't seem to stop crying. "There goes the faucet," her family say. "She's so sensitive . . . too sensitive." How lucky though for the rest of us that she was! It must be because Norma feels things so deeply that her writing is so full of feeling.

Rita Williams-Garcia, as we meet her in "Food from the Outside," is another case entirely. Her response to life is not to cry about it but to take action. Laughter, nerve, jive, and guile are how Rita, her brother, and her sister get around their strict, opinionated mother's rule never to eat at anyone else's house. Rita explains it with a comic's deadpan timing: "You see, our mother, known throughout the neighborhood as 'Miss Essie,' was still refining her cooking skills." The children's elaborate efforts to outsmart Miss Essie make their lives seem more fun and eventful than the situation comedies they watch on TV.

Paul Fleischman had no such obstacles to contend with. As he himself admits, "I lived in comfortable circumstances in beautiful Santa Monica, California, ten blocks from the beach, amid a loving family, in a time of peace . . ." *But* "all that meant nothing." Why? Because "throughout his school years he suffered from CSD, Chronic Stature Deficiency. Paul Fleischman was a 'shrimp.'"

I'm quoting from Paul's introduction to his story, "Interview with a Shrimp," which is set up in a journalistic question-and-answer format. To me, the fact that Paul has chosen such an approach to writing about his childhood confirms one effect of his shortness. Having a special vantage point, being *different,* helped to make him an original thinker—and eventually a writer.

Paul's story is also unusual in providing an overview of an entire childhood. Most of the stories in the book focus on a single dramatic incident, perhaps because that's the way experience is imprinted in our minds.

Things that were upsetting or unresolved at the time stay with us.

Jane Yolen's "The Long Closet" is just such a memory—it begins with a mystery and ends with a terrible discovery. One night when she is sleeping in her grandparents' house in Virginia, an insistent, sighing sound wakes her. In this story—a tale of suspense, really—we are with Jane every moment, afraid to find out what the sound is, yet pulled forward by it. Everything is described with nerve-racking slowness. "The room was filled with that lovely, scary early morning half-light you get in the South; shadows of the tall pines seemed to creep around and about the wainscoting on the walls. The sound came again, and I realized it was coming from the long closet."

How does a writer re-create the past and give it over to us fresh and new and shining in the present moment? I think detail of the senses—what is seen, heard, smelled, *felt*—is the only answer. Draw a picture in words and make it real. This is just what Howard Norman does in "Bus Problems," when he describes the bookmobile in Grand Rapids, Michigan, where he worked every weekday in the summer of 1959.

We know just by the quality of Howard's writing—and also because he does tell us so—that for him the bookmobile was an enchanted world, "a secure and peaceful place." We can see the leather benches mended with masking tape, and feel the heat of the day outside. It's as if the story has opened on an empty but familiar stage, then suddenly onto it leap the most amazing characters, and the drama begins.

If a child is lucky, there is always shelter, a place that is yours alone. For Michael J. Rosen, that place was on the back of a horse. "I'd climb in the saddle, and instantly, other riders, other horses in the ring, whatever it was I didn't want to do after camp or beginning in September . . . it all ceased to exist, along with the rest of my life on the ground, shrinking, fading behind the trail of dust the horse and I made heading to the horizon."

What I most appreciate though about Michael's story "Pegasus for a Summer" is the vulnerability and longing it conveys. He bravely wears his heart on his sleeve, letting us see so clearly his need for approval, for love.

All children certainly need these things, and the degree to which they get them, or don't, depends on their families. But children can sometimes be wrong about how their families feel about them, as E. L. Konigsburg wryly demonstrates in "How I Lost My Station in Life." There were two daughters in the family, Elaine (E. L.) and her sister Harriett, and it seems that Elaine's role was (1) to be the baby of the family and (2) to get all As in school. Everything was going along fine until (1) they moved in with relatives who had a child younger than she was and (2) she had to go to a new school, where the teacher ". . . asked the wrong questions for the answers I gave."

Behind the specifics of Elaine's plight is a bright child's need to do well—so that others will love her and also *for its own sake*. It is this latter aspect that can serve us, once we learn it, for our entire lives.

So many of the stories in the collection appear to be about achievement but aren't really. In Kyoko Mori's nearly bottomless "Learning to Swim" we easily understand her desire to please her wonderful mother by earning red or black lines on her bathing cap— each representing a certain number of meters swum in the school pool. The events in the story take place in Japan and there is a controlled, matter-of-fact tone to the writing that seems a part of this distant culture, yet we can still see in each speech and gesture all that her mother does for Kyoko and how deeply she is loved.

But what if a child's parents for some reason don't make the child *feel* loved? In that case, something truly amazing can still happen, as it does in Karen Hesse's "Waiting for Midnight." Unable to sleep at night, haunted by fears and her next-door neighbor's secrets, Karen turns to prayer. She witnesses what seems to be a miracle, and yet to me the *real* miracle is her own resourcefulness and the heartbreaking beauty of her imagination.

In "The Snapping Turtle" by Joseph Bruchac, beauty is outside and all around him. This is a story about nature, about a young boy's everyday intimacy with the world of plants and animals. Joe's grandparents, who raised him, gave him a good balance of things: his grandmother loved books and reading, and his grand-father schooled him in the ways of the forest and streams.

When he catches a snapping turtle one day while fishing for trout, his grandparents' response to his dilemma of what to do with the turtle makes it clear just how lucky he is in them: "My grandmother . . . looked at me. So did Grampa. It was wonderful how they could focus their attention on me in a way that made me feel they were ready to do whatever they could to help."

This response—to pay attention in a deep and careful way—is something that Joseph Bruchac and the other writers in this collection all seem to have learned as children. Their way of noting the details in a single moment and of feeling the pain and comedy and wonder of things are gifts to us.

As we read the stories, both moved and entertained, we may also be consoled. A girl who can't stop crying, three nervy kids in an African American family, a short boy growing up in California, a girl suddenly awakened in her grandparents' house, a midwestern boy with his first summer job, an elementary school scholar in the 1930s, a boy who loves horseback riding, a Japanese girl adrift, a lonely girl in Baltimore, a boy who is most at home outdoors—surely we recognize these children.

Surely they are like us after all.

— AMY EHRLICH

Norma Fox Mazer

In the Blink of an Eye

✦

NORMA FOX MAZER

I. Cigarette Butt

In the gutter, a lit cigarette butt catches my eye. I swoop for it, stick it in my mouth, and take a puff. It tastes like dirty straw; still, I suck deeply, as I've seen my father do. I choke and cough, and my eyes stream tears, as they so often do at home, but these are OK tears, the kind you get from doing something forbidden and tough. My mother hates smoking. She says it's a filthy habit; she calls cigarettes coffin nails, and every time my father lights up, she says, "Oh, Mike!" My sisters and I think she's prejudiced about cigarettes and wish that she'd leave my father alone.

My sisters are Adele and Linda. We all have modern names, American names, interesting names. My mother's name used to be Zlatckey. You can't even say a name like that. Zlatckey! That was her name when she came to this country as a tiny girl with her parents and brothers. Then Zlatckey became Slats, but that was almost as bad, so she picked a new name, Jenny. That became Jeannie and then, in time, Jean. An OK name. It goes with my father's name, Michael, which is the best name in our family.

I let the butt drag from a corner of my mouth, the way my father does. Humphrey Bogart, the movie star, does the same thing. I think my dad looks a little like Humphrey, and they can both talk with the cigarette hanging from their lower lip. "How do you do?" I say, jutting my chin to keep the cigarette butt stuck on my lip. "My name is Norm—"

The butt slides off my lip and lands in the gutter again. Just as I bend down to retrieve it, I have a thought that makes my stomach jump. What if, behind one of the windows of one of the houses on this street, which is First Street in Glens Falls, New York, someone is watching me? And what if this someone, who is probably another mother, tells my mother she saw me smoking—and smoking not just a cigarette, but a cigarette *butt* that I picked up not just from the sidewalk, but from the gutter? The *filthy* gutter.

I walk away fast, humming and looking around brightly, as if I don't even know what the word *cigarette* means. But my breath is hot and stinky, a dead giveaway. I fan my mouth over and over. Then, from the other end of the street, I hear my sister calling me to supper. "Norma," she yells, "Normaaaa!" She's six years older than me and thinks she's my other mother. I'm not ready to answer and dawdle past Bud the Bicycle Man's repair shop. It's really just another little single-family house, with a sagging porch jammed with bicycles and bicycle parts. Inside, more bicycles hang from the walls and the ceiling. And there's Bud, with his grease-smeared overalls, who never says anything except "Ay-yuh" when you ask him to fix the chain on your bike or raise the seat.

Two doors down is the candy store, which is also a house with the store in front where the living room is supposed to be. I check all my pockets on the off chance that there's a penny that I missed spending. Two sisters with rolled gray hair own the store. They stand so perfectly straight behind the counter that I think maybe they sleep like that, ready in an instant to open their eyes and sell the next customer a Tootsie Roll or six gumdrops.

"Nor-maaa . . . Norma Fox!" In the authoritative slap of my sister's voice, I hear the bad news that she might already know that I've been — smoking. She has a way of intuiting things like that. And now it's not just my smelly cigarette breath that's hot, but my whole face.

"Your sister's calling you," someone says behind me.

It's Herbie Sternfeld, giving me one of his strange grins that seems to involve only half his face.

Herbie, his parents, and their shaggy St. Bernard live downstairs from us. They're our landlords, and my mother says I have to be polite to them. It's not hard to be polite to Herbie's parents. I like them. Being polite to Herbie is different, though. I don't know if I don't like him, or if I'm just scared of him. I don't know if I'm scared of him because he is scary or because he's weird.

It's not just his double-thick glasses or his awkward, neck-forward walk, or even his stiff black hair that looks like cartoon hair that somebody shot electricity through. It's the way he talks in a loud, uninflected voice, and how he spends his time, doing experiments with chemicals in the shed behind the Sternfelds' kitchen. And it's how sometimes he looks at you and says hello, but sometimes he looks at you and yells at you to get away, and sometimes, the worst, he flashes his eyes.

I hate it when he flashes his eyes. They're big and round and black, and they dart around and hardly ever seem to look straight at you, but then suddenly they'll light up and do that flashing thing, as if he's sending an important message. A vital message. A message you better get.

I'm surprised to see Herbie on the street. Sometimes he sits on the front porch and yells at people passing by, but he hardly ever goes out. Me, I'm always outside, playing every minute I can. Like all the other kids, I race through backyards at dusk playing hide-and-seek, listening for the call of "Alleee alleee infree!" I climb the crab apple tree on the side of our house to eat the sour, wrinkled little fruits, and I roller-skate and bike everywhere. I jump rope and play ball with the girls, and marbles with the boys, crooking my thumb and crowing when one of the dark no-nonsense shooties hits the mark.

"I'm going to the store," Herbie says. Shouts, really. "Getting bread for my mother. You like that white bread, huh, Fox girl?"

It's true I like the mushy, store-bought white bread the Sternfelds eat, the kind of bread my mother won't allow in our house because, she says, it isn't healthy. I know she must be right, but I also know how good mushy, store-bought white bread tastes, because I've eaten it, taken it right from Herbie's sweaty hand. I only did it once, but I also read one of Herbie's comics at the same time, which makes two bad things I did simultaneously. We don't read comics in our house, either.

"Norma!" my sister calls again briskly. "Norma Fox! Norm*aaa*! Supp-*er*!"

"Com-*ing*!" I call back, but I don't move. Herbie's staring at me: it's almost an eye flash, and maybe that's the reason I tell him I've been smoking. To distract him. To fend off that eye flash.

"Smoking?" he says in his loud voice. "You have not."

"I have!" I say, and with two fingers next to my mouth I demonstrate how I held the cigarette just like a movie hero.

Herbie peers at me through his thick glasses, as if I'm one of his experiments. "Dirty liar," he says.

My cheeks go hot. This is almost the worst insult anyone can give me. I lean into his face. "*Huuuuh!*" I breathe, and blow hot cigarette breath at him. "*Huuuuh!*"

He reels back as if I've shot him, one shoulder up defensively, then gives me a hard shove, sending me back against a tree. I hit my head, and it hurts! I want to cry, but I can't, because I'm outside. "You dumb sissy," I choke.

Herbie makes an ugly grimace and walks away. Maybe he didn't hear what I said. I cross fingers on both hands and run the rest of the way home, holding back the tears.

In the house, in my family, I cry a lot. I get my feelings hurt all the time. I cry if someone says something mean to me. I cry when I hear a sad story. When dirty Billy Miner knocks me down in the snow, falls on top of me, and shoves his lips on mine, I cry — but not outside. I wait until I get home. Then I cry agonies of humiliation. I cry when I lose my turquoise ring. I even cry — but only at home — if I don't get a good mark on a test.

Nobody likes my crying. "She cries at the drop of a hat," they say. "There she goes again. . . . Here come the waterworks. . . . Turn off the faucet, somebody!" Just seeing my eyes fill and my face get set to crumple is enough to bring on exasperated sighs. Sometimes I'm almost like two different people, the tomboy outside my house and the crybaby inside.

My baby sister never cries. She doesn't even care if you say, "I'm going to tell Daddy on you!" Nothing can make her cry. She just sticks out her tongue and laughs at you. A spatter of reddish freckles arches across the bridge of her nose, her little blonde braids stick out at an angle from her head, and she says things that are so funny the grownups repeat them to each other. She's fearless, kisses dogs, and tells everyone in first grade the Facts of Life, which I have only recently learned about, myself, from a book our mother gave me called *Let's Talk About Life*. (The first story in the book is about chickens and eggs. The next one is about frogs and eggs. Nothing becomes too clear to me from reading that book.)

My uncle calls my little sister Dynamite. We all have names besides our given ones. Older sister is the Bright One, the Beautiful One, the Good One. I'm the Too Sensitive One, the Tomboy, the Faucet. Younger sister is the Brat, the Mouthy One, and Dynamite, the best name of all.

My older sister is pretty much dynamite, herself. She has already done many good things in her life, such as always getting on the Honor Roll and, even when she was only six years old, making breakfast every morning for my mother. Of course she has a boyfriend. His name is Will, he has a big nose, and he's handsome, with white blonde hair sticking up like a Marine cut. I want him to notice me, and he does now and then, but mostly not. That's why sometimes I go in my room and cry, even when nothing has happened. My eyes swell, my cheeks get hot and tight, and then come the tears. "Crying again?" my mother says, looking in. Which makes me cry harder.

Every night, I promise myself I'm going to stop crying. I won't ever cry again. But I do. I can't help it. Every time something happens, I cry. And cry and cry.

I have been crying my way through the days, the weeks, the months. I cry rivers, lakes, and oceans of tears. "There goes the faucet," I hear. "She's so sensitive . . . too sensitive!" I start to hate my crying. It leaves me feeling weak and helpless, but what can I do? I don't ask for tears. They just come.

IV. Wonder Woman

My sister is waiting for me, standing near the Sternfelds' front porch, a kind of concrete apron with two pillars. Upstairs, right above it, we have a better porch too, where my mother lets us eat in summer. My sister puts her hands on her hips. "Where were you? What were you doing?"

"Nowhere. Nothing." I talk through tight lips.

"I was calling you."

"I know."

"Mom is home from work. She wants you for supper."

"I know."

"Were you with someone?"

"Who?"

"That's what I asked you."

"What?"

"Don't be fresh. Who do you think you are, Wonder Woman?"

"Yes, yes, I'm Wonder Woman!"

I forget to keep my lips tight, and she leans close and sniffs, her nostrils drawing up in disgust. "What's that nasty smell?"

I run around her, up the wooden steps into our apartment, and down the hall: past the room that I share with my little sister, past the door to the back stairs, then the living room and the kitchen, and into the bathroom. I lock the door and rinse my mouth repeatedly with cold water. The encounters with Herbie and my sister have upset me. I was tough, but I wanted to cry. And now I do. First I cry just a little, rubbing my shoulder and my head, where it hit the tree. I think how mad my mother's going to be if she finds out I smoked. I shouldn't have done it, especially not a filthy butt from the gutter, and maybe I'm going to die from all the germs. I cry harder. It's comforting in a horrible sort of way to feel the hot tears on my cheeks.

My mother knocks on the bathroom door. "Are you in there? Are you crying again?"

"No," I choke, and think how sorry they will all be when I die. Sad and sorry. They'll be the ones crying then. They'll appreciate me at last — so young, so dead.

At supper, I'm especially quiet and polite, so no one will notice my red eyes and ask if I've been crying again, and then notice me some more and wonder why my breath is stinky. But it's OK, anyway, because my parents are upset, too, and not paying attention to me. They're talking about Mr. and Mrs. Sternfeld, who might want to raise our rent. I don't think they will, because they're too nice. They're not at all like Herbie. They're both old and small with white, fluffy hair. They're quiet little people, and they smile when they see me and nod their little white heads and say, "Nice girl! Nice girl!"

That night, through my bedroom floor, I hear Herbie talking to his parents in his loud, excited voice. My little sister is sleeping in the opposite bed. Nothing wakes her up. Herbie's yelling now, and I feel scared for his parents. I wish I could go down there and zap him, like Wonder Woman. One zap for shoving me, one for yelling at his nice little parents.

V. Eyes

Every morning in the cold weather, before my father leaves for work, he runs down the back stairs from our apartment to the unheated shed on the ground floor. Sometimes I get up early and run down the stairs after him. In the shed, he pulls up the trap door in the floor, and we go down another flight of stairs into the cellar. It's dark down there. As my father feeds the banked night fire shovelfuls of coal, it leaps and roars into life inside the furnace. If Daddy's not in too big a hurry, he lets me dig into the coal bin and feed the glowing heart of fire. It's hard, heavy work, but I don't ever cry when we do this.

Nor do I cry when I play with my girlfriend Eva in the shed in warmer weather. Eva's the crybaby, then. She's chubby and always wants to play stupid things like Tea Party and never anything good like Spies. It's a new game I've made up. We have to be very quiet, which Eva doesn't like. We can't giggle or snort or make any sounds. She doesn't like that, either. And we can only play the game in our shed, because right next to it is the Sternfelds' shed, and we can't play the game without the Sternfelds' shed.

The way you play is this: tiptoe to the wall that separates the two sheds and press your eye against the wall where the thin vertical slats meet. If you get the right angle, you can see into the Sternfelds' shed, and if you're lucky, you can catch Herbie across the room, near the little window, mixing things in jars and beakers. And then — and this is the point of the game — you can make up stories about him. Sometimes he talks to himself. He makes noises and grunts. Sometimes he laughs. He's crazy, or might be a genius. Or both, I think. In comics and movies, mad-genius-scientists' eyes always flash like his. Plus, I notice, his lips are very, very red.

"So what!" Eva says, when I point this out. "It's boring."

She won't play any more with me. I don't really care, because I'm never bored when I make up my stories or watch Herbie through the slats. Sometimes it crosses my mind that this game is something else my mother wouldn't like me to do. *Stop*, I tell myself, but I don't. I don't want to stop.

Once or twice, Herbie looks toward the flimsy wall separating us, and seems to look at almost the exact spot where I've got my eye. It scares me. *Stop*, I say to myself again. But I go on making up stories about Herbie. I go on playing Spies. It's almost like crying, something I tell myself not to do, but do anyway, except that Spies is better. It's stories, like the books I read, but what's so good is that they're mine. No one can say anything about my stories, because no one knows about them. They're all in my head, like the chant I do every time before I play Spies — *Herbie be there*. And he is there, day after day, almost as if he knows what I'm doing and is a willing part of my game and my imagination.

One day, when I put my eye to the crack between the boards and peer into the Sternfelds' shed, Herbie is there again, but not across the room. He is right there, standing by the wall, staring back at me, his face puckered with concentration. He has a hypodermic needle in his hand. Faster than I can take in what's happening, he raises the needle and pushes the plunger. A stream of hot liquid shoots between the slats and into my eye.

For an instant, there's a stillness, as if nothing has happened. Words form in my mind. *She froze with terror.* I'm making up a story about this. That is the way to do it, to keep things from hurting. In the next instant, my eye begins to pulse and then to burn and hurt more than anything has ever hurt. I stumble up the back stairs, calling for my mother—my mother, I want my mother.

She sits me in a chair in the living room, the best chair, my father's reading chair. She wraps ice in a dishtowel for me to hold against my eye and runs to the phone. My eye feels as if it's held in place by the frailest of threads, as if any wrong movement will snap it free. I sit like a ramrod in the chair, focused on holding my eye in my head and the pain far back in my mind, where I can almost see it—a rush of blazing white. If I can keep the pain back there, in that white place, then my eye might also stay in place.

Soon the doctor comes. He produces a light from his bag and looks into my eye with it for a long time. Then Mrs. Sternfeld is there, squeezing her apron between her hands, patting my head and my shoulder. "She's good, a good girl," Mrs. Sternfeld says.

No, I think. I'm not interested in being a good girl. What I'm interested in is *not crying*. Since I ran up the stairs, I haven't uttered a word of complaint or shed a single tear. I don't understand exactly why I'm not crying. Maybe I don't want to cry in front of strangers. Or maybe this is too important for tears. Tears are the easy way, the way I've always gone, and now I've chosen — or been allowed — to take another way. Silence. Quietness. Waiting. Watching.

"Well," the doctor says at last, "a fraction closer, and she would have lost her sight in that eye."

His words make an immediate, deep impression on me, deeper than the pain, deeper than the fear or the memory of Herbie's resolved expression as he released the acid. In years to come, I never forget those words or lose a sense of gratitude that my sight was spared.

It may be from that moment that I begin to take the world in through my eyes with a special intensity. It is from that moment that I stop crying. Although I don't know it then, sitting in that chair in our living room, I have passed over a line — the invisible line between childhood and whatever it is that comes next. Not adulthood, not that quickly, but the beginning of the long, long walk into another world.

✦ ✦ ✦

Notes from
NORMA FOX MAZER

"The years during which my family lived in a second floor apartment on First Street in Glens Falls, New York, stay in my memory as a series of sharp, brief snapshots. To write 'In the Blink of an Eye,' I collected a number of those snapshots and put them together to see how they connected to one another and what their greater meaning might be.

The events, both large and small, of the story, all took place. I picked up a cigarette butt from the gutter, played marbles with the boys, and ate raw rhubarb and crab apples. I climbed trees, had a friend named Eva, and went down into the cellar with my father in the winter, where he let me shovel coal into the furnace. My older sister called me to supper, and my younger sister kissed dogs, and my mother sure did hate smoking.

And, yes, our landlord's son shot acid into my eye through that thin vertical space between the boards separating our shed from his. And the doctor was called, and I didn't cry, and he said those words about my eyesight which I never forgot. The acid and the doctor happened in the same space of time, one morning or, more likely, one afternoon (I've forgotten which), but did everything in the story happen sequentially, one moment after another, the way things do in a story — in this story?

No. Our minds, our memories, are like erratic cameras. They snap quickly, this picture, not that one, another, then for days or weeks perhaps, not a single picture, then a whole series. It will be years after the moments we're all living through now before we discover which pictures were developed, which won't fade. And when we see these pictures in our mind's eye, we'll attach special significance to them.

I do, anyway. I think it means something that I remember the moment I stopped crying. And having written this story, I understand, for the first time, how that moment is linked to my having become a writer. Life is ultimately a mysterious unfolding of events. It's impossible for me, now, to imagine myself as anything but a writer. Still, I wonder . . . would I have become a writer if I'd gone on sobbing my way through life?"

Food from the Outside

✦

RITA WILLIAMS-GARCIA

My sister, brother, and I didn't have a dog, but we sure could have used one around dinnertime. Our dog would never have had to beg for table scraps, for we promised sincerely in our mealtime prayers always to feed Rover the main course. It wouldn't have been so much for love of dog, but for survival. You see, our mother, known throughout the neighborhood as "Miss Essie," was still refining her cooking skills. Until we could persuade our parents to let us have a dog, we sat at the dinner table with wax sandwich bags hidden in our pockets, especially when Miss Essie served "Hackensack," our code word for mystery stew.

"Rosalind, Russell, and Rita! Don't get up from that table 'til you eat every bit of that food," Miss Essie commanded. Then she'd stand there and not leave until we began eating.

Since we knew we'd be at the table for a long time, we came up with experiments to amuse ourselves while our parents watched television in the other room. Our favorite food test, the pork-chop drop, was devised by my eleven-year-old brother Russell, our resident scientist.

"Tonight we will continue our study on speed and density," Russell said, holding up his pork chop.

"I'll count, I'll count!" I volunteered, lowering my face to plate level.

Rosalind, the oldest at twelve, turned toward the living room to confirm that the coast was clear, then gave the "go ahead" for the pork-chop drop.

The object of the pork-chop drop was to compare the hardness of that night's pork chops to those of dinners past. Usually Russell would hold the chop about two feet above the plate and let it drop, while Rosalind or I counted the side-to-side reverberations of the pork chop as it hit the dinner plate. The thinner and harder the pork chop, the higher the drop count.

All we knew about food was what Mommy cooked, and the cold sandwiches and stewed spinach they served in the school cafeteria. Living in Seaside, California, we were separated by thousands of miles from our grandmothers, aunts, and cooking cousins who lived in New York, Virginia, and North Carolina. Eating in restaurants and fast-food places were frivolities we knew nothing of. Above all, we adhered to Miss Essie's firm rule, which was never to eat dinner at anyone else's house. She never gave a reason for her rule — other than the promise of a spanking, and we never thought to question her. As soon as our friends' fathers drove up to their driveways from work, we were to go straight home. Up until 1966, when we were twelve, eleven, and ten, Rosalind, Russell, and I believed that oil-soaked pork chops flattened to blackened sand dollars and cemented rice that defied separation was how food looked and tasted.

It was when Daddy replaced our black-and-white model with a color TV that we got an inkling about the texture and appearance of food from the outside, taste being the only missing component. We would sit in the dark before the glowing screen, oohing and aahing over a parade of McDonald's and Crisco Oil commercials, not to mention those sitcom dining-room scenes where platters of succulent meats and brightly hued vegetables graced the table.

"Mommy, how come our French fries don't look like that?" I'd exclaim, for ours were oily olive, dark brown, or black — certainly not golden brown and crinkled like the fries in the commercials.

"That's how white people cook," Mommy would reply, seemingly unaffected. Or, "That's not real — that's TV."

These answers worked initially, but being inquisitive

children, we began to ask our friends what they ate and how it tasted. We dared not ask them to smuggle out samples of their mothers' cooking—at least I didn't, believing Miss Essie was omniscient.

One thing was for certain. Daddy and Mommy didn't eat what we ate. They ate first and separately at some secret parent banquet where they drank Pepsi and laughed, and children were not allowed within earshot. To compound the mystery, Miss Essie did not permit us inside the kitchen while she was cooking their supper. We were to stay outside until she called us in for our own.

This only caused more speculation about what our parents ate and why we could not have any. Naturally we came up with a plan to investigate. The plan called for us to end our kickball game promptly at four-thirty in the afternoon. That was when Billie Holiday and Miss Essie sang "Ain't No Body's Business" while hot popping grease applauded in the kitchen.

"It's the only way," Rosalind insisted. "Me or Russell will do it. Pick one."

"Why *my* arm?" I wailed, limply offering it to her. "Why can't we use *your* arm?"

"Because you're the baby, and Mommy will do anything for her Rita Cakes."

I stuck out my tongue, rankled by a nickname that I had outgrown.

Rosalind yanked my forearm, then sucked hard until a red flower appeared on my skin. We stood back to admire it. Although it didn't swell as we had hoped, the red blotch was convincing.

Phase two of the plan then went into effect: As Agent X brought sobbing Agent Y in through the front door, Agent Z stationed himself at the back door, gateway to the kitchen. Just as Rosalind had predicted, Miss Essie dropped her potholder to attend to me.

"See, Mommy! A bee stung me."

Mommy, somewhat skeptical, inspected the fading wound, then took me into the bathroom for some first aid. This was all we needed to get our investigation of the grownups' food — or what Russell called the "fact-finding expedition"— under way.

We conferred at the dinner table that evening. Rosalind and I listened intently as Russell described the meats, vegetables, and starches he'd discovered.

"Sounds like chicken-fried steaks to me," Rosalind said.

"Chicken-fried steaks?" I gasped, unable to comprehend a two-meat dish or why anyone would want to eat it. All that chewing! I couldn't recall ever eating a steak, but was sure I wouldn't have liked it. And fried chicken always needed Kool-Aid to wash it down. I shuddered and asked my brother, "What else?"

"There were some beans in the small white pot."

"Yuck!"

"What color?" my sister wanted to know.

Russell put on his thoughtful face, imitating his hero, the colored engineer on *Mission: Impossible.* "I'd say, light brown with black round—"

"Black-eyed peas!" Rosalind cried, as if they were as good as pizza. "What else?"

"Vegetation of the dark green variety."

I loved the way my brother talked. He checked out almost every science book in our elementary school library and always entertained us with new facts and words.

"Boiled?" Rosalind asked.

"Beyond recognition," Russell replied. "With a piece of ham inside."

"Collard greens."

I grew nauseous. "Chicken-fried steak, black-eyed peas, and collard greens. Poor Daddy!"

"Yeah," Russell said.

Rosalind picked at her canned ravioli, then blurted, "I'd rather have that than this."

How could she say that? Ravioli was kid food with its own TV commercial. When was the last time you saw people on TV singing about chicken-fried steak and black-eyed peas?

. . .

The following evening we were not our usual selves at the dinner table. There was no talking, no food experiments, no laughter. Instead, we bit the bullet, quickly eating almost everything on our plates.

Once excused from the table, we reconvened in Russell's room. There, behind closed doors and out of earshot of our mother, we each produced a yellow school memo from our skirt pockets or shirt sleeves. These memos invited parents to bring their home cooking to our school's first ever International Food Fair.

Although we were veterans of Mommy's cooking, we did not want anyone else to sample those hardened pork chops and rice bricks. We would never live down our teachers' pity or our classmates' jokes. We agreed that Mommy could not know about the International Food Fair, let alone contribute a dish.

"Mommy won't find out about the fair unless *someone* squeals." Rosalind looked straight at me.

"If anyone squeals, I'll bet it's you," I said, convinced that my sister, the black-eyed pea lover, was becoming more adultlike every day. It was only a matter of time before she joined our parents' ranks and ate meals with them, leaving Russell and me at the kids' table.

Rosalind rolled her eyes, which Miss Essie expressly forbade. Eyeball-rolling was right up there with saying bad words and talking back.

"Ooh, I'm telling," I sang.

"I rest my case," she said. "Snitch."

"Red alert," Russell warned, hearing the thump of Miss Essie's bare feet as they headed toward the bedroom. Quickly Russell slid his school memo under his bed.

Rosalind and I sat on ours, arranging our skirts over our crossed legs.

Mommy opened the door without knocking. "There's cake on the table."

Normally those words created a rush for the door, but neither Rosalind nor I could get up. Russell, seizing his opportunity to choose the biggest slice of Mommy's pineapple pound cake, jumped up and bounded past Mommy for the kitchen. As soon as Mommy retired to her room, Rosalind and I raced after him for dessert.

"Why couldn't it be a bake sale?" Rosalind whined, for Miss Essie's cakes baked higher than Betty Crocker's and her rolls were softer than cafeteria rolls. "Why a food fair? An *International* Food Fair."

"We're not international," I said, trying to be helpful.

"We're colored," Russell told me, because that's what we called ourselves before 1968. That or Negro. "Everyone at school will expect Mommy to bring colored people's food."

"Maybe LaVerne's mother will do it. LaVerne is

always talking about her mother's barbecued chicken and ribs . . . how spicy and lip-smackin' good they are," Rosalind said, beaming.

Russell and I glanced at each other, then at her.

"You had LaVerne's mother's cooking!" Russell deduced.

"I'm telling!"

"You better not, or I'll get you, you little snitch!"

I mouthed "Oh, Mommeeee" at my sister, who flicked yellow icing at me, hitting me in the chest. I dabbed the icing with my finger and ate it.

Russell said, "Rachel's mother is making corned beef and cabbage."

"Rachel, Rachel, Russell likes Rachel," I sang.

Rachel O'Grady was a white girl in Russell's class with red hair and freckles all over her face. Russell was too dark to blush but his nostrils flared, making us laugh. That caused Miss Essie to holler, "All right in there!"

It was inevitable that one of us would flagrantly break the dinnertime rule and have to face Miss Essie. As it turned out, this was me. For our school's science exhibition I was paired with Yolanda Watson, the other colored girl in my class. We were at her house and had just finished constructing a weathervane to rival all weathervanes when her mother announced that it was dinnertime. Without thinking, I leaped up from the desk and grabbed my supplies.

"What are you doing?" Yolanda asked.

"I gotta be going," I said, as if Miss Essie was standing right there.

"Oh, but you must stay for dinner," her mother insisted.

"Oh no, I can't! Mommy said we can't eat no one else's cooking."

Mrs. Watson laughed and said, "Nonsense, child. I've made more than enough. Go wash up. I'll call your mother."

I could not wash my hands until I heard Mrs. Watson talking on the phone with my mother. Mrs. Watson was so hospitable, so insistent, that Mommy did the unexpected. She relented. I then washed my hands, certain of one thing: I was going to get a whipping that night. As clear as Miss Essie had always made herself about the dinnertime rule, I knew I wouldn't be able to sit for a week once I walked through our front door. But I was on the verge of tasting food from the outside, and that made me fearless. If I was going to get a whipping, it would be worth every snap of Mommy's belt.

We washed our hands and sat at the table. "What's for dinner?" I whispered to Yolanda.

When I heard the words, "fried chicken," my face

dropped. Yolanda and her mother exchanged "what's wrong with this colored child" glances, then asked what the matter was.

I knew better than to embarrass my mother with rude behavior and said, "Nothing, Miss Watson."

Yolanda's mother brought out a bowl of cooked cabbage, another bowl of mashed potatoes — the smell of butter wafting in the air — and a platter of golden-brown meat piled up in a pyramid.

"What's that?" I asked, pointing to the meat platter.

Yet another look was exchanged between the two. Yolanda poked me and said, "Fried chicken."

"Unh, unh," I disagreed, anxious to take my first bite. No sooner had "amen" sealed the blessing than my hand was all in the platter, reaching for a drumstick. I bit into it. The skin, a crunchy cornucopia of spices, set my palate a-dancing! I could not recall ever being so giddy at the dinner table. I tore into the golden-brown meat, savoring the juices, still remarkably in the tender white flesh.

Next I tried the peppered cabbage, surprising myself by stabbing and eating leaf after leaf. I wondered if the other cooked, soggy vegetables that I'd hated all my life could taste as delicious as the cabbage. My mind reeled.

"Gravy?" Yolanda offered, as I ate my first bite of the mashed potatoes.

"No way!" I exclaimed, knowing she could not possibly understand the sacrilege of pouring gravy over food as heavenly as this. Besides, I wanted to remember each distinct flavor of Mrs. Watson's mashed potatoes, which were creamy but not mushy, bathed in butter and dotted with bits of onion. I ate four more pieces of chicken, then marched happily home. After Yolanda and her mother moved away and those Kentucky Fried Chicken commercials began to air on TV, I was convinced Mrs. Watson was the *real* Colonel Sanders and my friend Yolanda was the KFC heiress.

That night, having gladly taken a beating for breaking the dinner rule, I earned my sister and brother's respect. I also earned their envy as I described every crunchy, spicy, tender bite of what I now knew was fried chicken. My only regret was that I could not have shared the meal itself with my sister and brother.

Finally my sister's envy turned to outrage. "If the squirt can get food from the outside, then all of us can get food from the outside," she said.

"And just how do we do that?" Russell asked.

"By going to the International Food Fair. It's our only chance to eat other people's food. *Good* food. Just imagine . . . barbecued spare ribs—the way they're supposed to taste."

"Corned beef and cabbage," Russell said.

"And fried chicken," I added. "But how can we get there?"

Rosalind said, "Mommy will take us."

"Are you crazy?" Russell and I exclaimed, one after the other.

Even though the door was closed, Rosalind felt the need to whisper. "Russell, do you still have your school memo? The one about the food fair?"

He found it underneath his bed.

"Good," Rosalind said. "Now, what is the one thing Mommy can make?"

I shot my hand up. "I know! I know! Rolls and cakes! Rolls and cakes!"

It was not long before we were huddled into planning formation, humming the *Mission: Impossible* theme.

In her best handwriting, Agent X drafted a new school memo announcing a shortage of dishes needed for the International Food Fair—biscuits, rolls, cakes, and Kool-Aid. At Agent Z's suggestion, Agent X added French and German dishes—entrees Miss Essie would not attempt. As agent Y, my part was to leave the "school memo" on the table along with our homework for our mother's inspection.

On the morning of the International Food Fair Miss Essie told us to keep our school clothes on all day because we were going to the program at the school.

My sister, brother, and I were as jubilant as looting thieves. We could barely contain ourselves, anticipating the tables of prepared dishes from all over the world. Our friends were equally eager to sample our mother's cakes and rolls, since we had spent a good part of the day bragging about Miss Essie's delicious baked goods.

We rushed home from school and finished our homework in record time. Instead of our usual kickball game, we played cards out on the patio to preserve our school clothes. In between hands of casino we talked of nothing but the food fair and which tables we would visit.

Then five o'clock came. Miss Essie called our names, and we came running. With no time to lose we washed our hands and lined up in the kitchen to help her with the cakes and rolls. Miss Essie was ready for us. In our hands she placed three warm aluminum pans, tightly wrapped with foil.

Somehow the shape of the tins did not seem right for cakes or rolls. I who had once earned the nickname Rita Cakes could not detect vanilla, coconut, frosting, or butter anywhere. I raised the aluminum pan to my nose, took a sniff, and said, "Mommy, this don't smell like butter rolls or cake."

"That's 'cause they're pork chops," Miss Essie said. "Now let's go."

✦ ✦ ✦

Notes from
RITA WILLIAMS-GARCIA

"'Food from the Outside' is one story of mine that Miss Essie will never read because its truth outweighs the fiction. Even now, my sister, brother, and I often relive those days of sitting at the dining-room table before plates of pork chops or heaping bowls of 'Hackensack,' conducting experiments.

When we weren't playing with our food, we dreamt about our futures. Rosalind wanted to be an artist, Russell, an aerospace engineer, and I wanted to write stories. My allowance went to purchasing notebooks, postage, envelopes, and erasable typing paper. By age twelve, I was sending out stories to magazines and book publishers. When the rejection letters came in, Rosalind and Russell amused themselves by reading them aloud at the table, substituting their own versions of the editors' polite words of rejection. (Older siblings can be cruel!)

A year later I sold my first story to *Highlights for Children*. My mother divided the money among the three of us, and we went shopping for school clothes. After that, Rosalind and Russell would ask me during dinner if I had sent out any more stories."

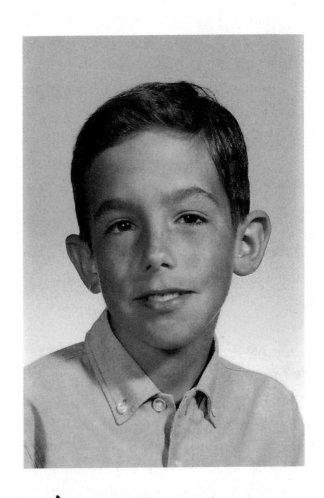

Paul Fleischman

Interview with a Shrimp

✦

PAUL FLEISCHMAN

He arrives wearing a maroon corduroy shirt and corduroy pants. Has he chosen this fabric for its vertical lines, in hopes of looking taller? We shake hands. He appears to be about five feet six. Though sitting down would soften our inequalities of height, he seems in no hurry to take his seat. His speech and manner are confident. One would hardly guess the secret he'd revealed to me by phone and which I've chosen as the focus of our chat — that throughout his school years he suffered from CSD, Chronic Stature Deficiency. Paul Fleischman was a "shrimp."

How small were you as a child?

I was the smallest boy in the entire first grade. Likewise, in the second, third, fourth, fifth, and sixth grades. When I went to junior high school, I was the smallest boy out of a student body of a thousand. The name *Paul* means "small" in Latin. My parents chose well.

Clearly, a severe case of CSD. How important was your size to you at the time?

It seemed the first and foremost fact about me, instantly known to all observers. It was my definition, my central quality — and I hated it. I felt myself to be a modern Job, punished by an inscrutable God. That I lived in comfortable circumstances in beautiful Santa Monica, California, ten blocks from the beach, amid a loving family, in a time of peace — all that meant nothing. I would have traded another world war for six inches.

Millions of young men forced back into service, cities in flames, the world economy disrupted?

Actually, it's not so far-fetched. Napoleon was a super-shrimp who tried to conquer all of Europe, at a cost of millions of lives, to prove to the world that he was really Mr. Big.

*And then there was Mussolini, the Italian dictator, in the
1930s.*

Another world leader who never tried out for the N.B.A.

*And then there was you — president of Roosevelt Elementary
School, vice president of your junior-high homeroom, then
president.*

With plans to take over all of southern California.

*Obviously, being small didn't hold you back. When did you feel
the disadvantages of your height?*

Staring at a tall adult's belt buckle. Standing at the
blackboard in math class, working a problem next to a
girl a foot and a half taller. Being placed in the front
row and at the end of the line in every group photo. At
my junior high school — grades seven through nine —
the ninth-graders had been granted a raised patio
called the Ninth Grade Walk. Any intruder from the
lower grades could be expelled from it — or, more
dramatically, thrown over the wall into the bushes
below. I *never once* set foot there, even when I became

a ninth-grader myself, for fear of being taken for a seventh-grader and hurled over the battlements.

The worst, however, was the humiliation that took place in junior-high P.E. at the start of every semester. All the boys sat in their underwear in the gym, waiting to be called forward to be publicly measured, weighed, and assigned a letter—*A* for the big kids, *B* or *C* for the moderately endowed, *D* for the runts like myself. Naturally, these vital statistics were read into a microphone so that the muscle-bound coach across the room could scrawl them on a card. It was a scene reminiscent of slave auctions and the inspections at Auschwitz. I dreaded these events for a month before-hand. They happened twice a year—six times alto-gether in junior high. "Only four more left," I'd tell myself.

Did your smallness loom as large to other kids as it did to you?

Yes and no. I've brought along my junior-high year-books. Have a look at the inscriptions.

"Stay out of dark bars and taverns, and grow a little this summer."

"You're one of the few who make me look big."

"Remember to stay out of tall grass (one inch high)

or you will get lost." Obviously, there was little public sensitivity to CSD at the time.

On the other hand, I had several friends who towered over me. Kids, it's often said, are cruel. But some kids can also be wonderfully oblivious of differences that rivet others. Mark Scott was a friend of mine whose stilt walker's stature probably derived from his habit of drinking an entire quart of milk in one gulp. People might have smirked seeing us side by side, but neither of us was bothered by the height difference. We were focused on the business at hand — skate-boarding, calling Dial-a-Prayer on the telephone, scouring the laundromat floor for dropped coins.

What were your defenses against teasing?

In the classroom, brains and wit. I was "the little guy with the big brain." I won my sixth-grade class's scholarship award. Brains earn respect, but I was liked for being funny. I wrote a joke book with a friend in third grade. I pored over *MAD* magazines like a Biblical scholar, even punching holes in them and carrying them in my binder. In junior high, where three elementary schools converged, I met a group of fellow *MAD* fanatics — the sharp, wisecracking pack of friends I traveled among all the way through high school.

What about out on the playground?

Speed and coordination were my compensations for being small and weak. I avoided football and concentrated on tennis, which I was good at. Stealing and passing were my fortes in basketball. My friends and I developed a style of play in which we controlled the ball for long stretches of time, pretending to shoot but passing at the last instant. Then, we'd sink a basket and win two to nothing. It drove opponents crazy.

And then there were the made-up games.

Can you explain?

Those were games my friends and I invented that were actually parodies of standard sports. The longest lasting was "skrugby," which was football played with the banana-shaped fruit of a plant that grew in one of my friends' yard. We used the sort of fancy terminology that goes with traditional sports — arcane names for maneuvers, cryptic signals, complex scoring systems. The great thing about skrugby was that only we — not the school jocks — knew how to play it. We were very selective about admitting new players. When we'd stripped all the fruit from the plants at my friend's, we began using two socks rolled into a ball. At the same time, we used the word "skrugby" for another made-up game, namely soccer played with a chalk eraser in front of the tennis backboards. In high school, when several of us founded an underground newspaper — another alternate, satiric world — we reported on skrugby games just as the official school paper reported on football.

Did you follow professional sports or only make fun of them?

I was a big Dodgers fan, not just because I lived in Los Angeles but because of their style of play. They used speed and brains instead of brawn. Maury Wills, my hero, was their leadoff hitter — small, fast, and an expert base-stealer. An infield hit, a steal, another steal, a sacrifice, and out of nothing they'd made a run. The Yankees, by contrast, were Goliath, with Roger Maris and Mickey Mantle bashing home runs. I loathed them. In football, the Los Angeles Rams had a player like Maury Wills, a short, squirmy running back named Dick Bass who slipped through tacklers' hands like a fish. It was a joy to watch him slither out of their grasps. It was the revenge of the small, the triumph of Charlie Chaplin over the hulking policeman.

One of the tragic side effects of CSD is loss of confidence regarding the opposite sex. How did your size affect your interaction with girls?

Grammar-school boys pay little attention to girls, but I did, for the simple reason that there was always one girl in my class who was shorter than I was. For several years Sally Stewart filled this role. I wasn't religious, but prayed she'd never move away. In junior high, when girls shot up like June cornstalks, the contrast between most of them and me became comical. I still remember hurrying out of a classroom, rounding a corner at a run, and smacking straight into an Amazon of a ninth-grader. She barely budged; the collision knocked me to the ground. I got up and tried to disappear, recalling the advice of Laurel to Hardy in one of their movies: "Act nonchalant."

I had no girlfriends during junior high. I went to a total of two or three school dances. Though I got good grades, I would have failed the test of sexual experience that kids used to give each other, awarding five points if you'd kissed (eight for kissing underwater, ten for French kissing), fifteen points if you'd—you get the idea. Strangely, not all short boys fell into my category. There were pint-sized tough boys, more muscled than I, who executed vicious tackles in football, smoked—despite tobacco's reputation for stunting—

and scored As on the sex tests. I listened to their accounts in awe. It was inspiring. Maybe the short could inherit a bit of the earth after all.

What happened when you reached high school?

Two things. Intelligence, creativity, life experience, political awareness — more and more, these out-shadowed looks. And then, when it no longer mattered so much, I grew. Not a lot, but enough so that I no longer stood out so much. I realized that I wasn't Job. Instead of being cursed, I'd actually been blessed with all the things that really mattered.

What advice do you have for today's vertically challenged?

Stand tall! You'll survive and prosper in the end. And you'll be much more comfortable in cramped airplane seats.

✦ ✦ ✦

Notes from
PAUL FLEISCHMAN

"Being short led naturally into being a writer for me. It was clear that I'd make my living with my brains, not my body. I wrote my first stories in grammar school—the adventures of two Chinese mice, the tale of an ice-age boy who thaws out in the present, a hilarious (so I thought) comedy titled *The Colonels on the Corn*. My father, Sid Fleischman, switched from writing adult books to children's books at this time. From his works—read aloud chapter by chapter, as they were written—I absorbed the pleasure of plot, the joy of playing with words, the stranger-than-fiction quirks of history.

Though my case of CSD lifted long ago, the experience casts a long shadow in my memory and has surfaced, in disguised form, in several of my books. Aaron in *The Half-A-Moon Inn* has a major physical problem to deal with, a different one than mine—he's mute. *Saturnalia* concerns a holiday in which the world is turned upside-down, with little children commanding their parents. It's a notion that appeals especially to the small and powerless. In *A Fate Totally Worse Than Death*, I took my gleeful revenge on the tall, wealthy, female aristocracy of my high school. Most recently, *Weslandia* stars a grammar-school misfit who develops his own alternate civilization in his backyard, exactly as my childhood friends and I invented our own games. Exactly as I still make up alternate worlds — short stories, novels, poems — today."

The Long Closet

✦

JANE YOLEN

At my grandparents' home there was a long closet that had two entrances. One was in the room my brother Stevie and I shared at the back end of the house; the other opened into my grandparents' bedroom in the front. You could sneak all the way through the closet, under my pinafores and Stevie's short pants without touching a thing. But at the other end it meant dodging around Grandma's dozen flowered cotton house-dresses that tended to wrap around your shoulders and hold you fast, or her muzzy, full-length fur coat that was like some large animal waiting to pounce. And it meant stepping over Grandpa's ugly work boots that were larger than any shoes I had ever seen, with their leather strings turned black with wear.

We played in that closet during our long Virginia sojourn, my brother and cousins and I. Some games were familiar ones that I knew from New York City like Hide-and-Seek, Sardines, and Tag. There was also a game we made up on the spot called Split, which had rules that changed whenever friends came to visit. Split was Hide-and-Seek in pairs, and the only thing unchangeable about it was that Michael and I, who were the oldest cousins, were not allowed to pair up together. We were too canny, too familiar with the hiding places, and too stubborn to be found.

The long closet smelled of cedar and mothballs, and something else, a heavier, homier smell that I realized years afterward had been my grandfather's sweat. My grandmother didn't have any particular smell, except perhaps a sweet talc scent; it was not a strong recognizable smell at any rate. Only later, when she was all alone and had taken up sucking on lemons, did she have a signature odor. To this day I smell a lemon and I think of her. But not then, not in the long closet. Not in the time I am going to tell you about.

We often visited Grandpa Dan and Grandma Fanny's little two-story brick house under the whispering sycamores, staying for ten days in the summer. It was a wonderful place for a holiday, with the Hampton Roads, a part of Chesapeake Bay, just a short walk away. There were many children close to my age living up and down the block. On soft summer nights you could hear their mothers calling them home, the names like a southern anthem sung into the dusk. Across the street was a family with four girls:

Mary Beth, Mary Louise, Mary Alice, and Alice. Several houses down were Frances, Willard A, and Bubba. I developed a southern accent, just to fit in, losing it as soon as we got home again.

But the time this story begins was in the 1940s, during World War II. My father had joined the army as a Second Lieutenant and was being sent overseas. So we moved down from New York City to Hampton, Virginia, to the house where my mother had grown up. We would be spending the war years there, safe with Grandpa Dan and Grandma.

It had not been an easy decision. My mother—a small and darkly beautiful woman, who was shy with strangers but forthright with friends—had to pack up all our belongings in the sunny apartment overlooking Central Park, and cart us down to Virginia on her own. Daddy was off in boot camp and not able to help settle us in. As the third child of six, Mommy had long ago carved out her own life away from her close-knit and confining southern family. Returning home was for her a kind of defeat. But the war meant sacrifices of a much greater sort for other people. She never let us know how much she longed to be back in the great brawling city she had adopted for her own.

Daddy came to visit for a week and then shipped overseas. We went to see him off on a big boat from Newport News, and then settled in happily with our grandparents. Only Mommy seemed to miss Daddy horribly from the start; Stevie and I were too pleased to be surrounded by our extended family, all of whom indulged us more than our absent father ever had. In fact, Daddy seemed more present now that he was away, because he sent letters home every week that Mommy read aloud to us. She pretended the letters were for all of us, but I could read the greeting. It always said "Dear Isabelle." It never mentioned Stevie or me.

Daddy wrote how he was winning the war single-handedly. I mistook this story-telling ability for the truth. It was ten years before I understood he hadn't even been in the fighting. He was a foreign correspondent, a newspaperman in khaki. When he came back to Virginia with a shoulder wound because he had been in London during the German buzz bomb attacks, it was convincing evidence of what a great warrior he had been. He played it for all it was worth, wearing his uniform for days after returning home, and keeping his arm in its sling long past any medical necessity. In fact, he never got to shoot a gun.

Grandpa Dan was a handsome, smiling man who always had time for his grandchildren — Michael and Linda one town over, and Stevie and me right there in his house. He owned a clothing store downtown, working long hours. But whenever he was at home, he enjoyed showing us how to use the tools in the garage, telling us stories, fixing the tree house in the yard. Grandma, with her white braids piled up on her head like a crown, was several years older than Grandpa Dan, but hated anyone knowing it. So we were never sure when she had actually been born. It made birthday celebrations odd to say the least. She was a bit more distant than Grandpa Dan, and she never told stories, but she walked the long block every evening. Anyone who wanted to walk with her or to work with her in the kitchen would get her full attention, but otherwise she was not exactly attentive.

After two tries at going around the block with her—she was the fastest walker I had ever known—I took the kitchen route. My favorite chore was chopping the apples for applesauce in Grandma's big wooden bowl. The chopper had a wooden handle and a dark, curved knife, like a scimitar I thought, like ones I'd read about in stories from *Arabian Nights*. *Chop, chop, chop.* I was Ali Baba and Sinbad and Sheherazade, sitting on the kitchen table and bending over the bowl. *Chop, chop, chop.* Friday night my cousins and Aunt Cecily and Uncle Eddie came for Sabbath dinner. *Chop, chop, chop.* We got to sit in the dining room at the big mahogany table with the grownups. *Chop, chop, chop.* And afterward we played outside in the limpid summer nights, the fireflies winking on and off. It stayed light in the summertime till past nine.

During the warm days, the neighbors' children and I played Chase-the-Dog, teasing a long-suffering mutt called Wowser. Wowser would take our pokes and whistles for a long time; he really had a lovely disposition. But finally he would have enough, rising heavily onto stubby legs to chase after us, whuffling like the Jabberwock out of Wonderland. At that we would all scatter, running and screaming with terror and delight. The older kids could climb a low projecting branch of one of the sycamores to get away from Wowser. But I was too short to get up without help. Mary Louise had to lean down and haul me up before Wowser got there. No one was ever bitten, though Wowser certainly had ample time and opportunity.

The one time I ever remember Mommy, Grandpa Dan, and Grandma acting together was the day Stevie got his first haircut. Mommy and Grandma protested because he had the sweetest head of golden curls imaginable. But he was already almost three years old and Grandpa Dan insisted. "This is no boy!" he said.

Grandpa sat Stevie on a silver-colored washtub that was upended on the lawn and, kneeling down next to it, proceeded to sheer off Stevie's curls. Mommy started crying, and Grandma wept as if her heart were broken, but the little golden curls floated down like angel wings to lie nestled in the green grass.

Stevie's lower lip began to tremble, not because the haircut hurt, but because Mommy and Grandma were making such a fuss.

"There!" Grandpa Dan remarked. "A proper boy." He picked Stevie up and carried him around on his shoulders for several minutes, calling out, "A proper boy! A proper boy!" Stevie loved that part and began giggling.

I gathered up the curls, as many as I could that had not been blown away by the breeze. My mother kept one in her wallet for years.

And then one morning everything changed.

I woke up early because I heard a funny sound in my bedroom. It had intruded itself into my dream: a kind of sighing, like the wind through the sycamores. And it repeated and repeated, with a peculiar insistence — an awful sound.

I thought at first Stevie was having a nightmare, but he was fast asleep in the bed across from mine, his snores coming in little *pop-pop-pop*s.

The room was filled with that lovely, scary early morning half-light you get in the South; shadows of the tall pines seemed to creep around and about the wainscoting on the walls. The sound came again, and I realized it was coming from the long closet.

I began to tremble.

Now I was not normally a frightened child. My daring in games, in running last from the dog, in following the older children wherever they led, was already a legend all the way up to Kicoughtan Road. "Dare Janie," the local children would tell one another. "See what she's gonna do." But this sound made me shiver. There was something almost inhuman about it.

I knew it couldn't possibly be a ghost or a monster. I didn't actually believe in such things, though I loved reading about them. And besides, it was morning, not midnight. But it was a sound that had such desperation, such loneliness, such sorrow in it, as if the house itself were weeping, that I knew — without really understanding why — that shivering was the only reasonable response to it.

I don't know how long I lay in bed, hoping that Stevie would wake up so we could listen to the sound together. Then I could play big sister and calm his fears and mine at the same time. But he didn't wake. He just slept on and on, with that quiet little *pop-pop-pop* snore.

"I dare you . . . ," I whispered to myself. And then I got up. Slowly I walked over to the long closet, my bare feet dragging along the splintery wooden floor. When I reached the closet — ten long steps from my bed — I put my ear against the door.

The sound was louder there—a moaning, a groaning so powerful it seemed to shake the wood.

Trembling so hard I thought I might actually faint, I eased the closet door open and went in.

Cedar and mothballs and that heavier, mustier smell enveloped me. Silently I walked under Stevie's clothes and mine, pulled along by a curiosity that was greater than fear. I came to the long winter coat that marked the beginning of my grandparents' things. Grandma's fox stole that I so loved to stroke brushed my face. This time it brought me not the slightest bit of pleasure. Grandpa's heavy serge suits, two of them that he wore only on the High Holy Days when he went to synagogue, stopped me for a moment. I pushed them aside and stepped carefully over his work boots.

The awful sound was coming in waves now. I pushed past my grandmother's soft, silky crepe Sabbath dress. Then I got tangled for a moment in one of her cotton housedresses.

It was pitch dark in the long closet because my grandparents' door was closed, but I knew where I was by the feel of every dress and suit. Dragged along by that heavy rope of sound, by the rise and fall of it, I pushed open the door.

And blinked in the sudden light. The sound was coming from the window. I turned to see my grandmother sitting in the rocking chair, staring out at the dawn. Her white braids hung down her back. She was wearing a flowered housedress. The awful moaning cry was coming from her. I didn't know what it meant.

Grandpa was still lying on his side of the big double bed, where the nubbly white chenille spread hung neatly over the end. I walked to the foot of the bed and waited for him to tell Grandma to stop crying.

He didn't move.

I went over to wake him, touching his shoulder. He was cold and stiff.

It didn't occur to me to scream. Or to speak. I had energy for only one thing.

I turned and ran.

I ran faster than I had ever run from Wowser. Faster than in any of the games of Hide-and-Seek, Sardines, Tag, or Split. I ran out of the bedroom door, into the hall, and back to my own room where I jumped into the bed with Stevie. I wrapped myself around him, big spoon around little spoon, and listened to his little *pop-pop-pop* snores till Mommy came in and told us both that Grandpa Dan was gone.

"Gone?" Stevie asked. "Gone where? Can we go with him?"

Stevie didn't understand what she meant. But I knew. I had known it the minute I touched him.

Gone. Not like Daddy who was *gone* overseas. Not *gone* like us from New York.

Gone. Like in dead. No more stories. No more tree house. No more cut curls.

Gone. Like in forever.

Grandma cried in her bedroom for nearly a month. Mommy brought her meals up there, sat with her, tried to reason her back to herself. Aunt Cecily came over and tried the same. But Grandma had to cry that sorrow out, I guess. There was so much in her, I couldn't imagine it all.

Stevie would sometimes go and sit on her lap and they would rock together for a long time in silence, staring out of the window till he got bored and left.

But I couldn't bring myself to cross the threshold of the bedroom. I would stand in the hall and call out, "Grandma, please. Please, Grandma." Until one day she saw me standing there, and stood up, smiling.

"I think we need to make some applesauce," she said.

I followed her like a little shadow down the back stairs. That day I chopped apples in the wooden bowl till my hand was sore. But I wouldn't stop, afraid — I think — that only my chopping kept her in the kitchen, kept her out of the crying room.

I never went into the long closet again.

✦ ✦ ✦

Notes from
JANE YOLEN

"My father's family, the Yolens, are liars, but more politely call themselves storytellers. If it's a choice between what really happened and what makes a better story, they go for story every time.

My mother's family, the Berlins, always tell the truth. Except about important things. Like age. Like death.

I guess I am a bit of both.

But all families have stories that change and grow over the years. Stories that start with a kernel of truth and get bigger. My own children stand behind my back when I tell these kind of stories, making their fingers into quotation marks and whispering to anyone who is listening, 'Author Embellishment.'

So I suppose the story of the long closet, a Berlin story told by a Yolen, has been embellished by time and by memory. What I have written is how I remember the story of my grandfather's death, except that I couldn't recall Wowser's real name and so had to make that up. And I couldn't recall the other games we played as children, so I made that part up, too. And while I remember Grandma's flowered housedresses vividly, as well as the fox stole and the crepe dress, the rest of what was in the long closet is pretty hazy.

I called my Aunt Cecily after I finished writing this

story. 'Tell me,' I asked, 'what really happened the night Grandpa died.' Interesting that in fifty years I had never asked that particular question.

She said Grandpa had been working hard at the store. He came home, lay down in bed, had a massive heart attack, and died. He was fifty-four years old, younger than I am right now. 'If you kids and your mother hadn't been living there,' Aunt Cecily added, 'I do believe Grandma would have died, too. She would have mourned herself to death.'

For years after Grandpa died, my mother tried to write stories. But she was a Berlin, not a Yolen. Stories to her were just lies. She felt that they had to be entirely made up, and so she did not put the truth in any of them. She sold only one story in her lifetime, to *Reader's Digest*, a piece that she wrote with a friend under the pseudonym Yolanda Field about not being able to have children and then—miraculously—having twins. My father, on the other hand, wrote magazine and newspaper stories that had only a nodding acquaintance to reality. He made up 'facts' with abandon, but was always, somehow, true to the core of what he was reporting.

Luckily, I got the Yolen genes in good number and I tell tales that are true, not true, and somewhere in between.

Author embellishment indeed!"

Left to right:
Elaine*- Sherry - Harriett

E.L. Konigsburg

How I Lost My Station in Life

✦

E. L. KONIGSBURG

Except for the time I want to tell about, the year
and a half when we lived in Youngstown, Ohio, we
always lived over the store. When my father managed
Harris's Men's Clothiers in Phoenixville, Pennsylvania,
we did, and then when he went into business for himself and opened a ladies' dresses and dry goods store
just two blocks down the street, we did again.

Living over the store had its advantages. For one
thing, we were always downtown, and every important
thing was nearby. As soon as I was allowed to cross
the street by myself (look both ways, even after waiting
for the light on the corner to change) I could walk to
school, to the library, to Sunday school, and I could
walk to the Colonial for the Saturday movie matinee
with my sister Harriett — two Ts.

Harriett and I shared a bedroom at our new place

over the store. A door in our bedroom led to a little balcony that hung over the narrow space between our building and Troxell's Jewelry Store next door. We had orders not to set foot on it. It was not safe. So there it was, as romantic as Juliet's balcony when she was wooed by Romeo and as useful as a hangnail. I didn't mind too much. I was a basic indoor child. I had my reasons.

I was not very good at sports.

Awkward would be a kind term.

Clumsy would be accurate.

The sidewalk was our playground. I was not good at any of the sidewalk games. *Hopscotch:* Drew the lines better than I could stay off them. *Jump rope:* Never could jump in. Always had to stand in. (Double dutch is still a mystery.) *Roller-skating:* Fell a lot. Never learned to brake. Had to run into something to stop myself. *Bicycling:* Still bear a scar under my chin from when I finally learned to ride a two-wheeler and went straight into a fire hydrant.

I was also hopeless at music. Once a week Miss Klinger came into our classroom to teach us music. She divided our class into redbirds and bluebirds. The bluebirds were allowed to sing; the redbirds listened. I was a redbird. At Christmas redbirds were allowed to sing, but all Miss Klinger offered were carols. Being

Jewish, I did not think I should, but I wanted to, so I did. But I never sang all the words. When I came to Jesus or Christ, I hummed.

Fortunately, gym and music were never given letter grades. (How could anyone give a redbird a grade when she was never allowed to sing?) So those subjects never interfered with one of my two best things: Getting As. My other best thing was being the baby of the family.

Although there were occasions, like music days, when I did not enjoy school, I always enjoyed—really, really enjoyed—being the baby of the family. There were only two of us. Although Harriett was smart and responsible, these things were expected of her, for she was the older sister. The baby of the family is never expected to do things as well as the older ones do— and when you are the baby of the family, they are all the older ones. The baby of the family is always in training. She gets the kind of attention that is some-thing between being a daughter and being a household pet. And she feels slightly adorable even when she isn't. There is an *unexpected* quality to everything you do when you are the baby of the family.

Phoenixville was a mill town. The mill was called Ajax. I don't know what was manufactured there, but I do know that when the mill closed down, people stopped buying dresses and dry goods. My parents had to close up shop, and we had to move from over the store.

I was in the middle of fifth grade. I was in the middle of learning about decimals in math and in the middle of learning about the middle of Europe in geography. Before we left, my school principal gave my mother two envelopes for my new school principal. One had my school records and the other had a "To Whom It May Concern" letter. My mother never let me see that letter because it contained my IQ and standard test scores, which were big secrets back then, especially to the person whom they most concerned— me. I had overheard my mother and father whispering about that letter, and I knew they were proud of whatever it said.

We packed up the family Plymouth four-door and went west, all across the width of Pennsylvania, and moved in with Aunt Rozella in Youngstown, Ohio.

Compared to Phoenixville, Youngstown was big. Last year's geography book printed **Youngstown** in boldface and gave it four lines of text. Phoenixville was not even mentioned.

Compared to our place over the store, Aunt Rozella's house was big. Aunt Rozella's husband was so successful that I was sure that if he ever appeared in a textbook, **Uncle Iz** would be printed in boldface and be given at least four lines.

Although this was to be only a temporary arrangement until we could find affordable housing, I think my mother did not like being beholden to her younger sister; and I think having a whole family move in must have felt like a minor invasion to Aunt Ro. She had a big house, yes, but she had her own uses for it. There was Aunt Ro herself, **Uncle Iz**, Dorothy, their live-in maid, and their adorable little boy, my cousin Morley. Morley was smart for his age — not smart enough to get As in school, but only because he was too young to go.

Except for Morley, who paid attention to no one, and my father, who was on the road in the Plymouth four-door, none of us was very comfortable during the week in Aunt Ro's big house with the live-in maid.

Weekends were another matter. On weekends we went to Farrell, just over the state line in Pennsylvania, where my father would meet us. There we stayed with my father's sister. Aunt Wilma worked in a bakery, and she lived over the store, and her children — she had two — were older than I was, older than Harriett, and one of them was old enough to drive us from Youngstown to Farrell. At Aunt Wilma's we were much more crowded and much more comfortable.

But on Mondays it was back to Youngstown.

Right across the street from Aunt Rozella's house was Warren G. Harding Elementary School, and a few blocks farther on was Rayen High, the only public high school on the entire Northside. A lot of kids from lesser neighborhoods went there. Harriett registered at Rayen. Once enrolled, she could remain there even after we found affordable housing.

Warren G. Harding Elementary School, on the other hand, did not have kids from lesser neighborhoods; so when my mother marched across the street to register me for the fifth grade, she knew that I would not be there when we moved into our affordable housing in a lesser neighborhood. I would be there for a few weeks at most. It was the time of year between the end of Christmas break and the start of a new semester, and both Mom and Dad had promised that by the start of the new semester, we would leave Aunt Ro's. So even though my mother knew that going to Harding would be a temporary thing, she took that "To Whom It May Concern" letter over to the principal and enrolled me in their fifth grade.

By this time I had observed that my cousin Morley, who paid attention to no one, needed a lot of attention himself. Furthermore, whenever attention was to be paid, he always needed to be the center of it. I had also observed that as adorable as he was, when Morley didn't get his way, he was not. Furthermore, as the new family pet, he was treated as extremely adorable even when he wasn't even slightly.

As long as we lived at Aunt Ro's, I would be expected to do things as well as the older ones — because I was one of them now. As long as we lived at Aunt Ro's, I would have to make do with only one of my two best things; and that was getting *A*s.

But there was a problem. Fifth grade at Warren G. Harding Elementary School was not in the middle of the middle of Europe in geography. They were in the middle of the United States. And, within the first week of my being there, they would be having a semester test. I was determined to pass that test, and not only pass it, but get an A. Maybe an A–plus.

I had to. I had to show everyone, Aunt Rozella and Uncle Iz — and most especially me, myself — that I could do what was expected — whatever that "To Whom It May Concern" letter had said I could.

When I got my A — maybe an A–plus — my new principal could announce it over the public-address system that, against all odds, Elaine Lobl had gotten an A — maybe an A–plus — on the semester test in geography. And when I walked into the classroom, the new teacher and all the students could give me a standing ovation — whatever that was.

I crammed. I made my mother ask me every question at the end of every chapter. I practiced spelling the names of all the cities I was to know about, and when I went to bed, the only thing that kept me from having nightmares was the dream of that teacher leading the applause as I went up to collect my perfect paper.

She passed out the corrected test papers, starting with the highest score. Not mine. Second highest, not mine. Third, not mine. I was about two-thirds of the way down the list. (I still remember one of the questions: What is the chief food fed to pigs in Virginia? I didn't know the answer then, but I do now.)

When you have lost your home, when you have a "To Whom It May Concern" letter to live up to, when you are no longer the baby of the family, when you think that getting an unexpected A is all you can do to restore your place in the family, being two-thirds down the list is as good as failure.

I carried my test paper across the street. Aunt Ro asked me how I did, and swallowing hard, I answered, "She asked the wrong questions for the answers I gave."

Finally, we had a house to rent. And not a minute too soon. I was happy to leave Aunt Ro, Cousin Morley, and Warren G. Harding: Displaced, replaced, and out of place.

A new semester was starting, and I would be going

to William McKinley Elementary School. My teacher would be Miss Frances Thompson, and neither she nor the principal, Mr. Perkins, would see the "To Whom It May Concern" letter because I begged my mother not to show it to them.

William McKinley Elementary did not have a lunchroom. My dad was still looking for work, selling notions out of the back of his car to make expenses, so he did not come home during the week and certainly not for lunch. My sister was at Rayen High, which had a school cafeteria, so she did not come home for lunch either. I did. It was just Mama and just me. Just canned soup and good rye bread. We were as poor as we would ever be, but those lunch hours were rich magic. My mother would have lunch on the table and the radio on our favorite soap opera when I came home. We would listen to *Mary Noble, Backstage Wife* while we ate lunch, and then we would redd up and talk. ("Redd up" is what Pennsylvanians say instead of "tidying up.")

My mother and I loved the same radio programs and Franklin D. Roosevelt. We loved the same movie stars and hated the same ones, too. We both loved clothes but couldn't afford any. My mother seemed to want for me exactly the same things I wanted for myself. She was proud of me, and I was proud of her. I thought my mother was perfect, and she made me feel that I was almost. We had a kind of easiness with each other, and I couldn't think of living anywhere that she was not. I loved her achingly.

When Miss Thompson passed out report cards for that first six weeks' grading period, she announced that she was giving out the best report card she had ever made out in all her years of teaching: All *A*s and one A–minus. And that report card was mine. I was back where I belonged — at the head of the class at William McKinley Elementary School and the baby of the family at 1507 Florencedale Avenue.

When I got to sixth grade, I had two new teachers, Mrs. Clark and Miss Mayer, both of whom I loved — although I probably loved Mrs. Clark more. I was getting *A*s from both of them, and I was sometimes allowed to sing even when it wasn't Christmas.

Then a few months before my eleventh birthday, on a day that will go down in infamy, my mother announced that she was going to have a baby. My mother, who would not even consider letting us have a puppy because we couldn't afford another mouth to feed, this same mother announced that she was about to have a baby.

I was to be replaced again. I was outraged.

And I was embarrassed. By then, I knew what it took to get pregnant, and I thought that my mother ought to be ashamed of herself, that at her age — she was thirty-four years old — she had done it.

Neither my father nor my mother ever used the word *pregnant*. He said that my mother "was in the family way," and she said that she "was expecting."

My father was still having a lot of trouble finding steady work, still traveling, still coming home only on the odd weekend, and I suspected that he was no more pleased than I was about having a new baby in the family, but I supposed he felt partly responsible. My father asked Harriett and me to take care of her. Knowing how responsible Harriett was, he asked her to arrange to double up on her classes so that when the semester was over, she could skip the rest of the school year and stay home to take care of our mother. Harriett agreed.

Only weeks later, I was told that we couldn't pay the rent at 1507 Florencedale. I was told that we would be moving to cheaper housing in a lesser neighborhood. Still Youngstown. Still the Northside. Still Rayen High for Harriett. But not William McKinley for me. Our new place would be in a different elementary school district. I was to be displaced again.

Mr. Perkins, the school principal, called my

mother in to school and told her that he and both my teachers, Miss Mayer and Mrs. Clark, thought I would be out of place at the new school. They wanted me to stay at William McKinley, and if my mother would allow me to be bused, they could get an out-of-district permission for me. She agreed.

So every morning, Harriett and I caught a city bus, using school bus coupons. I got off at the Thornton Street stop on Fifth Avenue and walked the few blocks to the big yellow brick building that said "McKinley School" carved in stone above the door. Harriett rode on to Rayen High. I carried my lunch and ate alone in Mrs. Clark's classroom.

When her doubling-up semester was over, it was Harriett who had those magic lunch hours with my mother. I was left out.

I no longer thought that my mother was perfect, and she no longer made me feel that I was almost.

I helped with the supper dishes, and I learned to help with the ironing, but I still felt left out. I felt as if I had not only lost my lunch companion, I had lost my place at the table. We no longer had a kind of easiness with each other, I began to think of my mother as "She."

She who was expecting was not feeling too healthy most of the time. She developed a terrible rash on her arms and chest, and her gums bled when she brushed her teeth. She was anemic even though she had the appetite of a sumo wrestler. She craved strange foods out of season. Every time she had to stand for any length of time, the veins in her legs swelled and turned blue, and as her stomach grew, so did the size and number of blue swollen veins. The veins had a name: *Varicose,* but my mother was a *She,* and the baby was an *it.* Not even a capital *i.* Just *it.*

Harriett and I walked with her to Dr. Kaufmann's office downtown because we didn't have money for bus fare. Our new apartment was closer to town than Florencedale Avenue had been, but since we lived on the second floor, she who was in the family way did a lot of huffing and puffing getting up that flight of stairs. We had no health insurance, and Medicaid had not yet been invented, and we had neither friends nor family in the medical profession, so Dr. Kaufmann agreed to deliver it at a lowered fee because he was Aunt Rozella's doctor and personal friend, a fact she reminded us of even though Dr. Kaufmann didn't.

My father found a job in Farrell. And he found us affordable housing. As soon as school was over, we would once again be living over a store. We would have a kitchen downstairs and a living room, two bedrooms, and a bath upstairs — over the store. The store itself was empty. The windows were not boarded up, but were whited out with a paste made from Bon Ami cleanser.

We had hardly moved our furniture into the new place when my father said, "her time is near," and we had to move her back to Aunt Rozella's so that she could be near the hospital and Dr. Kaufmann.

I thought to myself, "It better be a boy." A baby brother would allow me to be The Baby Sister, a secondary role, but one that would certainly have more status than being The Middle Child.

She delivered it on June 12, right on schedule.

It was a girl.

She named it Sherry Hope.

She actually thought that she had invented the name Sherry.

I found out that she was nursing it instead of giving it a bottle, and that was just more proof of how she was just too old and too old-fashioned to be having babies. To myself, I called it Sherry Hope-There's-No-More.

Back then, Southside Hospital in Youngstown, Ohio, kept women who had just given birth for two full weeks, and they would not allow anyone under the age of fourteen to set foot inside. So Harriett, who was fifteen and a half, got to see it, and so did Aunt Rozella.

Uncle Iz could have gone if he had wanted to. Even Aunt Ruth was allowed to go. Aunt Ruth was about to have a baby herself, but Southside let her in regardless of what she might be carrying. Not me. They wouldn't let me see it. Everyone who did said that it was as beautiful as its name.

Since Dad's new job meant that he had regular working hours, he went every night, and guess who he took along with him? Harriett, his fifteen-and-a-half-year-old daughter. He told me that even though he, too, had wanted a boy, he had to admit that it was beautiful.

So on the fifteenth day after it was born, Harriett and my father went to the hospital to bring them home. I had to stay behind to redd up the house. I waited by the window until I saw the car pull up. I was outside by the curb waiting when she stepped out of the family Plymouth and handed me a bundle in a pink flannel receiving blanket. She told me to support its neck.

I pulled the blanket back.

And I saw.

I saw the most beautiful baby in the whole world. A gorgeous, golden baby girl.

This was no "it." This was Sherry. Sherry Hope Lobl. This was my baby sister, as bright and as golden as the wine of her name.

From that moment on, I didn't want to let her go, and I never have. The new baby of the family became the girl who is my sister who became the woman who is my lifelong friend.

Sherry and I are both grandmothers now. She lives in southern Ohio, and I live in north Florida, but we talk to each other on the phone every day — sometimes a couple of times a day — and we have the phone bills to prove it.

✦ ✦ ✦

Notes from
E. L. KONIGSBURG

"In those Youngstown days when my father was out of work and trying so hard to find a job, I didn't know that what was happening to our family was happening to a lot of other families, too. That period of history is so famous that it has a name: The Great Depression.

When I was your age, the only way I could relate to the world at large was by reading books, but what I found there never matched what I saw around me. If the kids were poor, they lived in England a long time ago. If they had adventures, they didn't live in landlocked places like Farrell, Pennsylvania, or Youngs-town, Ohio. And if their mothers were having babies, no one mentioned varicose veins or children who felt they were being replaced.

I was a grown woman and a mother of three before I even thought about becoming a writer. After the third of my three children started kinder-garten, I decided to write. I was prompted to do so more by incidents that happened in their lives than by incidents that happened in mine. I wanted to write something that reflected their kind of growing up because when I was your age, I never felt that the books I read reflected me.

My sister Harriett lived in Farrell until last year, when she moved to nearby Hermitage. Both of her married children live near Youngstown.

I don't think you would call my cousin Morley cute now, but you would call him handsome. He is still smart for his age. He is a **federal judge** in Ohio.

The yellow brick building that was William McKinley Elementary School is boarded up, and the little patch of yard around it is littered and unkempt. Towns change. Memories don't. In my mind, those yellow bricks are golden."

Howard Norman

Bus Problems

✦

HOWARD NORMAN

In the summer of 1959, I spent every weekday as an assistant to Mr. Pinnie Oler, librarian and driver of the bookmobile. This was in Grand Rapids, Michigan. It was a very hot summer. In fact, on the day I want especially to tell about, July 23, WGRD radio announced that it was the hottest day of the decade so far: 103°.

The bookmobile was an old, rickety school bus painted blue. It was fitted inside with bookshelves and two leather benches you could sit on to read. The benches were repaired with small strips of masking tape. There was a fan screwed to the dashboard, and a second fan was nailed to the back shelves, so that air circulated nicely and helped cool things down.

Mr. Oler was, I would guess, about forty. He had a slight Dutch accent. There were a lot of Dutch Reform churches in town. He was about five feet eight inches tall, the same height as my father. Mr. Oler had a thin face, a sad face, I thought. He had sandy brown hair combed straight back. He always wore tan-colored slacks, white socks, black high-topped tennis shoes and a long-sleeved white shirt. He *never* rolled up the sleeves, not even on the hottest day of the 1950s.

In the *Grand Rapids Press,* the job had been listed as a "volunteer position." The day after school got out, June 9, my mother, Estelle, took me to the book-mobile and said, "My son's interested in the job." After shaking my hand and scarcely looking me over, Mr. Oler said, "He'll do fine." I started work the very next morning. My job included repairing torn pages with Scotch tape, spraying books with a special solution that killed dust mites, writing out overdue notices, and other odds and ends. From the get-go, I took my job seriously. When I stepped into the bookmobile at 8:45 on the corner of Giddings and Market Street, Mr. Oler would say, "Good morning, kid," then hand me a list of chores. Also, he kept an ice chest near his seat and gave me a bottle of Ne-Hi orange soda to go with my lunch every noon. Actually, in the Midwest we called it "pop," not soda. I remember this job as being the first thing I was truly proud of.

I had only one friend—one was enough. His name was Paul Amundson. I would have hung out with Paul after work and on weekends, no doubt about it, but that summer he was visiting his grandparents in Norway. I wrote him a letter:

Dear Paul,

I'm working on the bookmobile this summer.
See you this September.

Your friend,
Howard

It was the first letter I ever wrote. A few weeks later, I got Paul's return postcard from Norway; it had a stamp showing the head and antlers of a reindeer.

Let us say that you were standing next to the driver's seat of the bookmobile and facing the back. Filling the right-side top three shelves were books about zoology, astronomy, medicine, all under the category of SCIENCE. The bottom three shelves held GOVERNMENT/SOCIAL SCIENCE. The shelves along the back wall contained SPORTS/RECREATION/HOBBIES. Now, along the left side of the bookmobile: the top three shelves held FICTION/POETRY, whereas the bottom three were reserved for children's books, under the sign that said JUVENILE. The wooden card catalogue was in the back left corner. On top of the catalogue was a slotted box: BOOK REQUESTS.

The bookmobile was a secure and peaceful place.

My father was away somewhere mysterious and unknown to me that summer. He was what I would call a ghost in our house, someone who once belonged but no longer did, yet insisted on showing up now and then, causing a disturbance, getting everyone upset, then disappearing to who knows where. I had three brothers. My older brother was at a disciplinary camp for juvenile delinquents; he had stolen a car. My two younger brothers were at home with my mother. I was happy to not spend my days at home. All in all, the bookmobile gave me a lot of privacy. And I had ample time to carry out my most private passion, which was looking at photographs (in the SCIENCE section) and reading (in SCIENCE and FICTION) about the Arctic—the most remote and barren region of the world. Eskimos, polar bears, icebergs. In the bookmobile I read all the books written by Jack London. *White Fang* was my favorite. From such novels I understood that the far north was a place where serious once-in-a-lifetime adventures were taking place. Though I also remember thinking that if I lived in the Arctic I would miss trees. I loved the big shady maple and oak trees in Michigan.

Like any kid footloose on the weekends, I more or less killed time. I rode my bicycle. I fished for crappies and sunfish in Reed's Lake and the Thornapple River. But the bookmobile was my weekday home that summer.

Engine-wise, the bus was dilapidated, and often broke down. Mr. Oler would just shrug and say, "We've got a bus problem." The bus might stall out in the middle of the street, the radiator might spout steam and water like a geyser, or oil might spill out beneath the bus. When we had a bus problem, Mr. Oler would find the nearest telephone and call his wife, Martha, who was a mechanic for the Grand Rapids school system.

Martha Oler was a very beautiful woman. I'd guess she was at least ten years younger than Mr. Oler. I saw her about five times that summer. I thought that she looked confident and interesting in her mechanic's overalls. When she pulled up in her pickup truck, Mr. Oler was always happy to see her. She would park the truck and carry her toolbox to the bookmobile. But before looking at the engine, she always kissed Mr. Oler. I mean, they took a long moment to hold and kiss each other. Martha Oler had dark red hair and was an inch or so taller than Mr. Oler. She had a quick smile.

Whenever she came to fix the bookmobile, she poked her head inside and said, "Fancy seeing you here!" Which of course was a little joke, since I was *always* on the bookmobile. A couple of times she could not fix the bus problem and had to call a tow truck. Waiting for the tow, she and Mr. Oler would hold hands, lean against her truck, and talk. Mr. Oler would pop open a Ne-Hi orange and share it with his wife without wiping the rim on his sleeve, the way us kids were taught to do.

Besides stops for bus problems, there were what Mr. Oler called "unscheduled stops." He was truthful with me about this. "Howard," he said, the first time he parked the bus in front of his and Martha's apartment in the middle of an afternoon, "I'm making an unscheduled stop. My wife and I are trying to have a baby." That is all he said or needed to say. I was too young to think about it in any detail. I only knew that he and Martha needed to see each other privately. At such times, Mr. Oler carried out the same routine. He would step out of the bookmobile, pop open the hood as if the radiator had boiled over, then disappear inside his apartment building. I would keep myself busy.

And so it was, on July 23 at about 3:00 p.m., that Mr. Oler made an unscheduled stop. He propped open the hood and went into his building. Using a world atlas open on my lap as a table, I wrote out the overdue notices. But it was no more than five minutes after Mr. Oler had gone inside that a surprise visitor stepped on board. I recognized Tommy Allen right away. He was what my mother called a "JD," which stood for Juvenile Delinquent. Still, she fed him supper three or four nights a week. I had seen a magazine photograph of Sal Mineo in the movie *Rebel Without A Cause,* and had heard my brother and Tommy call the actor "very cool." I think Tommy modeled his look after Sal Mineo: slicked-back black hair, black jeans, black tee shirt. He was my older brother's best friend.

When he got inside the bookmobile, he said, "I was walking to downtown. I see the hood's up. You got a breakdown?"

"Yeah. Mr. Oler had to make a phone call," I said, trying to protect Mr. Oler's privacy, since the truth was none of Tommy's business, I felt. "He's in his apartment. He'll be out pretty soon."

"That's convenient, the bus breaking down in front of his apartment," Tommy said. "Oh well. I'll just wait here with you. Maybe Pinnie Oler'd give me a lift toward downtown a ways. It's a scorcher out, ain't it?"

"Hottest day of the decade."

"Says who?" Tommy said.

"Says WGRD."

"WGRD," Tommy said, "oh, well, then. Sure it's true."

"Can you really cook an egg on the sidewalk on a day like this?" I said.

"I cooked one this morning," Tommy said. "Right out in front of my house."

"I wish I could've seen that," I said. "What'd you do with the egg?"

"I ate it, dummy," Tommy said. "If it's this hot tomorrow, come on by. I'll cook one on the sidewalk for you."

I looked out the window and saw a young woman, about age fifteen, riding her bicycle across the field opposite the apartment building. As she got closer, I could see that she wore a one-piece black bathing suit with a short-sleeved white shirt over it, and flip-flop sandals. She had a fancy new-looking bicycle. She rode right up to the bookmobile, got off her bike, opened the kickstand, propped up the bicycle, and stepped into the bookmobile. She was about Tommy's height. She had dark brown hair; you could see comb tracks in it. Tommy took one look at her and said, "Hello, baby," but he said it in a fake television-actor kind of way, I thought.

"Baby, baby, baby, *wah wah wah*," the young woman said, as though she was a baby in a crib. "Do I look like a *baby* to you?"

"No, I guess not," Tommy said.

Things happened in a strange and quick order now. She took out a comb from her shirt pocket, stood in front of the rear-view mirror above the driver's seat, crouched a bit, and combed her hair. Then she turned and said, "What are you boys doing inside on a day like this? Just across the field's a pond. Nobody else is there. Oh, my mom would kill me if she knew I went swimming with two boys and no lifeguard around. She'd be so mad."

But I don't think Tommy heard past the word "pond." A look of horror crossed his face.

The pond the girl had spoken of was known in our neighborhood as the "polio pond." It was a small pond at a gravel quarry gouged out of a vast rocky field. The quarry was about a quarter-mile from Mr. and Mrs. Oler's apartment. Anyway, this was a time in which polio, a really frightening disease that paralyzed you, was on everyone's mind. Staring out from posters all over town were a lame boy and a lame girl, both on crutches. The posters were designed to raise money to fight polio. In *Life* magazine I'd seen pictures of a girl who had to spend her childhood trapped inside an iron lung in a special hospital.

In our neighborhood, rumor had it that you could catch polio from getting even one single drop of the polio pond in your mouth. I don't know how such a stupid and false rumor got started and then became a more powerful truth than real truth, but I believed this rumor with all my heart. I knew that Tommy and my older brother believed it, too, because they had a curse, "I hope you fall into the polio pond!" which they used only on their worst enemies. True, the pond *looked* normal. It was very pleasant looking, actually, with frogs and tadpoles and cattails waving along the edges, and lily pads. But hidden in its waters was polio, and God help the person who dared swim or fish or even dip a toe in that pond.

". . . pond . . ." said the girl, and Tommy was fast out the bookmobile door.

He ran to the front and slammed down the hood. Then he raced back inside, sat in the driver's seat, turned the key in the ignition, started up the engine, and yelled back at me, "A breakdown, huh? You lied to me!" He shifted gears, and we hurtled forward. The bus jerked a few times, but Tommy was handy with vehicles — my brother had called him "a genius with cars"— and he quickly got the hang of driving the bus.

"Hey, what're you doing?" the young woman shouted, and then broke into a nervous laugh.

"Getting you to the hospital!" Tommy shouted, then concentrated on the road.

I threw myself onto a reading bench and hung on for dear life.

"You idiot!" the girl screamed at Tommy. "My new bike's back there!"

Blodgett Memorial Hospital was only five or six blocks away. Tommy pulled up to the EMERGENCY entrance. He turned off the ignition, yanked up the emergency brake, opened the door, and ran inside. In a minute he returned with two attendants, a nurse, and a doctor. They all piled into the bookmobile. By this time the girl was standing straight-backed against the card catalogue. "There she is," Tommy said, pointing.

"What seems to be the trouble with her?" the doctor asked Tommy in a very gruff, doubting voice.

"She . . . she . . . she swam in a pond that's got polio germs in it. The quarry pond. She's probably caught it."

The doctor's face stiffened and he looked furious. "There's nothing wrong with that girl, is there? This hospital, son, is *not* a place for practical jokes. Polio is not a practical joke." Without another word, he nodded to the two attendants, who grabbed Tommy and me and took us into the hospital. The nurse escorted the young woman from the bookmobile. She was laughing and crying. Inside a room marked SECURITY we were watched over by an attendant.

Two policemen soon arrived. They took down our names and telephone numbers. Then they went out into the hallway to consult with each other. One policeman came back and said, "Okay, you and you,"—he pointed to me and the young woman— "my partner's calling your parents to come and get each of you. You,"—he pointed to Tommy—"you come with me." Tommy followed the policeman out to the police car.

In the hour or so that we waited in the room, the girl only said, "My name is Marcia."

When I got home, I told my mother the whole story.

A few weeks later, we all met again in a courtroom. My mother stood next to me. Tommy's uncle Will stood with him. Marcia had both of her parents with her. The judge said, "Now, Mr. Thomas Allen, for the offenses listed here today, you could be charged as an adult. You don't, however, have any previous record. And your uncle suggests there was actually a reason *why* you stole a bookmobile, and then foisted some far-fetched story having to do with"—the judge looked at his notes—"*polio* to the emergency-room doctor. What in the world possessed you to concoct such a tall tale, Mr. Allen?"

Tommy's uncle pressed Tommy's lower back with his hand, making Tommy stand in a respectful, upright posture. "Well," Tommy said, "this girl rode up on her bicycle. She said she'd been swimming in the polio pond."

"Which you actually believe threatened Marcia's life?" the judge said.

"Yes, I did believe it," Tommy said.

"And *still* believe it?" the judge said, shaking his head slowly back and forth, as if suggesting that Tommy say "No."

Tommy looked at Marcia.

"If you swim in that pond, you definitely could catch polio," Tommy said. "Marcia, there, swam in it, and I think you should order her to have a checkup, just in case."

"I see," the judge said. "Well, stupidity and good intentions notwithstanding, I am sentencing you, Mr. Allen, to sixty days at the Kent County Camp for Delinquents. It's not jail, mind you. It could have been jail."

"Thank you, your honor," Tommy's uncle said.

Tommy's uncle pressed Tommy's back hard. "Yes, thank you, your honor," Tommy said, half mumbling.

"And as for you, Mr. Norman," the judge said. "You should not have been left alone on the bookmobile in the first place. I have already reprimanded Mr. Oler for such an oversight. Mr. Oler and I have settled this matter. I hope your mother's already given you a good talking-to, as well."

The judge struck his gavel. As the court officer led him from the room, Tommy turned and gave me a nice, forgiving smile, which I thought was the most generous thing anyone had ever done for me. He was forgiving me, I felt, for not shouting out, "He tried to save the girl's life!" Because I knew that was the truth.

I was allowed to go back to work on the book-mobile. Mr. Oler never mentioned the incident to me. I never mentioned it to him, either. Later, I heard that the place they sent Tommy to was a farm about twenty minutes south of Grand Rapids. Tommy had to slop pigs and feed cows and chickens, and rake out a barn. I heard that he wore his black tee shirt, black jeans, and black shoes every day. Plus, he wore sunglasses, even in the farmhouse at night. It is true that he took the tractor out for a spin when he was not supposed to even touch it. They added a week onto his sentence for that. I also heard that everyone at the correctional farm got to like him a lot.

Mr. and Mrs. Oler had a baby girl.

✦ ✦ ✦

Notes from
HOWARD NORMAN

"I chose this particular story to tell because I really never forgave myself for not speaking up in court that day, and because I feel that sometimes life just sparks moments of great drama. Such moments haunt you, and if you can detail and animate them on paper in a way that emboldens and honors the memory, you have become a writer. I never much wanted to write about my childhood, though I like to tell stories of what happened when I was young, especially to my daughter Emma, who is always saying, 'Okay, tell me what happened to you when you were —,' and then picks an age. In the case of 'Bus Problems,' what I wanted most to do was show how one minute day-to-day life can be so familiar, and then suddenly everything changes! Also, I wanted to write about Tommy Allen, who more than any TV or movie character, was a real 'action hero.'"

Pegasus for a Summer

✦

MICHAEL J. ROSEN

This is a true story about a horse. It's also a mostly true story about the horse's rider, me, but I can hardly distinguish what I remember from what I'd *like* to remember — or to forget — about myself the summer that ended as I entered seventh grade.

Outside school, I did two things better than most kids (and doing better probably meant as much to me as it meant to everyone else): swimming and horseback riding. Yet without a pool or a stable at school, I could never prove those talents to anyone. But the day camp I attended each summer provided for both.

Oh, one year, I did compete on a swim team with my best friend Johnny. I swallowed a teaspoon of honey-energy before each event with the others in my relay. All season, my eyes bore raccoon rings from the goggles. Ribbons hung from my bedroom corkboard.

But I hated it, hated it just as I hated every sport that had fathers barking advice from the sidelines, or hot-shot classmates divvying the rest of us into shirts and skins, or coaches always substituting in their favorite players, and team members who knew every spiteful name for someone who missed a catch, overshot a goal, slipped out of bounds, fouled, fumbled, or failed them personally in any of a zillion ways.

But I didn't give up swimming, as I had baseball, football, and basketball. (Their seasons were so brief, how could a person master one skill before everyone switched to the next sport?) And I devoted myself to horseback riding.

The whole idea of camp, which represented the whole idea of summer, hinged on those few hours each week at the camp stable, just as the whole of the school year merely anticipated the coming summer vacation. At camp, it was simply me against—against no one. It was me *with* the horse. The two of us composed the entire team, and we competed with greater opponents than just other kids. We outmaneuvered gravity, vanquished our separate fears, and mastered a third language: the wordless communication of touch and balance.

Still, I never completely lost my fear of this massive, nearly unknowable animal who was fifteen times my weight, and l don't know how many times my

gawky human strength. "Keep in mind, the horse per-
ceives *you* as the bigger animal," our riding instructor
Ricki would always remind us, though not one of us
believed her.

I had taken lessons from Ricki during five previous
summer camps — how to read a horse's ear positions,
conduct each movement with the reins, maintain posture and balance through each gait — yet the only thing
I remember is that I loved riding. Maybe I loved it
because I excelled. Maybe I excelled because I loved
it. I'd climb in the saddle, and instantly, other riders,
other horses in the ring, whatever it was I didn't want
to do after camp or beginning in September at junior
high — it all ceased to exist, along with the rest of my
life on the ground, shrinking, fading behind the trail of
dust the horse and I made heading to the horizon.

Curiously, most of the obnoxious kids, the ones
who did the harassing and teasing during baseball or
football practice, spent their hours on horseback jerking the reins to stop their horses from munching
ground clover, or thumping their boots into the sides
of their uninspired horses. Not that I deliberately rode
circles around them, but . . .

On those Mondays, Wednesdays, and Fridays when
we rode at camp, I insisted my mother pack carrots
for my lunch (for my horse — I hated carrots). I pulled
on long pants and boots even when the temperature

soared into the nineties. I slipped dimes in my pocket just to buy a soda in the tack room after lessons. And most mornings, I bugged my favorite-counselor-of-all-time Mitch: Can I skip capture-the-flag and go help the younger kids saddle their horses? Can our group have our lunch at the stables? In short, can I exchange everything else camp offers for more time with the horses?

Since I was turning thirteen, this was my last summer of camp. Ricki allowed us, her senior riders, to choose our own horses. She guided us along the line of readied, haltered horses, describing each animal, hinting at its possible challenges:

"Now, Smoky, here—he's a Tennessee walker, pretty gentle, though a bit hard-mouthed. Good for one of you stronger boys. Maybe you, Allen?"

Mitch would nod in agreement, or look down the row for a more suitable match. He'd ridden most of the horses. He'd even owned a horse of his own before coming to Ohio for college.

Appaloosas, quarter horses, pintos, buckskins. Braided manes, palomino coats, legs with white stockings, faces marked with moons or stars—but really, personality was all that mattered: skittish, poky, docile, bullheaded, rascally, distracted. Some horses kicked when another horse came too close; some had to be neck-reined, others tightly reined; some wouldn't put up with a rider's mixed signals, and some, well, you couldn't always predict.

It was up to each of us to say how much spirit or obstinacy we could handle. Twenty-four riding sessions lay ahead. Almost seventy-five hours with that one chosen horse.

"Now Sparky's a girl who likes to move," Ricki said, as she swatted flies from another horse's eyes. "Used to be a jumper, too. Needs someone to keep her in check, who'd enjoy her spunk." Maybe because Ricki looked straight at me, remembering me from other summers; or maybe because of the horse's color (a flecked white coat that Ricki called "flea-bitten gray—and, no, that doesn't mean she has fleas"); or maybe because of Sparky's blue eyes that sparkled as the sun shined in (was that how she got her name?): whatever the reason, I walked right up and took Sparky's halter. Mitch gave me a quick pat on the back of my neck, which I took to be his approval.

For each riding session, we'd saddle and bridle our horses with the stable assistants' help, and then ride into the ring to practice figure eights, pivoting, cantering left and right—whatever maneuver Ricki had planned. Then it was out the gate and over a long plank bridge that spanned a marshy, spring-fed creek. As if walking a giant xylophone, the horses' hooves struck each board, and the hammered notes echoed through the hollow. Then, single file, we'd follow forest trails barely wider than a horse. Mitch would call over his shoulder to point out a horned owl's nest or the sort of tree from which baseball bats are made, or to warn us of an especially slippery embankment. Across hoof-muddied creeks, through shallow ravines, over rotting white pines and oaks, the horses performed almost without us. We simply leaned forward going under trees and backward heading down hills.

Eventually, we'd arrive at the meadow for "open practice," which mostly meant a chance to break loose. Though Ricki hadn't instructed us in any gait faster than a canter, some horses, Sparky included, just longed to gallop—it seemed more natural. Suddenly the *one, two and three, four* of her cantering hooves vanished into a lift-off, a levitation I could feel the way you can feel the instant a plane lifts off or a roller coaster dips, and I'd be weightless, hardly resting in the saddle, my heart clop-clopping its own rapid gait as I hovered at a velocity only the tears that the wind jerked from my eyes revealed. In those moments—how long did they last? No more than a minute or two— Sparky and I flew and the earth vanished entirely beneath us. She had become Pegasus, the winged Greek horse, and I, a twelve-year-old mortal, by some miracle, had been chosen to ride her.

And then, by accident, honestly, when we'd be

heading back toward the barn, some horses (Sparky included) would shift from a gallop to a dead run, which, of course, was absolutely forbidden. It was too uncontrolled, too dangerous even for us advanced kids. It was too risky to allow a charging horse to stampede into the yard, careening into the barn and startling the tethered horses and the bystanders. And it was too thrilling — countless times more thrilling than anything else I'd ever experienced — to stop.

Lessons ended inside the stables, heaving loose the impossibly heavy saddle, slipping out the grassy, frothy bit, brushing and carding the horse. It meant coming down to earth and I could clearly recognize the odors: the horse's short damp hair, scratchy wool saddle blankets, the warmed worn leather, sun-parched manure, sweet hay and oats.

And finally, before leaving, I took my own reward: a bottle of orange soda from the tack room cooler.

Sparky performed like no other horse I'd ever ridden. Even Ricki told my mother on parents' night, "Those two have a special rapport." At every session, I sensed improvement. Sparky's trot smoothed out, though that probably meant I was learning to settle into her stride. She understood the instant I reined, leaned, and thumped my heel to move us into a canter. With Sparky, I finally understood what Ricki meant about how the horse and rider work in such harmony that they merge powers and thoughts to become a single creature. On the other hand, almost every lesson Ricki would pull me aside to say something like, "The two of you ought to try a little more this or that." I knew that "the two of us" actually meant the one of me.

Every day of the July Fourth week, it thunder-showered and lessons had to be held indoors. The horses liked this as little as we did, but even worse, the storm distracted them, unsettled them — Sparky's ears continually flicked forward and back, fixing on whatever the wind knocked, wherever the thunder cracked.

That Friday, riding our horses into the stalls, this one kid Brett let his appaloosa named Choco drink at the trough with two other horses, though Brett knew that crowding made his horse nervous. And sure enough, another horse nosed in, and Choco bolted backward, and started bucking. The nearby horses jolted away, whinnied, and toppled a cart of straw.

"Stop, you idiot son-of-a-bitch horse!" Brett shouted in panic. (While only the counselors minded the cussing, the horses, we all knew, did not like shouting.)

"Clear out," Mitch said, as he pulled campers from the area. "Brett! Quit screaming!"

Brett hunkered down, both hands clinging to the saddle horn, both feet flopping free of the stirrups. Then Choco's hooves fired into the stall door, knocking the gate from its hinges, and Brett toppled to the floor, wedged between the wall and his spooked horse.

Mitch snatched at Choco's whipping reins, which stopped the bucking for a moment. Ricki inched along the wall to help Brett slide out of the way. Mr. Olmstead, the stable owner, appeared, too, and seized Choco's bridle, while Ricki darted in to grab Brett. But then Choco reared, trying to yank his head free, and he did, his front legs boxing in the air. But since Mitch still tugged at the reins, Choco was off-balance and heaved himself backward, battering the rear of the stall, ramming his flank right into Ricki's chest, and pinning her momentarily against the wall.

And then there was screaming—whose? Brett's, no doubt, since he'd just missed being crushed. And probably everyone else's, too, as we crowded around. Ricki slumped to the straw floor as Mr. Olmstead and Mitch yanked Choco out of the barn.

Another counselor ran to call the ambulance. The stable hands hurried the horses into stalls or out into the field to make room for the medics. Mitch treated Ricki for shock—he draped a saddle blanket over her body and pulled bits of straw from her hair. Ricki squinted from the pain. Her mouth stayed open as though trying to get the air back into her lungs. I crouched beside her and talked in a low voice, repeating over and over—*everything will be all right, the ambulance is coming, just relax*—trying to keep her from nodding off. People were always doing that on television. Our bus idled right outside the door, ready to take us home. But we were going to be late. We had to wait, find out what was going to happen. A horse had hurt not just someone, but *Ricki*. We were in a different kind of shock.

A dazed weekend ended with Mitch's announcement at flag-raising, Monday morning. "It could have been much worse. That horse could have crushed more than a few ribs. She's got four broken ribs—did you know you don't wear a cast for ribs? But it also means no riding for Ricki, and probably no camp for her."

A few of us made Ricki cards or wrote letters. Mitch gave us her address and brought stamps to camp. It turned out that she lived on the same street as my grandmother, so I biked over three days that week to visit. There were always different cars in Ricki's driveway, so I'd ride over to Grandma's and have one of her ice-cream floats, then ride around the block a few more times, and then, convinced that Ricki was busy and didn't really want camp kids bothering her, race home for dinner. I also thought I'd tell my parents I wanted to stop going to camp; I circled that topic for three days as well, before dropping it.

The owner's youngest son, Gibby, took over for Ricki. We sort of knew him—he was the one who slapped the horses' rears to move them in or out of their stalls. Gibby didn't know our names. He didn't bother to use the horses' names. For three straight sessions, Gibby had us circle him in the ring while he pelted dirt clods at the horses that weren't keeping in step, until the time ran out.

Then someone besides us kids must have complained, because with only a few sessions left, Gibby brought out his own horse, Striker, told us to march behind him "in a perfectly straight line, one horse's-length apart," and led us to the meadow.

"You're on your own," he said. "Just don't run 'em." Then he dismounted and gathered dirt clods.

Mitch and I and a few other kids turned our horses away from the group, just as Gibby called out to someone, "Keep that blind mare to a trot." I leaned into a canter, and Sparky responded as though she, too, had been waiting for free practice. Behind us, Gibby shouted his warning again: "I said, don't race her. Take the field at a trot."

Just as I completed one half-circle, passing Mitch on his horse Paintbrush, a dirt clod whizzed past my chest. "You, for crying out loud! Listen to me!"

"You want me?" I called back as I jerked the reins to bring Sparky to a halt. Horses crisscrossed the field between Gibby and me.

"No, I want to talk to myself all day!" he shouted,

even though he'd come close enough to just talk. "Yes, you. Too many holes and burrows to be running a blind animal! Trot her. Got it? Trot."

"What do you mean? Sparky's not blind."

"Right. *She's* not blind, and *you're* not stupid. Look, kid, just keep it slow, got it?" And then Gibby turned to yell at another kid who'd dropped his reins over his horse's grazing head.

I hopped down and stood in front of Sparky. Her enormous eyes gazed to each side, blinking, wondering, no doubt, why we weren't flying, what I was doing on the ground. I moved to stare into her right eye, at the sun breaking from clouds that were as much in her eye as in the sky. And I shuffled over and stared into her left eye, at the herd of tiny horses and riders veering toward the woods. I pressed my face to her velvet muzzle, and I held my breath, trying not to cry, trying not to let my eyes water or my breath leak even a sob, but I couldn't. How many times had Sparky walked me through those woods, never once stumbling as she lifted her hooves across the gullies and rotting trees? She had always dodged slower horses and obstacles in the ring. She recognized me. Even Ricki said she did. A blind horse could do all that?

Before long, Mitch came to see what was wrong. I shook my head to answer his questions. *No,* I wasn't hurt. *No,* I wasn't scared. *No,* nothing happened. *No,* I'm not going to just hop on and ride on home. *No,* I don't care if the other kids see me crying. Ultimately, I said that I hated Gibby, I hated him, I hated camp, and everything else because how could I like anything if, if Sparky was blind! If the whole world was this unfair! Blind? How could I not have known that? Seen that? Felt that? Gibby was right: I was stupid — *and I was blind.*

I wanted to stand in that field and I wanted to cry at least until camp ended, and maybe until summer ended, and maybe until I turned thirteen or nineteen or thirty and this sadness, this overpoweringly sorry feeling — about Sparky, about myself — had run dry like the tears.

But it didn't take that long. The bus was waiting back at the stables. "Come on, I'll help you up," Mitch said and cupped his hands beside the stirrup as though I'd ever needed a boost from him or anyone else. I took Sparky's reins and led her across the field and into the woods, retracing a path that my own two feet had never before touched.

The next week, my last week of camp, Ricki felt well enough to return. Laughing made her chest hurt, and so did talking loud, so she couldn't do more than sit outside the ring and watch us perform for her final evaluation.

I packed carrots for Sparky and sugar cubes and every apple we had in our fruit bin. I didn't know how else to say good-bye. Instead of watching the other campers execute the set routine that Ricki had rehearsed with us, I brushed Sparky until her coat gleamed and Mitch called for the *R*s in the alphabet of camper names. And then Sparky and I executed the specified maneuvers because, really, they only required my two eyes and her four legs. She didn't fidget in place when I lifted each of her hooves, removed the halter and bridled her, mounted, dismounted, and then mounted again. She both walked and trotted in figure eights along the flagged poles, never brushing a single one. Sparky backed up, turned circles, left and right, cantered at the first signal, and stopped exactly along-side Ricki in the bleachers. I didn't have to ask her twice to do anything. And yet, instead of being pleased or proud, I felt only relief as I dismounted. How could I ride Sparky as though her blindness didn't matter?

On Friday, after the awards in boating and camp crafts and nature studies, Ricki presented her awards. The newer kids became Colts; some attained Yearling status; and some of the advanced riders, Thoroughbred. Moving very slowly, Ricki presented each of us a certificate and a card for a wallet, which, of course, none of us had. Maybe because I already had two

Thoroughbred cards from previous summers, Ricki left me out of the roll.

Then Ricki returned to her seat, gathered her backpack, and walked over, maybe to explain. But when she stood in front of me, instead of a whisper she announced, "This year, we have a special achievement honor, The Pegasus Award . . . " My heart beat so loudly I couldn't hear any of her words, let alone my name. As Ricki pressed a blue-ribboned card and a small trophy of a winged horse into my hands, I heard her say, "Just don't hug me. Congratulations!" I couldn't keep my eyes from filling with tears again, the happy kind, at least in part. The clapping grew loud, like the horse hooves echoing from the planks of our ravine bridge.

"Ricki," I forced myself to say her name. "Ricki, did you know that Sparky is blind?"

"Of course, yes."

"But—but *I* didn't. I cantered all those days in the field, and she could have fallen in the, in the holes, and Gibby—"

"Any horse can fall. But most always, they don't. You're a good rider, a careful one, and Sparky's eyesight is just about as important as her saddle color when it comes to riding. But . . . well . . . maybe I should have pointed that out."

The applause had stopped by now, and Mitch, crouching behind my knees, had pulled me onto his shoulders and stood.

"Bravo, Pegasus!" he exclaimed, while the other kids in my group leaped up to smack my butt as though I'd scored the final point in some important game.

Before we left the stables, I went to Sparky's stall. Under the dim overhead bulb, I waved my hands in front of one eye, then the other. Her ears flickered with attention. Her nostrils flared as they gathered a scent she clearly recognized. What did I expect to see? Each wide-open eye had any other horse's gaze.

And that was it. I never saw Sparky again. I never rode another horse. As for Ricki and Mitch, and even some of my friends from that day camp—they, too, remain within that one particular summer.

Curiously, it's Gibby I continue to see. Not in person, but when I obsess about the cruel things that seem so natural to us as people—cruelties to animals, including our own kind—it's Gibby, just a blurry image of him that reappears, shouting the word "stupid," and firing dirt clods.

One other thing does reappear every now and then. This image of myself, stunned and weeping in the middle of that meadow. And while that twelve-year-old boy and, no doubt, that mythic horse, are long gone, I now can see — rather than the sun, woods, or other riders — my own reflection in that cloudy, uncomprehending, sparkling eye of my horse. It's not so different from who I am today.

✦ ✦ ✦

Notes from
MICHAEL J. ROSEN

"That fall, something else — writing, in fact — took the place of riding (funny, how close the sound of the two words), although it might have been any number of other things, since the vacuum within me had to fill.

I began to keep a notebook of poems, reveries, impressions of moods and seasons. There were drawings, too, washes with a rapidograph — a very fancy and troublesome pen that I'd seen some of the older kids in the art room using. And because this was the Sixties, my recorded thoughts alluded to the monumental issues of the era: the ongoing war in Vietnam, hunger in Biafra, drug abuse. Not that I had anything to *say* about those oppressive issues, but I'd found some way to *listen* to what was being said about them, and that was by putting words on paper. There, I could study, in revision after revision, one lingering image, as if taken by a camera's flash, of an overwhelming, complicated, faster-than-I-could-process world.

Perhaps that summer, giving up not only riding but the realm of childhood that accompanied it, is where I might trace not my talent for writing, but my need for it. The very next summer, I began to work at that same camp, as a counselor-in-training for the youngest children, and I remained at the camp, eventually becoming the director for the eleven- and twelve-year-olds, until I was twenty-six.

For more than twenty years, summer camp provided my happiest times. Yet, somehow, I've allowed this story to make me sound friendless and broody. Where is my family, who have been the steadiest, most loving part of my life? I suppose that to tell a story is to create another kind of vacuum, removing so much of the real, taken-for-granted world in order to pull the reader into one that can be knowable, and I hope kindred, in a few thousand words."

Learning to Swim

◆

K Y O K O   M O R I

I was determined to swim at least twenty-five meters in the front crawl. As we did every summer, my mother, younger brother, and I were going to stay with my grandparents, who lived in a small farming village near Himeji, in Japan. From their house, it was a short walk through some rice paddies to the river where my mother had taught me how to swim when I was six. First, she showed me how to float with my face in the water, stretching my arms out in front of me and lying very still so my whole body was like a long plastic raft full of air. If you thought about it that way, my mother said, floating was as easy as just standing around or lying down to sleep. Once I got comfortable with floating, she taught me to kick my legs and paddle my arms so I could move forward, dog-paddling with my face out of the water.

Now I was too old to dog-paddle like a little kid. My mother had tried to teach me the front crawl the previous summer. I knew what I was supposed to do — flutter kick and push the water from front to back with my arms, while keeping my face in the water and turning sideways to breathe — but somehow there seemed to be too much I had to remember all at once. I forgot to turn my head and found myself dog-paddling again after only a few strokes. This summer, I thought, I would work harder and learn to swim as smoothly and gracefully as my mother. Then I would go back to school in September and surprise my class-mates and my teachers. At our monthly swimming test, I would swim the whole length of our pool and prove myself one of the better swimmers in our class.

At our school, where we had monthly tests to deter-mine how far each of us could swim without stopping, everyone could tell who the best and the worst swim-mers were by looking at our white cloth swimming caps. For every five or ten meters we could swim, our mothers sewed a red or black line on the front of the cap. At the last test we had, in late May, I had made it all the way across the width of the pool in an awkward combination of dog paddle and front crawl, earning the three red lines on my cap for fifteen meters. That meant I was an average swimmer, not bad, not great. At the next test, in September, I would have to try the length of the pool, heading toward the deep end. If I made it all the way across, I would earn five red lines for twenty-five meters. There were several kids in our class who had done that, but only one of them had turned around after touching the wall and swum farther, heading back toward the shallow end. He stopped halfway across, where the water was up to our chests. If he had gone all the way back, he would have earned five black lines, meaning "fifty meters and more." That was the highest mark.

All the kids who could swim the length of the pool were boys. They were the same boys I competed with every winter during our weekly race from the cemetery on the hill to our schoolyard. They were always in the first pack of runners to come back—as I was. I could beat most of them in the last dash across the schoolyard because I was a good sprinter, but in the pool they easily swam past me and went farther. I was determined to change that. There was no reason that I should spend my summers dog-paddling in the shallow end of the pool while these boys glided toward the deep end, their legs cutting through the water like scissors.

My brother and I got out of school during the first week of July and were at my grandparents' house by

July 7 — the festival of the stars. On that night if the sky was clear, the Weaver Lady and the Cowherd Boy would be allowed to cross the river of Heaven — the Milky Way — for their once-a-year meeting. The Weaver Lady and the Cowherd Boy were two stars who had been ordered to live on opposite shores of the river of Heaven as punishment for neglecting their work when they were together.

On the night of the seventh, it was customary to write wishes on pieces of colored paper and tie them to pieces of bamboo. On the night of their happy meeting, the Weaver Lady and the Cowherd Boy would be in a generous mood and grant the wishes. I wished, among other things, that I would be able to swim the length of the pool in September. Of course I knew, as my mother reminded me, that no wish would come true unless I worked hard.

Every afternoon my mother and I walked down to the river in our matching navy blue swimsuits. We swam near the bend of the river where the current slowed. The water came up to my chest, and I could see schools of minnows swimming past my knees and darting in and out among the rocks on the bottom. First I practiced the front crawl, and then a new stroke my mother was teaching me: the breaststroke.

"A good thing about this stroke," she said, "is that

you come up for air looking straight ahead, so you can see where you are going."

We both laughed. Practicing the front crawl in the river — where there were no black lines at the bottom — I had been weaving wildly from right and left, adding extra distance.

As we sat together on the riverbank, my mother drew diagrams in the sand, showing me what my arms and legs should be doing. Then we lay down on the warm sand so I could practice the motions.

"Pretend that you are a frog," she said. "Bend your knees and then kick back. Flick your ankles. Good."

We got into the water, where I tried to make the motions I had practiced on the sand, and my mother swam underwater next to me to see what I was doing. It was always harder to coordinate my legs and arms in the water, but slowly, all the details that seemed so confusing at first came together, so I didn't have to think about them separately. My mother was a good teacher. Patient and humorous, she talked me out of my frustrations even when I felt sure I would never get better. By mid-August, in both the front crawl and the breaststroke, I could swim easily downstream — all the way to the rock that marked the end of the swimming area. My mother thought that the distance had to be at least fifty meters. When I reached the rock, I would turn around and swim against the current. It was harder going that way. I had to stop several times and rest, panting a little. But swimming in a pool where the water was still, I was sure I could easily go on for twenty-five meters.

Our grandparents' house was crowded during the summer because all our uncles and aunts visited, bringing their children. My mother had three brothers and one sister. My brother and I thought of our aunt's husband and our uncles' wives as being our uncle and aunts as well — never making a big distinction between who was and wasn't related to us by blood. Our cousins, though, did not think of our father as their uncle. He had never visited in the country with us, and even when my mother and her brothers or sister got together in town, he was out with his own friends or else he would retire to another room, scarcely acknowledging their presence. My cousins never called him "Uncle Hiroshi," the way my brother and I called their mothers "Aunt Michiyo" or "Aunt Saeko." Even to my brother and me, our father seemed less like family than our uncles, aunts, cousins, and grandparents.

That summer, during the third week of August, two of my uncles, their wives, and my mother decided to take a trip to the Sea of Japan for the weekend, bringing my brother, our cousins, and me. All of us kids were excited about going to the seacoast. It was on the less populated side of our country, which faced China, Korea, Russia, and other faraway northern places.

I had never been to that sea, though the river we swam in ended there. When my mother warned me not to swim past the rock that marked off the swimming area—because the current got strong—she said, "We don't want you carried past Ikaba, all the way to the Sea of Japan." Ikaba, a village to the north, got its name, which meant "fifty waves," because the river was so turbulent and wavy there. I imagined the water tumbling down rocky mountains from Ikaba to the faraway sea.

Our three families took a bus to the seacoast, arriving shortly after dusk. We checked into an old-fashioned inn, where all of us kids were to sleep in one big room. My uncles and aunts—the two couples—had their own rooms, and my mother stayed alone, as she always did on these trips since my father never came along. If she felt lonely or odd, she never said anything—as always, she was cheerful and talkative. At supper, she said that she could hear the sea in the dark, but I thought she was imagining it. Lying down on my futon later I heard only my cousins—younger than I—laughing and screaming as they rolled around on the floor or threw pillows at one another instead of going to sleep the way we were supposed to.

The next morning after breakfast, we dressed in our swimsuits and walked to the beach, which was just down the road from the inn. On a narrow strip of white sand, a few families were clustered around bright red, blue, and pink beach towels. Some people were already in the water. Even a long way out, the water came only to their waists or chests. Big waves were hitting the rocks on a piece of land that jutted out to the sea to our left. Maybe my mother had heard the waves hitting that desolate, rocky shore the night before, I thought. They pounded and crashed, muffling all the other sounds on the beach.

While my uncles and aunts and their kids spread out their beach towels on the sand, my mother and I walked to the water's edge, leaving my brother behind with my cousins. I had never swum in the sea before, but I had seen pictures in my geography book of people floating on the Dead Sea. The writing underneath said that the salt in the water made it easier for people to float.

The sea was cold as my mother and I walked in—much colder than the pool or the river—but it was a hot sunny morning. I knew I would get used to it soon. We went in and splashed around for a while; then I started practicing my front crawl.

I couldn't tell if it really was easier to float. A big

wave came and hit my face sideways just as I was turning my head to breathe. I stood up coughing. The water didn't taste like the salt water that I gargled with when I had a cold. Instead, it had a strong bitter taste that stung my nostrils and my throat. My eyes burned.

"Try floating on your back," my mother suggested, flopping back and closing her eyes. "It's easy."

She was right. In the pool, I could float on my stomach, but never on my back. But in the sea, my legs and head didn't start sinking while my chest and stomach stayed afloat. All of me was floating; I could almost take a nap.

Once we got tired of floating, my mother and I started jumping the waves. Side by side holding hands, we treaded water, each paddling with one arm instead of two, waiting for the next big wave to come surging our way. If we stopped moving at just the right time, we could crest over the top and glide down to the other side, falling slowly down the gentle slope till another wave came and lifted us up. All around us, other grownups and kids were doing the same thing. There were so many waves coming and going. Sometimes we couldn't see people who were only a few feet away until a wave lifted us up and dropped us almost on top of them. Laughing, we would apologize before another wave swept us away.

I don't know how long we were riding the waves

before I noticed that my mother and I hadn't seen anyone for a long time. I thought of another thing, too. When we first started, my feet had brushed against the sand bottom almost every time we came down. In the lull between the waves, I'd be standing in the water only up to my chest. That hadn't happened for a while. My feet hadn't touched bottom for at least twenty waves now. I stretched my body as straight as I could, trying to touch bottom with my toes. Nothing. Just as I opened my mouth to point that out to my mother, a big wave came, my head went under, and my hand was swept loose from hers. When I came up again, I was turned around, facing the shore for the first time. I couldn't believe what I saw. The people on the beach looked so small that I couldn't tell our family from anyone else's.

Before I really understood what this meant, another wave rose, my head went under again, and I came up coughing and spitting. My mother, to my relief, was right beside me, treading water.

"Mom," I tried to warn her, but the look on her face told me that she already knew. Her eyes were wide open and there was a big frown between her eyebrows.

"Turn around and swim," she said. "It's not as far as you think."

"I can't," I gasped before a wave pounded me, filling my mouth with a burning, bitter taste.

My mother was beside me again, treading water. She couldn't reach out and hold my hand now, I realized suddenly, because even she needed both of her arms to stay afloat. The water was moving underneath, pulling us sideways. The beach looked farther and farther away. It was all I could do to keep my head from going under.

My mother started flinging her hand upward, trying to wave it from side to side. She was calling for help. That meant we were drowning.

Before the next wave hit us, I kicked my legs as hard as I could and lunged toward my mother, making up the short distance between us. The wave hit. We came up, both of us coughing and spitting, my arms clutched tightly around her neck.

"Listen," my mother said, in a choked-up voice. "You have to let go."

"But I'll drown," I wailed.

She stopped moving her arms for just a moment — long enough to put them around me and draw me closer. I could feel my shoulders, wet and slippery, pressed against her collarbone. "Let go," she said in a voice that sounded surprisingly calm. "Now, or we'll both drown."

By the time the next wave went over my head I was swimming alone, flailing my arms and legs to come up for air, and my mother was beside me. If it weren't for me, I thought, she could easily swim back to the shore. She was a strong swimmer. We were drowning because of me.

"Stay calm," she said, "and float."

We treaded water for a while, and between the waves my mother looked around, no doubt trying to measure the distance we had to swim.

"Look over there," she said, turning away from the shore and pointing toward the piece of land jutting into the sea. "We can't swim back to the beach, but we can make it to those rocks."

The waves had been pushing us sideways, toward the rocks, as well as farther from the shore. From where we were now, the tip of that land was about as far away as I could swim in the river without stopping if the current was with me. That piece of land was our last chance. If I couldn't make it there, I would surely drown: Heading toward the rocks meant turning away from the beach completely, swimming farther out to sea. If I drifted too far to the side and missed the tip of the land, there wouldn't be anywhere else. Every time I came up for air, I'd better be looking at those rocks, making sure they were still in my sight. The only stroke that would allow me to do that was the breaststroke.

I took a big breath and started kicking my legs with my knees bent, flicking my ankles the way my mother had taught me in the river. The arms, I told myself, should draw nice big arcs, not a bunch of little frantic circles that would make me tired. My mother swam right beside me in her easy graceful breaststroke — she was between me and the rest of the sea, guiding me toward the rocks, showing me how I should swim.

The waves we had been fighting were suddenly helping us. In just a few minutes, my mother and I stood on the rocky ground of that slip of land, looking back toward the shore. My legs felt wobbly, and I was breathing hard. The two of us looked at each other, too stunned to say anything. For a while we just stood trying to catch our breath, listening to the waves as they continued to crash at our feet. Then we started walking. The rocks formed a steep cliff above us, but at the bottom, there was enough room for us to walk side by side. Cautiously we picked our way back to the beach, trying not to cut our feet or slip back into the sea. On the way we noticed a group of people gathered on the sand, watching us. When we got there, they came rushing toward us. They were my uncles and several other men we had never seen.

"I waved for help," my mother said to them.

"We thought you were just waving for fun," one of

my uncles said. "We didn't know anything was wrong until we saw you walking on those rocks."

One of the strangers, an old man in a shirt and trousers, shook his head. "You got caught in a rip tide," he said. "A fisherman drowned there a few years ago."

Several people were talking all at once, saying how lucky we were, but I wasn't listening very carefully. My brother was running toward us. Behind him, the beach was more crowded than when we had first started swimming. For the first time, I noticed an ice cream stand not too far away.

"Mom," I said. "My throat hurts from the seawater. I would love some ice cream."

When my mother told people the story of our near drowning, that was the detail she always emphasized — how I had calmly asked for ice cream as soon as we were back on the beach. Every time we remembered this incident, she said to me, "You are a brave girl. You let go of me when you had to."

The way she talked about it, our experience in the Sea of Japan was a great adventure that proved my courage: If I could swim well enough not to drown in a place where a fisherman had died in a rip tide, then I never again had to worry about drowning. I did not question her logic — though years later I realized that my mother had said just the right things to prevent me from becoming afraid. If she had told stories of a near disaster, a close call—instead of the story about my courage—I might never have been able to swim again. Instead I believed that I had conquered that sea for good. All I had to do was be more careful and watch out for the rip tide. My mother and I swam at the same beach again the same afternoon and the two following days; we returned to my grandparents' house and continued our swimming lessons. I was getting so good, she said, that the following year she would teach me the butterfly.

Back at school in September, I swam the length of the pool in the breaststroke without stopping. When I got to the end, I touched the edge of the pool and turned around. The other side of the pool didn't look nearly as far away as the shore had from the sea the day I had almost drowned. The water wasn't moving or trying to pull me under. It was nothing. I started swimming back, past the first five meters where the pool was deep, then past the ten-meter mark, past the halfway mark, where the only other student from my class had stopped. I took a deep breath, changed to the front crawl, and swam all the way to the end. My hand hit the wall; I stood up. My mother would be pleased, I thought, to sew five black lines on my cap.

• • •

Though I did not know it then, that winter, when my mother turned thirty-eight, she began to be overcome by her unhappiness — not about me or my brother, but about her life in general and especially about the way my father seldom came home to spend time with her. In the next three years, this unhappiness grew heavier every day — till it was something she could not bear alone. My father stayed away more once he sensed her unhappiness. My brother and I were too young to fully understand what was happening, though we both knew deep down that something was terribly wrong. My mother had been the oldest of five children, the one who always took care of her younger siblings and helped her parents. She could not imagine confiding in her family and burdening them.

When I was twelve, my mother decided to die rather than to live the rest of her life crippled by unhappiness, unable to stir from the chair where she spent her afternoons weeping. She left me a note in which she told me these things and more. "You are a strong and cheerful person by nature," she wrote to me. "The way I am, with my unhappiness, I am no good to you. I'm afraid I would only hurt you by being around. You must go on alone without me. At first you will be sad, I know, but you will overcome your sorrow. Be strong. Be happy for me."

Her choice is not one I would make now if I ever found myself drowning in unhappiness. I would try everything to live. But I understand my mother, too. She had told me to let go of her when we were both drowning in the sea. Though I wanted to cling to her then, I knew that I could not. When she decided to die, she must have remembered that time. She was asking me, again, to let her go — to let her float deeper out to the sea, where she could be at peace, while I swam with all my strength back to the rocks. She wanted me to live and to be brave. Swimming now in the clear-water lakes of Wisconsin, where I live, I sometimes imagine my mother riding the waves of the sea, cresting over the top and falling gently without ever hitting bottom, laughing her easy musical laugh. She could be right next to me: We are separated only by glimmering water.

✦ ✦ ✦

Notes from
KYOKO MORI

"I decided to write about my experience in the Sea of Japan because it was by far the most dramatic thing that happened in my childhood. I have changed a few details of geography, and the 'real' experience happened in another language, but otherwise, the details are close to the facts from my past. Even when the facts are 'true,' though, our minds shape our memories. No matter what we write about, the distinction between fact and fiction, memory and story, is as elusive as the constantly moving wall of water that separates one swimmer from another.

I have always wanted to become a writer. In those summers that my mother, brother, and I stayed at my grandparents' house, my grandfather and I used to sit side by side every morning, writing in our diaries. In first and second grades, I had a diary that was divided in half: The top half was for pictures, the bottom half for words. As I grew older, words replaced all the pictures—*became* the pictures, which was just as well. Although I loved to draw and paint, and I still love to look at art, even in third or fourth grade I knew that words came easier to me than lines and angles.

My mother and her family encouraged me to write. My grandfather had been a schoolteacher, though he was retired by the time I was born. My mother, like her father, kept a diary and wrote weekly letters home to her parents during the year, describing the flowers in her garden, the cookies she and I had baked, the new clothes she was making for us, some funny thing my brother had said. Two of my uncles — my mother's younger brothers — are teachers. Because I am the oldest of all the children in my extended family, I remember the things my brother and cousins were too young to remember: When I was young, our grandfather was still strong enough to go walking in the mountains with me; my grandmother grew more flowers and vegetables than she did years later when my cousins were in grade school. So in a way, I always thought it was my duty — as well as my pleasure — to write down the family stories: To record, describe, and re-create the past so that it will never be lost."

Waiting for Midnight

✦

KAREN HESSE

In the early 1960s, I lived in a neighborhood in Baltimore city where everyone pretty much knew everyone else.

Our parents gathered on weekends for community barbecues while we kids, in shifting patterns, flocked from one friend's yard to another. In good weather, seven or eight of us would park our behinds on the corner stoop and put on a talent show. And every night, up and down our block, fathers would come out on their porches and call their children home.

"Harry!" That was Mr. Izzy.

"Bonnie!" That was Mr. Maish.

"Howard Brucey!" Howard Bruce's father had a voice so deep, he might have been calling Howard Bruce all the way from heaven.

My father didn't call me. I came home after my last friend vanished from the block.

Maybe my father's day job as a collection man exhausted him too much to come looking for me; maybe the constant battles between my parents kept them from noticing that it had grown dark and I hadn't yet come home. Whatever the reason, I didn't mind. I hated when evening came. I dreaded going to bed, because in my bedroom, at night, voices haunted me.

They whispered to me, whispered secrets, secrets I couldn't tell anyone.

Secrets about myself.

Secrets about my parents.

Secrets about the woman in the house next door. I was an unwilling conspirator in my next-door neighbor's secret. Her secret was so big, so cruel, it filled her own house and spilled over into mine. The secret of the woman next door was that every night, somewhere around midnight, she'd lock her children in an upstairs closet and wouldn't let them out again 'til morning.

Our row houses, on West Garrison Avenue, mirrored each other. The closet in the house next door was an exact reflection of my own. Those closets were small, too small for me to stay in for very long, much too small for the kids next door to spend each night in. All through the long hours, those children stood, jammed together inside that dark, airless closet, pleading with their mother to be let out. "Please," they would whisper. "Please, Mommy. We'll be good. Pleeease."

I heard every cry they uttered, every rise of panic, every whimper. Sleepless, I listened in my room, my bed pressed against the common wall between our two houses.

The secret of those children I kept along with all my other secrets. That's the way things were back then. You didn't interfere in anyone's private stuff, and no one interfered in yours.

I found ways to get through the night. I read under the covers using a flashlight; I made up stories inside my head, retelling those same stories at our neighborhood talent show the next day. I never told the truth about how things were for me or for the kids next door. Instead I kept my friends riveted to the stoop as I spun tales born out of my nightly need to escape the whispering.

Through most of my childhood my mother worked as a receptionist at Margo-Lynn Beauty Parlor. My father drove down the dusty back roads on the outskirts of Baltimore, collecting weekly payments from the poorest families, as they purchased, a dollar or two at a time, a new refrigerator or a new stove. When I got sick, neither of my parents could stay home from work. I went to school every day, regardless of how I felt. But on the days the school nurse sent me back home again, I stayed with Bubi Hannah.

Bubi Hannah lived with her daughter and son-in-law, in the row house two doors down from ours. Once, after coming home midway through the morning, I threw up all over Bubi Hannah's sofa. She never even got upset. She just cleaned it up, flipped the cushions over, and patting them smooth said, "Shirley'll never notice."

When I stayed at Bubi Hannah's house, sometimes I could hear the woman next door. She would pace, muttering to herself. I would look to Bubi Hannah, to see if she heard, too. Bubi Hannah would gaze into my face, her eyes moist. I wondered if Bubi Hannah knew about the children and the closet, too, but I couldn't bring myself to ask.

When I was ten, I read a story.

The story took place during Shavuos, a Jewish holiday that falls somewhere around the end of May. The hero of the story, K'Tonton, a Jewish Tom Thumb, plans to make a wish for himself at midnight on Shavuos, when he believes the sky will open and his wish will be granted. At the climax of the story, the sky does open, however K'Tonton doesn't spend the wish on himself. In the end, he uses it to help another.

It was a simple, moralistic tale, but arresting nonetheless, because it gave me hope that God might intervene if only I spoke out at just the right moment, in just the right way. I had plenty to speak out about: The way my parents were with each other, the way my mother was with herself, the way it was for the kids next door, the way it was for me.

I rarely saw the children next door, except occasionally when they twitched open their living-room curtains and peered out. They didn't attend public school. Their mother had made other arrangements. She had once taught school herself. My mother said she had been brilliant. But she had suffered a nervous breakdown and received no help, and that was supposed to explain everything.

We were told not to go trick-or-treating at her house, but never told why. We wouldn't have gone anyway. She scared all of us. Me, because I knew what she did to her children; the others, because she was so strange. Being near her felt like standing too close to a high-voltage wire.

It was impossible to avoid her, though. She would come out on her porch while I played jacks on mine.

"Hello, Karen," she'd say.

I'd feel myself stiffen as I said hello back.

"Have you read the newspaper today, Karen?" she'd ask.

I'd shake my head.

"How do you expect to learn?" She'd sound almost calm, but there was something in her voice that made my skin crawl.

"You'll never get anywhere if you aren't informed," she'd say. She'd stare at me, force me to look back at her.

I would slip off the porch as soon as I dared and race up the block, away from her, thinking all the while that her own children couldn't do what I had just done. They couldn't race up the block, they couldn't get away from her, not ever.

When I did catch a glimpse of her children — the girl, a few years older than I was, the boy, a year or two younger — the whiteness of their skin startled me. So pale, they were completely untouched by the Maryland sun, completely untouched by anyone or anything that wasn't in that house. No one knew them. I knew only their voices, only their desperation.

Meanwhile in my own house my mother sickened; dark circles under her eyes, no appetite, so thin a slight wind might blow her over. Her illness seemed connected to her unhappiness with my father, though I didn't understand how. Twice my mother went to the hospital. Each time she nearly died. Her doctor instructed me to take care of her: Do nothing to upset her; say nothing to upset her.

Each morning before I left for school, and each afternoon when I returned home, I would scramble eggs for my mother. I learned to make them moist, the way she liked them. From the time I left until the time I returned, and all through the evening and the long nights, my mother ate only those eggs. As I stood over the frying pan twice a day, I'd try to think good things, healing things, hoping those thoughts would enter the eggs and make my mother better.

"When is Shavuos?" I asked my father one evening.

On Shabbos and the holidays, my father served as cantor at a Reform synagogue in Baltimore. He sat on the bimah with the rabbi and led the congregation in song. I was approaching the age of thirteen, when Jewish children are admitted as adult members to the religious community, but my parents never mentioned my studying Torah or having a bas mitzvah.

"Shavuos?" my father said. "It's next week. Why? You want to come to services?"

"No," I said.

I couldn't go to services. I had to be home and awake when the sky opened at midnight, to wish for my mother and father, to wish for the children next door, to wish for myself.

The night of Shavuos I sat in the living room alone, watching television. My father left for services early; my mother had already shut herself in her bedroom for the night.

I climbed the stairs to my room around ten, washed, and changed into my pajamas. I listened for sounds from next door. The closet was quiet.

Closing my bedroom door, I turned out the light and stood at the dressing table in front of my window. *Less than two hours 'til midnight,* I thought, gazing into the sky. Surely I could stay awake for two hours.

My father came home a little after eleven.

As soon as their bedroom door shut, my parents started fighting. The air in the house prickled with their anger. The fight was a short one though. Within a few minutes the house grew quiet again; I heard only the occasional pop of a floorboard and the drip of the kitchen sink.

I thought everyone in the world had gone to sleep. It was just me and God now, on either side of the sky, waiting for midnight.

Still quiet next door. Maybe tonight, maybe just for tonight, it would stay quiet. I looked over my shoulder at my closet. My mother used to hang a calendar on the door and put gold stars on it for the days I didn't cry. I rarely earned more than a handful of gold stars in any particular year. She eventually gave up on the gold stars. I eventually stopped crying.

On that night of Shavuos, my feet grew cold as I stood waiting. My legs ached. I decided to climb into bed.

But I feared falling asleep and missing my appointment with heaven. To stay awake, I put my day clothes back on. I pulled my shirt back over my head, slipped into my pants, and sat upright in bed, leaning my cheek against the cool white wall. The time crept slowly forward. Once, I nodded off and started back awake. Rubbing my eyelids with the knuckles of my thumbs, I made myself stand and walk to the dressing table under the window.

I didn't need a flashlight. I could read my watch by the moon. The time was 11:39.

I wanted it to happen. I wanted the sky to open. I wanted to see inside heaven.

As I stared up into the night, a dog came down the alley and turned over a garbage can across the way. I shifted my eyes from the sky for a moment, down to he dog pawing trash, then quickly back up again. I didn't dare risk looking away any longer.

At five minutes to midnight, I tucked my chair in under my dressing table and leaned toward the window.

That's when, next door, the voices started.

"Please," the girl whispered. "Please. Let us out. We'll be good. I promise. We'll be good. Please let us out, Mommy. Pleeeease."

She sounded like a ghost, her voice coming softly through the closet wall. I turned toward the sound.

And that's when it happened. I sensed the change.

Quickly turning back toward the window, I saw it.

The filmy black of the night split open, and streaming out through the opening were the most exquisite colors. They swirled around and around, a dazzling display of radiance.

Out of that shimmering brightness, ladders unfurled. I could not see them clearly, and yet I knew they were ladders. And down those ladders, beings descended. Brilliant beings of light. They were angels. I was seeing angels.

I don't think I breathed. I don't think I blinked. My eyes wide, I took in every detail.

And then, just like that, the ladders disappeared, the colors vanished, and the night returned to its filmy blackness.

The entire scene had taken place in a heartbeat.

And I had not made any wish at all.

I had not wished for my parents to stop fighting, I had not wished for my mother to be well, I had not wished for the end of the children's suffering next door, I had not wished for the end of my own torment. I had stood before the face of God and wished for nothing.

K'Tonton, at least, had made a wish.

I wanted to cry, and yet my eyes stayed dry and round with wonder. I stood watching the black sky for a long time.

Next door, the pleading of the children grew quieter and quieter.

And finally, during a stretch of silence, I curled up on my bed and dozed off.

Suddenly I awoke. A different kind of light ricocheted off my bedroom walls. The light from heaven had filled me with awe, but this light filled me with terror. It paced around and around my room, like a caged animal.

Still dressed, I crept to my window, my heart thrumming in my neck. I saw two police cars in the alley below, lights rotating on their roofs, the low squawk of their radios crackling into the night. And then I saw the shadowy figure of a child, wrapped in a blanket, being brought out of the house next door and placed into one of the cruisers. A second child already sat huddled in the same cruiser's back seat. Alone, in a cruiser in front of theirs, rigid, unflinching, sat their mother.

Bubi Hannah stood inside her gate, her arms wrapped around herself. She wore a coat over her nightgown. Her hair, in a long white braid, hung down her back.

The police cars pulled away at last, and as their lights vanished, I realized my closet was silent. Completely silent.

I felt almost weightless.

The rest of that night I slept sweetly, peacefully, for the first time in I couldn't remember how long. I slept deeper than the voice of Howard Bruce's father, a sleep that might have come all the way from Heaven.

✦ ✦ ✦

Notes from
KAREN HESSE

"This was a hard story to share. But I chose to relate this moment in my life because it marked a turning point for me. On that night, the night that I've transformed into the climax for this story, a flame of faith was kindled in my soul. During that night, for the first time, I saw that no matter how desperate and unrelenting things seemed, in a moment the situation could change and there could be respite, comfort, hope. I have modified the story a bit; left pieces out, put pieces in; but the core of this story is true.

I learned at a very early age the reward of retreating into fictional worlds. Not only did reading give me an escape from a difficult childhood, but the characters shared their survival skills with me, skills that I could then mold, shape, and apply to my own life.

My roots as a writer extend all the way back to those long Baltimore nights. I never imagined that the stories I told myself in that little room on West Garrison Avenue would blossom into a life's work. I simply wove those tales to console myself.

I am still awed by the things people survive, how people can turn their most crippling trials into soaring triumphs. Telling their stories is what compels me to write."

The Snapping Turtle

✦

JOSEPH BRUCHAC

My grandmother was working in the flower garden near the road that morning when I came out with my fishing pole. She was separating out the roots of iris. As far as flowers go, she and I were agreed that iris had the sweetest scent. Iris would grow about anywhere, shooting up green sword-shaped leaves like the mythical soldiers that sprang from the planted teeth of a dragon. But iris needed some amount of care. Their roots would multiply so thick and fast that they could crowd themselves right up out of the soil. Spring separating and replanting were, as my grandmother put it, just the ticket.

Later that day, I knew, she would climb into our blue 1951 Plymouth to drive around the back roads of Greenfield, a box of iris in the back seat. She would stop at farms where she had noticed a certain color of iris that she didn't have yet. Up to the door she would go to ask for a root so that she could add another splash of color to our garden. And, in exchange, she would give that person, most often a flowered-aproned and somewhat elderly woman like herself, some of her own iris.

It wasn't just that she wanted more flowers herself. She had a philosophy. If only one person keeps a plant, something might happen to it. Early frost, insects, animals, Lord knows what. But if many have that kind of plant, then it may survive. Sharing meant a kind of immortality. I didn't quite understand it then, but I enjoyed taking those rides with her, carrying boxes and cans and flowerpots with new kinds of iris back to the car.

"Going fishing, Sonny?" she said now.

Of course, she knew where I was going. Not only the evidence of the pole in my hand, but also the simple facts that it was a Saturday morning in late May and I was a boy of ten, would have led her to that natural conclusion. But she had to ask. It was part of our routine.

"Un-hun," I answered, as I always did. "Unless you and Grampa need some help." Then I held my breath, for though my offer of aid had been sincere enough, I really wanted to go fishing.

Grama thrust her foot down on the spading fork, carefully levering out a heavy clump of iris marked last fall with a purple ribbon to indicate the color. She did such things with half my effort and twice the skill, despite the fact I was growing, as she put it, like a weed. "No, you go on along. This afternoon Grampa and I could use some help, though."

"I'll be back by then," I said, but I didn't turn and walk away. I waited for the next thing I knew she would say.

"You stay off of the state road, now."

In my grandmother's mind, Route 9N, which came down the hill past my grandparents' little gas station and general store on the corner, was nothing less than a Road of Death. If I ever set foot on it, I would surely be as doomed as our four cats and two dogs that met their fates there.

"Runned over and kilt," as Grampa Jesse put it.

Grampa Jesse, who had been the hired man for my grandmother's parents before he and Grama eloped, was not a person with book learning like my college-educated grandmother. His family was Abenaki Indian, poor but honest hill people who could read the signs in the forest, but who had never traipsed far along the trails of schoolhouse ways. Between Grama's books and Grampa's practical knowledge, some of which I was about to apply to bring home a mess of trout, I figured I was getting about the best education a ten-year-old boy could have. I was lucky that my grandparents were raising me.

"I'll stay off the state road," I promised. "I'll just follow Bell Brook."

Truth be told, the state road made me a little nervous, too. It was all too easy to imagine myself in the place of one of my defunct pets, stunned by the elephant bellow of a tractor-trailer's horn, looking wild-eyed up to the shiny metal grill; the thud, the lightning-bolt flash of light, and then the eternal dark. I imagined my grandfather shoveling the dirt over me in a backyard grave next to that of Lady, the collie, and Kitty-kitty, the gray cat, while my grandmother dried her eyes with her apron and said, "I told him to stay off that road!"

I was big on knowledge but very short on courage in those years. I mostly played by myself because the other kids my age from the houses and farms scattered around our rural township regarded me as a Grama's boy who would tell if they were to tie me up and threaten to burn my toes with matches, a ritual required to join the local society of pre-teenage boys. A squealer. And they were right.

I didn't much miss the company of other kids. I had discovered that most of them had little interest in the living things around them. They were noisier than Grampa and I were, scaring away the rabbits that we could creep right up on. Instead of watching the frogs catching flies with their long, gummy tongues, those boys wanted to shoot them with their BB guns. I couldn't imagine any of them having the patience or inclination to hold out a hand filled with sunflower seeds, as Grampa had showed me I could, long enough for a chickadee to come and light on an index finger.

Even fishing was done differently when I did it Grampa's way. I knew for a fact that most of those boys would go out and come home with an empty creel. They hadn't been watching for fish from the banks as I had in the weeks before the trout season began, so they didn't know where the fish lived. They didn't know how to keep low, float your line in, wait for that first tap, and then, after the strike that bent your pole, set the hook. And they never said thank-you to every fish they caught, the way I remembered to do.

Walking the creek edge, I set off downstream. By mid-morning, my bait can of moss and red earthworms that Grampa and I had dug from the edge of our manure pile was near empty. I'd gone half a mile and had already caught seven trout. All of them were squaretails, native brook trout whose sides were patterned with a speckled rainbow of bright circles — red, green, gold. I'd only kept the ones more than seven inches long, and I'd remembered to wet my hand before taking the little ones off the hook. Grasping a trout with a dry hand would abrade the slick coat of natural oil from the skin and leave it open for infection and disease.

As always, I'd had to keep the eyes in the back of my head open just as Grampa had told me to do whenever I was in the woods.

"Things is always hunting one another," he'd said.

And he was right. Twice, at places where Bell Brook swung near Mill Road I'd had to leave the stream banks to take shelter when I heard the ominous crunch of bicycle tires on the gravel. Back then, when I was ten, I was smaller than the other boys my age. I made up for it by being harder to catch. Equal parts of craftiness and plain old panic at being collared by bullies I viewed as close kin to Attila the Hun kept me slipperier than an eel.

From grapevine tangles up the bank, I'd watched as Pauly Roffmeier, Ricky Holstead, and Will Backus rolled up to the creek, making more noise than a herd of hippos, to plunk their own lines in. Both times, they caught nothing. It wasn't surprising, since they were talking like jaybirds, scaring away whatever fish might have been within half a mile. And Will kept lighting matches and throwing them down to watch them hiss out when they struck the water. Not to mention the fact that I had pulled a ten-inch brook trout out of the first hole and an eleven incher out of the second before they even reached the stream.

I looked up at the sky. I didn't wear a watch then. No watch made by man seemed able to work more than a few days when strapped to my wrist. It was a common thing on my Grampa's side of the family. "We jest got too much 'lectricity in us," he explained.

Without a watch, I could measure time by the sun. I could see it was about ten. I had reached the place where Bell Brook crossed under the state road. Usually I went no further than this. It had been my boundary for years. But somewhere along the way I had decided that today would be different. I think perhaps a part of me was ashamed of hiding from the other boys, ashamed of always being afraid. I wanted to do something that I'd always been afraid to do. I wanted to be brave.

I had no need to fish further. I had plenty of trout for our supper. I'd cleaned them all out with my Swiss Army knife, leaving the entrails where the crows and jays could get them. If you did that, the crows and jays would know you for a friend and not sound the alarm when they saw you walking in the woods. I sank the creel under water, wedged it beneath a stone. The water of the brook was deep and cold and I knew it would keep the flesh of the trout fresh and firm. Then I cached my pole and bait can under the spice bushes. As I looked up at the highway, Grama's words came back to me:

"Stay off the state road, Sonny."

"*Under,*" I said aloud, "is not *on.*"

Then, taking a deep breath, bent over at the waist, I waded into the culvert that dove under the Road of Death. I had gone no more than half a dozen steps before I walked into a spider web so strong that it actually bounced me back. I splashed a little water from the creek up onto it and watched the beads shape a pattern of concentric circles. The orb-weaver sat unmoving in a corner, one leg resting on a strand of the web. She'd been waiting for the vibration of some flying creature caught in the sticky strands of her net. Clearly, I was much more than she had hoped for. She sat there without moving. Her wide back was patterned with a shape like that of a red and gold hourglass. Her compound eyes, jet black on her head, took in my giant shape. Spiders gave some people the willies. I knew their bite would hurt like blue blazes, but I still thought them graced with great beauty.

"Excuse me," I said. "Didn't mean to bother you."

The spider raised one front leg. A nervous reaction, most likely, but I raised one hand back. Then I ducked carefully beneath the web, entering an area where the light was different. It was like passing from one world into another. I sloshed through the dark culvert, my fingertips brushing the rushing surface of the stream, the current pushing at my calves. My sneakered feet barely held their purchase on the ridged metal, slick with moss.

When I came out the other side, the sunlight was blinding. Just ahead of me the creek was overarched with willows. They were so thick and low that there was no way I could pass without either going underwater or breaking a way through the brush. I wasn't ready to do either. So I made my way up the bank, thinking to circle back and pick up the creek farther down. For what purpose, I wasn't sure, aside from just wanting to do it. I was nervous as a hen yard when a chicken hawk is circling overhead. But I was excited, too. This was new ground to me, almost a mile from home. I'd gone farther from home in the familiar directions of north and west, into the safety of the woods, but this was different: Across the state road, in the direction of town; someone else's hunting territory. I stayed low to the ground and hugged the edges of the brush as I moved. Then I saw something that drew me away from the creek: The glint of a wider expanse of water. The Rez, the old Greenfield Reservoir.

I'd never been to the Rez, though I knew the other boys went there. As I'd sat alone on the bus, my bookbag clasped tightly to my chest, I'd heard them talk about swimming there, fishing for bass, spearing bullfrogs five times as big as the little frogs in Bell Brook.

I knew I shouldn't be there, yet I was. Slowly I moved to the side of the wide trail that led to the edge of the deep water, and it was just as well that I did:

Their bikes had been stashed in the brush down the other side of the path. They'd been more quiet than usual. I might have walked up on them if I hadn't heard a voice.

"Gimme a drag," a voice said, just over the edge of the bank. I slid back, my heart pounding so hard I knew that it sounded like a drum solo.

"You let it go out, jerk," answered another voice that I could barely hear over my deafening heartbeat.

"I'll light it."

I'll light it. Not, There he is. Let's kill him? I hadn't been heard or seen! I was still safe. But I was as curious as I was afraid. What were they doing? I had to see.

I picked up some of the dark mud with my fingertips and drew lines across my cheeks. Grampa had explained it would make me harder to see. Then I slid to a place where an old tree leaned over the bank, cloaked by the cattails that grew from the edge of the Rez. I made my way out on the trunk and looked. What I saw shocked me. Pauly and Ricky and Will were worse boys than I'd thought. They were really bad! They had a cigarette and they were smoking it.

"Gimme," Ricky said again. "I'm the one who brought it."

"Stole it from your Mommy's handbag, you mean." Pauly held Ricky at arm's length as he puffed and then coughed. "An whyn't you get more than one?"

"If I stole a fresh pack, she would've known for sure. Gimme! I'm the one's gonna be in Dutch if she finds out."

No, I thought. *You're wrong. All of you are going to get in trouble after I tell Grama what I've seen and she gets through calling all your parents.*

As I watched, they shared the cigarette, alternately puffing at it, coughing, dropping it, and relighting it. Finally, when Ricky had puffed down to the filter, the last to get it, their smoking orgy was over. Ricky flicked the butt into the Rez and stared out at the water. "It's not gonna come up," Ricky said. He picked up something that looked like a makeshift spear. "You lied."

"I did not. It was over there. The biggest snapper I ever saw." Will shaded his eyes with one hand and looked right in my direction without seeing me. "If we catch it, we could sell it for ten dollars to that colored man on Congress Street. They say snapping turtles have seven different kinds of meat in them."

"Crap," Pauly said, throwing his own spear aside. "Let's go find something else to do."

One by one, they picked up their fishing poles and went back down the path. I waited without moving, hearing their heavy feet on the trail and then the rattle of their bike chains. I was no longer thinking about going home to tell Grama about their smoking. All I could think of was that snapping turtle.

I knew a lot about turtles. There were mud turtles and map turtles. There was the smart orange-legged wood turtle and the red-eared slider with its cheeks painted crimson as if it was going to war. Every spring Grama and Grampa and I would drive around, picking up those whose old migration routes had been cut by the recent and lethal ribbons of road. Spooked by a car, a turtle falls into that old defense of pulling head and legs and tail into its once impregnable fortress. But a shell does little good against the wheels of a Nash or a DeSoto.

Some days we'd rescue as many as a dozen turtles, taking them home for a few days before releasing them back into the wild. Painted turtles, several as big as two hands held together, might nip at you some, but they weren't really dangerous. And the wood turtles would learn in a day or so to reach out for a strawberry or a piece of juicy tomato and then leave their heads out for a scratch while you stroked them with a finger.

Snappers though, they were different. Long-tailed, heavy-bodied and short-tempered, their jaws would gape wide and they'd hiss when you came up on them ashore. Their heads and legs were too big to pull into their shells and they would heave up on their legs and lunge forward as they snapped at you. They might weigh as much as fifty pounds, and it was said they could take off a handful of fingers in one bite. There wasn't much to recommend a snapping turtle as a friend.

Most people seemed to hate snappers. Snappers ate the fish and the ducks; they scared swimmers away. Or I should say that people hated them alive. Dead, they were supposed to be the best-eating turtle of all. *Ten dollars,* I thought. *Enough for me to send away to the mail-order pet place and get a pair of real flying squirrels.* I'd kept that clipping from *Field and Stream* magazine thumbtacked over my bed for four months now. A sort of plan was coming into my mind.

People were afraid of getting bit by snappers when they were swimming. But from what I'd read, and from what Grampa told me, they really didn't have much to worry about.

"Snapper won't bother you none in the water," Grampa said. If you were even to step on a snapping turtle resting on the bottom of a pond, all it would do would be to move away. On land, all the danger from a snapper was to the front or the side. From behind, a snapper couldn't get you. Get it by the tail, you were safe. That was the way.

And as I thought, I kept watch. And as I kept watch, I kept up a silent chant inside my mind.

Come here, I'm waiting for you.

Come here, I'm waiting for you.

Before long, a smallish log that had been sticking up

farther out in the pond began to drift my way. It was, as I had expected, no log at all. It was a turtle's head. I stayed still. The sun's heat beat on my back, but I lay there like a basking lizard. Closer and closer the turtle came, heading right into water less than waist deep. It was going right for shore, for the sandy bank bathed in sun. I didn't think about why then, just wondered at the way my wanting seemed to have called it to me.

When it was almost to shore, I slid into the water on the other side of the log I'd been waiting on. The turtle surely sensed me, for it started to swing around as I moved slowly toward it, swimming as much as walking. But I lunged and grabbed it by the tail. Its tail was rough and ridged, as easy to hold as if coated with sandpaper. I pulled hard and the turtle came toward me. I stepped back, trying not to fall and pull it on top of me. My feet found the bank, and I leaned hard to drag the turtle out, its clawed feet digging into the dirt as it tried to get away. A roaring hiss like the rush of air from a punctured tire came out of its mouth, and I stumbled, almost losing my grasp. Then I took another step, heaved again, and it was mine.

Or at least it was until I let go. I knew I could not let go. I looked around, holding its tail, moving my feet to keep it from walking its front legs around to where it would snap at me. It felt as if it weighed a thousand pounds. I could only lift up the back half of its body. I started dragging it toward the creek, fifty yards away. It seemed to take hours, a kind of dance between me and the great turtle, but I did it. I pulled it back through the roaring culvert, water gushing over its shell, under the spider web, and past my hidden pole and creel. I could come back later for the fish. Now there was only room in the world for Bell Brook, the turtle, and me.

The long passage upstream is a blur in my memory. I thought of salmon leaping over falls and learned a little that day how hard such a journey must be. When I rounded the last bend and reached the place where the brook edged our property, I breathed a great sigh. But I could not rest. There was still a field and the back yard to cross.

My grandparents saw me coming. From the height of the sun it was now mid-afternoon, and I knew I was dreadful late.

"Sonny, where have you . . . ?" began Grama.

Then she saw the turtle.

"I'm sorry. It took so long because of . . ." I didn't finish the sentence because the snapping turtle, undaunted by his backward passage, took that opportunity to try once more to swing around and get me. I had to make three quick steps in a circle, heaving at its tail as I did so.

"Nice size turtle," Grampa Jesse said.

My grandmother looked at me. I realized then I must have been a sight. Wet, muddy, face and hands scratched from the brush that overhung the creek.

"I caught it at the reservoir," I said. I didn't think to lie to them about where I'd been. I waited for my grandmother to scold me. But she didn't.

"Jesse," she said, "Get the big washtub."

My grandfather did as she said. He brought it back and then stepped next to me.

"Leave go," he said.

My hands had a life of their own, grimly determined never to let loose of that all-too-familiar tail, but I forced them to open. The turtle flopped down. Before it could move, my grandfather dropped the big washtub over it. All was silent for a minute as I stood there, my arms aching as they hung by my side. Then the washtub began to move. My grandmother sat down on it and it stopped.

She looked at me. So did Grampa. It was wonderful how they could focus their attention on me in a way that made me feel they were ready to do whatever they could to help.

"What now?" Grama said.

"I heard that somebody down on Congress Street would pay ten dollars for a snapping turtle."

"Jack's," Grampa said.

My grandmother nodded. "Well," she said, "if you

go now you can be back in time for supper. I thought we were having trout." She raised an eyebrow at me.

"I left them this side of the culvert by 9N," I said. "Along with my pole."

"You clean up and put on dry clothes. Your grandfather will get the fish."

"But I hid them."

My grandmother smiled. "Your grandfather will find them." And he did.

An hour later, we were on the way to Congress Street, the heart of the colored section of Saratoga Springs. In the 1950s, Congress Street was like a piece of Harlem dropped into an upstate town. We pulled up in front of Jack's, and a man who looked to be my grandfather's age got up and walked over to us. His skin was only a little darker than my grandfather's, and the two nodded to each other.

My grandfather put his hand on the trunk of the Plymouth.

"What you got there?" Jack said.

"Show him, Sonny."

I opened the trunk. My snapping turtle lifted up its head as I did so.

"I heard you might want to buy a turtle like this for ten dollars," I said.

Jack shook his head. "Ten dollars for a little one like that? I'd give you two dollars."

I looked at my turtle. Had it shrunk since Grampa wrestled it into the trunk?

"That's not enough," I said.

"Three dollars. My last offer."

I looked at Grampa. He shrugged his shoulders.

"I guess I don't want to sell it," I said.

"All right," Jack said. "You change your mind, come on back." He touched his hat with two fingers and walked back over to his chair in the sun.

As we drove back toward home, neither of us said anything for a while. Then my grandfather spoke.

"Would five dollars've been enough?"

"No," I said.

"How about ten?"

I thought about that. "I guess not."

"Why you suppose that turtle was heading for that sandbank?" Grampa said.

I thought about that, too. Then I realized the truth of it.

"It was coming out to lay its eggs."

"Might be."

I thought hard then. I'd learned it was never right for a hunter to shoot a mother animal, because it hurt the next generation to come. Was a turtle any different?

"Can we take her back?" I asked.

"Up to you, Sonny."

And so we did. Gramp drove the Plymouth right

up the trail to the edge of the Rez. He held a stick so the turtle would grab onto it as I hauled her out of the trunk. I put her down and she just stayed there, her nose a foot from the water but not moving.

"We'll leave her," Grampa said. We turned to get into the car. When I looked back over my shoulder, she was gone. Only ripples on the water, widening circles rolling on toward other shores like generations following each other, like my grandmother's flowers still growing in a hundred gardens in Greenfield, like the turtles still seeking out that sandbank, like this story that is no longer just my own but belongs now to your memory, too.

✦ ✦ ✦

Notes from

JOSEPH BRUCHAC

"When I think back on my childhood and the old house that I lived in with my grandparents, two images always come to mind. The first is books. Shelves and bookcases in every room filled with everything from leather-bound sets of Kipling and Dickens, Sir Walter Scott and Mark Twain and the Romantic poets to *Reader's Digest* condensed volumes which arrived in the mail every month. The books were my grandmother's, but as soon as I could read — and I was reading everything I could get my hands on by the time I was in second grade — I thought of them as mine, too. Grama was glad to share them with me, first by reading them aloud and then later by knowing just the right book to pull down from a high shelf and put into my hands.

The second image is of the little piece of forest behind our house — 'The Woods' as my grandfather called it. Although Grampa Jesse could barely read a newspaper, he knew how to read the woods better than anyone I ever knew. The trees, the birds, the trails the animals made, he saw them all and shared them with me. Sometimes he did it without saying anything, just directing my attention the right way at just the right time — so I would see the robin's nest deep inside the spruce tree, its eggs as blue as a clear sky, so that I would realize those twigs and stones at the bottom of the stream were really the movable camouflaged homes of caddis fly larvae. He taught me to be careful about how I walked, about never taking too much of anything — whether it was the May flowers we picked to make bouquets or the trout from Bell Brook — and always to give something back. It might just be a word of thanks, but even a small gift meant something. It kept the balance.

My grandmother loved the outdoors, too, but her love was for the gardens she kept, the gardens I mention in this story. She always kept those gardens overflowing with flowers close to the roadside where everyone could see them and enjoy their beauty, so carefully planted that they were patterned like a patchwork quilt.

I think it was those two worlds — the world of books and the natural world that surrounded me as a child — that made me a writer. I wanted to share the things I saw and heard, the things I imagined. My grandparents were always sharing, and it just seemed like the natural thing to do. And whenever I wrote a poem or a story, both Grama and Grampa were eager to hear it and quick to tell me they had never heard anything quite like it before. So I kept on sharing and always trying to give something back.

That is why I chose to tell this story, a story that shows a little of those roots my grandparents nurtured."

AUTHOR BIOGRAPHIES

AVI has written more than seventy books for all ages and across genres. He is the author of the Newbery Honor Books *The True Confessions of Charlotte Doyle* and *Nothing But the Truth*; the Newbery Medal winner *Crispin: The Cross of Lead*; *The Fighting Ground*, which won the Scott O'Dell Award for Historical Fiction; and two sequels to *Crispin* titled *Crispin: At the Edge of the World* and *Crispin: The End of Time*. Avi lives in Colorado with his wife.

FRANCESCA LIA BLOCK is best known for her groundbreaking Weetzie Bat novels, many of which have been named as American Library Association Best Books for Young Adults. She also received the American Library Association's Margaret A. Edwards Lifetime Achievement Award. Her most recent works include *The Frenzy, House of Dolls,* and *Wood Nymph Seeks Centaur: A Mythological Dating Guide.* Francesca Lia Block lives in California.

JOSEPH BRUCHAC is an author, storyteller, and editor who has drawn on his Native-American heritage throughout his writing career. He has edited more than thirty books and has written more than sixty books of his own, including *The Faithful Hunter;* the Keepers of the Earth series; *The Boy Who Lived with the Bears,* a *Boston Globe–Horn Book* Honor Book; *Dog People,* winner of the Paterson Children's Writing Award; and *Many Nations: An Alphabet of Native America,* an International Reading Association Teachers' Choice. The cofounder of *Greenfield Review Press,* he lives with his wife in upstate New York.

SUSAN COOPER was born and raised in England and has written books for children and young adults, a Broadway play, and several screenplays, two of which earned Emmy nominations. Of her many books, the best known are the five fantasy novels in the young adult series The Dark Is Rising, which have won numerous awards, including the Newbery Medal. Her most recent work, *The Magic Maker,* is a biography of John Langstaff, creator of the Christmas Revels, and was published in 2011 by Candlewick Press. Susan Cooper lives in Massachusetts.

PAUL FLEISCHMAN is the award-winning author of many books for children and young adults, including *Joyful Noise: Poems for Two Voices*, winner of the Newbery Medal; *Graven Images*, a Newbery Honor Book and a *Boston Globe–Horn Book* Honor Book; *Bull Run*, winner of the Scott O'Dell Award for Historical Fiction; *Saturnalia*, a *Boston Globe–Horn Book* Honor Book; *Dateline: Troy*, an American Library Association Best Book for Young Adults; *The Dunderheads*; and *The Dunderheads Behind Bars*. He lives in California.

KAREN HESSE grew up in Baltimore, Maryland, and now lives with her family in Vermont. She is the author of the Newbery Medal–winning *Out of the Dust*, which was also named a Best Book by *School Library Journal*, *Publishers Weekly*, and *Booklist*. Her other books for young readers include *Phoenix Rising; Letters from Rifka; The Music of Dolphins*, named an American Library Association Best Book for Young Adults and a Best Book by *Publishers Weekly* and *School Library Journal*; and *A Time of Angels*, named an International Reading Association Young Adults' Choice. In 2006, Karen was selected to receive the Kerlan Award for her contributions to the Children's Literature Research Collection at the University of Minnesota.

JAMES HOWE has written more than seventy books for children and young adults, including the Sebastian Barth mystery series, the Pinky and Rex series, and such highly acclaimed picture books as *Horace and Morris but Mostly Dolores* and *There's a Monster Under My Bed.* Best known for his award-winning Bunnicula series about a vampire rabbit, he received the E. B. White Read Aloud Award for *Houndsley and Catina,* the first book in a series. James Howe lives in New York State.

E. L. KONIGSBURG, the author of novels, short stories, and picture books, won her first Newbery Medal for the second novel she ever wrote, *From the Mixed-Up Files of Mrs. Basil E. Frankweiler.* That same year her first novel, *Jennifer, Hecate, Macbeth, William McKinley, and Me, Elizabeth,* was named a Newbery Honor Book. With *The View from Saturday,* published almost thirty years and more than fifteen books later, she won her second Newbery Medal. Born in New York City, E. L. Konigsburg lives in Florida.

REEVE LINDBERGH is the daughter of aviator Charles Lindbergh and author Anne Morrow Lindbergh, and has written many picture books and adult novels. Her novels include *Johnny Appleseed; The Awful Aardvarks Shop for School; View from the Air: Charles Lindbergh's Earth and Sky; The Circle of Days; Homer, the Library Cat;* and *My Little Grandmother Often Forgets,* published by Candlewick Press. She received the *Redbook* Children's Picture Book Award for her books *Benjamin's Barn* and *The Midnight Farm.* She lives in Vermont with her husband, their children, and an assortment of animals.

NORMA FOX MAZER wrote many highly acclaimed novels for young adults, including *After the Rain,* a Newbery Honor Book; *Taking Terri Mueller,* winner of the Edgar Allan Poe Award for Best Juvenile Novel; *A Figure of Speech,* a National Book Award Finalist; and *Dear Bill, Remember Me? and Other Stories,* a *New York Times* Outstanding Book of the Year. Many of her novels have also been named Best Books for Young Adults by the American Library Association. She passed away in 2009.

NICHOLASA MOHR was born in Manhattan's El Barrio and raised in the Bronx. She has written numerous books for children and young adults, including *Nilda; El Bronx Remembered,* winner of the American Book Award and a National Book Award Finalist; and *Growing*

Up Inside the Sanctuary of My Imagination, a memoir. She has been honored with a number of prestigious awards, including the Raúl Juliá Award by the Puerto Rican Family Institute. Nicholasa Mohr moved back to El Barrio, where she continues to write books and plays for people of all ages.

KYOKO MORI was born in Kobe, Japan. She moved to the United States at the age of twenty, originally to finish her undergraduate college degree. Her books for young adults include *One Bird* and *Shizuko's Daughter,* which was named an American Library Association Best Book for Young Adults, a *New York Times* Notable Book, and a *Publishers Weekly* Editors' Choice. Her most recent books for adults include *Polite Lies: On Being a Woman Caught Between Cultures; Stone Field, True Arrow;* and *Yarn: Remembering the Way Home.* Kyoko Mori currently teaches creative writing at George Mason University.

WALTER DEAN MYERS is a pioneer of young adult fiction and is considered one of the preeminent writers for children. His novels about urban teens and the challenges they face have won him dozens of awards, including the first Michael L. Printz Award for *Monster,* five Coretta Scott King Awards, and two

Newbery Honors. He wrote *Autobiography of My Dead Brother,* a National Book Award Finalist, and *Jazz,* an American Library Association Notable Children's Book, illustrated by his son, Christopher Myers. Walter Dean Myers lives in New Jersey.

HOWARD NORMAN has translated and edited two collections of stories for young readers: *Trickster and the Fainting Bird,* and *The Girl Who Dreamed Only Geese and Other Tales of the Far North,* which won a Parents' Choice Silver Honor and the Anne Izard Storytellers' Choice Award and was nominated for the Dorothy Canfield Fisher Award. In addition, it was named a *New York Times Book Review* Best Illustrated Children's Book of the Year. Two of Howard Norman's novels for adults, *The Northern Lights* and *The Bird Artist,* have been chosen as National Book Award Finalists. He and his wife, poet Jane Shore, and their daughter, Emma, divide their time between Washington, D.C., and Vermont.

MARY POPE OSBORNE is the author of many highly acclaimed novels for young readers as well as picture books, middle-grade biographies, and collections of myths and fairy tales. Her most recent works include the Magic Tree House series, *Tsunamis and Other Natural*

Disasters, the Spider Kane mystery series, and the Tales from the *Odyssey* series. She worked on and traveled with *Magic Tree House: The Musical,* which was written by her husband, Will Osborne. She and her husband live in New York City.

KATHERINE PATERSON left China just before the United States entered into World War II. Since then she has lived all over the United States and in Japan. She has received numerous awards for her writing, including National Book Awards for *The Master Puppeteer* and *The Great Gilly Hopkins,* as well as Newbery Medals for *Jacob Have I Loved* and *Bridge to Terabithia.* Katherine Paterson is vice president of the National Children's Book and Literacy Alliance. In 2010, she was selected as National Ambassador for Young People's Literature by the Library of Congress. Her most recent work, *The Flint Heart,* was written with her husband, John Paterson, and published in 2011 by Candlewick Press. She lives with her husband in Vermont.

MICHAEL J. ROSEN has written, edited, or illustrated more than thirty books for children and adults, including *Elijah's Angel,* winner of the National Jewish Book Award; *Speak! Children's Book Illustrators Brag About*

Their Dogs; The Heart Is Big Enough: Five Stories; and *The Dog Who Walked with God.* Additionally, he has worked as literary director at the Thurber House, the writers' center in the restored home of James Thurber. Born and raised in Columbus, Ohio, he now lives in a forested area of central Ohio.

RITA WILLIAMS-GARCIA was raised in Seaside, California, and Jamaica, New York, where she currently lives. Her first novel, *Fast Talk on a Slow Track,* was named an American Library Association Best Book for Young Adults and an American Library Association Quick Pick and won the PEN/Norma Klein Award and a Parents' Choice Silver Honor. Her second novel, *Like Sisters on the Homefront,* is a Coretta Scott King Honor Book. Her most recent work, *One Crazy Summer,* won numerous awards and honors, including the 2011 Coretta Scott King Award, a Newbery Honor, and the Scott O'Dell Prize for Historical Fiction, and was also named a National Book Award Finalist.

LAURENCE YEP was born and raised in San Francisco. He is the award-winning author of more than sixty books for children and young adults, including the Golden Mountain Chronicles, for which he received two Newbery Honors, for *Dragonwings* and *Dragon's Gate*. He is also the author of *The Star Fisher,* winner of a Christopher Award, and *Child of the Owl,* which won the *Boston Globe–Horn Book* Award, as well as the Tiger's Apprentice series and the City series. He received the Laura Ingalls Wilder Award in 2005 for his contributions to children's literature. He lives in California.

JANE YOLEN has written and edited more than two hundred books and anthologies—for all age levels and in genres ranging from picture books to fantasy to science fiction. Her numerous awards include a Christopher Award for *The Seeing Stick;* the National Jewish Book Award for *The Devil's Arithmetic;* the World Fantasy Award for *Favorite Folktales from Around the World;* and three honors for her body of work in children's literature: the Kerlan Award, the Keene State College Children's Literature Festival Award, and the Regina Medal. She divides her time between western Massachusetts and Scotland.

AMY EHRLICH, the editor of *When I Was Your Age,* volumes one and two, notes that "writing begins with observation. The authors in this collection, like all children, felt things deeply. But they also were able to observe their feelings and therefore to remember them as well. Those memories are a writer's most durable tool." Amy Ehrlich has been an editor and a writing teacher and is the author of more than twenty-five books for young readers. She lives in Vermont.